FAREWELL, MY CUCKOO

An absolutely gripping British cozy murder mystery

MARTY WINGATE

A Birds of a Feather Mystery Book 4

Revised edition 2024
Joffe Books, London
www.joffebooks.com

First published in Great Britain in 2018

This paperback edition was first published in Great Britain in 2024

© Marty Wingate 2018, 2024

This book is a work of fiction. Names, characters, businesses, organizations, places and events are either the product of the author's imagination or are used fictitiously. Any resemblance to actual persons, living or dead, events or locales is entirely coincidental. The spelling used is American English except where fidelity to the author's rendering of accent or dialect supersedes this. The right of Marty Wingate to be identified as author of this work has been asserted in accordance with the Copyright, Designs and Patents Act 1988.

Cover art by Imogen Buchanan

ISBN: 978-1-83526-478-2

To Leighton

CHAPTER 1

The cuckoo comes in April,
And sings its song in May,
In June it changes tune,
And July it flies away.

The sun poured through the tall Gothic windows of St. Swithun's, backlighting the vases of cornflowers and columbine on each deep sill and illuminating the towering altar arrangement — a glowing mass of deep-pink roses, china-blue delphinium spears, and lacy cow parsley. Although a gorgeous June day outdoors, the sun's warmth had yet to penetrate the thick flint-and-stone church walls, and my bare arms were peppered with gooseflesh. Not the best look, and it was all I could do not to edge over to a pool of sunshine just to my right. But of course, I couldn't move an inch. Not now.

"Marriage is a blessed event."

As he spoke, Reverend Eccles spread his arms wide to include not only those of us at the altar, but the entire congregation.

"It is a gift from God that as man and woman grow together in love and trust, they shall be united . . ."

I paid great attention to what the vicar said, but still stole a glance at Michael, who stood across from me. He ignored Reverend Eccles and had his eyes — the color of midnight studded with stars — locked on me. He looked gorgeous in his dark suit with his black hair, always a bit shaggy and tousled. The corner of his mouth tugged up into a smile. I blushed, a warmth rushing through me that banished my gooseflesh skin.

". . . if anyone present knows a reason why these persons may not lawfully marry . . ."

As if. I cut my eyes out to the congregation and saw my dad, Rupert Lanchester, and stepmum, Beryl, beaming. My dad winked at me. They had been married not three years ago and so, they understood what this day meant.

"The vows you are about to take . . ."

The flower girl, only four years old, had tired of the affair, plopped herself onto the stone step at the vicar's feet, and overturned her basket, shaking the remaining rose petals onto the floor. She bent over her treasure, showing off the details of her hat — a thin gold circlet onto which was attached a tiny robin fashioned out of dried mushrooms and painted in bright colors. An arts-and-crafts project from the mind and fingers of Willow Wynn-Finch, of course. The flower girl began to stack her petals, counting to herself as she did so. "One, two, five, elevens." She was precious.

"Julia?"

I jerked to attention.

"Julia," Reverend Eccles repeated. "The ring."

The ring? What happened to the vows? My thoughts had wandered, and now I looked round to see that all eyes were on me.

"Sorry," I whispered, shifting the wedding bouquet with its dripping tendrils of honeysuckle to my other hand as I slipped the loose gold band off my right pinkie finger and gave it to the vicar.

Holding up the Bible, he continued. "Let these rings be a symbol . . ."

It was too beautiful for words. My eyes blurred with tears, and I only hoped I could finish the ceremony without making a fool of myself. At last, came the glorious end.

"And now," Reverend Eccles proclaimed, "Akash Kumar and Vesta Widdersham, I pronounce you husband and wife."

* * *

Yes, all right, it wasn't my wedding, but love was in the air, as they say, and so high time that I, Julia Lanchester, and my boyfriend of two years, Michael Sedgwick, took that next step. The feeling had been building between us all week as Vesta and Akash's wedding approached. It occupied my every waking moment, and had caught Michael up, too. I could see it in his swift glances toward me, as if assessing the situation and his chances. But he must know his chances were extremely good. We had been dropping the heaviest of hints to each other, saying how Vesta and Akash, both well into their sixties, knew they couldn't let life pass them by, and how a commitment in front of God and the village meant a strengthening of a relationship. All comments concerned the happy couple, but the subtext was clear: It was time for us, too. Weddings. They'll do that to you.

* * *

"You look the perfect bride," I said to Vesta as we walked into the garden at the Stoat and Hare pub, just down Church Lane. She'd found a lovely linen suit, a blue that matched the delphinium and complemented the pearly pink frames of her glasses and the subtle pink tint to her pixie haircut.

"You're not so bad yourself," Vesta replied.

My dress, polished cotton with cap sleeves, a princess neckline, and a short bell skirt, was a riot of flowers in purples, blues, and pink. I loved it, even though I did feel as if I were a garden on the move. "I hope it wasn't too much. At least I matched the altar arrangement."

"It was so good of His Lordship to let you close the TIC on a Saturday," Vesta said as she laid her bouquet next to the guest book and straightened the jacket on her dress.

I gave her a hug and a kiss on the cheek. "Linus knows what's important."

Although I was manager of the Tourist Information Center in our village, Smeaton-under-Lyme, and Vesta was my second-in-command, it was Lord Fotheringill — Linus — who called the shots. It was, after all, his estate, comprising not only the village, but also his home, Hoggin Hall, several outlying hamlets, the abbey ruins, along with various farms, fields, orchards, and woods. Not the largest estate in Britain or even in Suffolk, but still, a considerable responsibility, and yet he knew the lives of his tenants came first.

"And your husband looks gorgeous," I commented, nodding to the bar where he stood chatting with the vicar. Over dark trousers, Akash had worn a kurta — a men's collarless shirt that came to his knees and traditional in India. Made from a red jacquard overlaid with black brocade, it set off his dark hair shot through with silver.

The groom's day off had not been a problem, either. Akash ran the village shop, where we could buy everything from a pint of milk to freshly prepared lasagna in the cold case. He had left his assistant manager, Gwen Gunn, behind the till for his wedding day and honeymoon weekend.

Reverend Eccles lifted a glass for the first toast. He and his wife were on the threshold of a two-week fishing holiday in the Highlands — he fished, she painted landscapes — but had stayed an extra day at home just for the nuptials. I'd seen their packed car at the curb, and knew they were eager to be off.

After each glass had been refilled, I gave Vesta a nudge. "Go on now. Nuala's cake awaits."

Nuala Darke, proprietor of Nuala's Tea Room and baker extraordinaire, stood chatting with Linus as she hovered over the three-tiered beauty she had spent the past fortnight creating. Just the sight of the cake induced "oohs" and "aahs." Heavy with spices and sultanas, each tier was encased in marzipan, and covered in filigreed royal icing with candied violets circling the edges, and a dome of fresh roses at the top. I'd been dreaming about it all week and intended to be first in line for a slice. After the bride and groom, of course.

"Aren't they the most incredibly lovely couple you've ever seen?" Willow sighed as she stood next to me and we watched friends queue up to congratulate the bride and groom. "It's a truly happy beginning for them."

Willow, who had a strong, but unique sense of style, had dressed with a decided wood-fairy appeal, wearing several gauzy layers in shades of green. Amid her brown curls, she set her own thin circlet of gold, this one decorated with bits of moss and a tiny nuthatch, also made from a dried mushroom and painted in sleek lines. She'd offered such a creation to me, but I had begged off, saying it might not stay well in my chin-length dark blonde bob.

"You and Cecil will look just as lovely when your turn comes," I assured. Willow and Lord Fotheringill's son, Cecil, had become officially engaged a few months ago and had set the wedding date for two years hence.

She smiled, revealing a small gap between her front teeth, and scrunching up her freckled face. "And you and Michael?"

I blushed. "Oh, I don't know." I tried for a cavalier tone, but it sounded false even in my own ears.

Willow waved across the garden to Cecil and her aunt Lottie Finch who ran Three Bags Full, the village wool shop, and departed to join them. Willow ostensibly still lived with her aunt, but I'd say there were a fair number of overnights at the Hall these days, and everyone concerned seemed delighted with the situation.

I stayed where I was as Michael sidled up to me and handed over a glass of champagne. When I'd taken it, he slipped his free hand round my waist, resting it on my hip, and squeezed.

We'd both been asked to stand up for the wedding couple, because Vesta's daughter lived in New Zealand and

Akash's son had just been posted to Los Angeles. We had been proud to do so. Now, having completed our duties for the day, we stood quiet for a moment and observed the scene. The bride and groom hadn't wanted the usual sit-down dinner reception during which each of us gave a speech and a toast. Instead, they had preferred a quiet gathering at the pub.

"Are we staying long?" Michael asked.

"Why?" I gave him a sly look.

"Because," he said, his lips close to my ear, "when we get back to the cottage, there's something I want to ask you."

"Oh." The sound caught in my throat, and I took a sip of champagne but overshot, and a stream of fizz dribbled out of the corner of my mouth and down my chin. I wiped it away with the back of my hand. "We can leave any time. It isn't as if we're the hosts. Of course, we should stay for the cake, don't you think?"

"God, yes," Michael replied. "We wouldn't want to miss that."

It was something he'd learned early on — never get between me and cake.

* * *

Just gone seven o'clock, and the sun hung low in the sky. We'd left the reception later than we'd planned, but no matter, because we had the evening ahead of us. A pied wagtail darted ahead on the pavement, keeping us company as we walked hand in hand from the pub and down the high street toward Pipit Cottage, which sat middle in a row of what had been housing for flax weavers in centuries past. Accommodations were part of my pay package as manager of the TIC, and Michael had moved in with me a year ago autumn. The cottage was cozy, to say the least. It had a tiny sitting room with fireplace, kitchen you could barely turn round in, and bedroom and bath up a steep set of stairs, but it suited us, because we didn't mind bumping elbows. French doors led to a stone terrace big enough for a bistro table and two chairs, and a deep back garden, which I let get a bit wild, as it suited the birds that way. I kept the seed table well stocked and fat balls in the wire feeder.

Pausing at the corner where Westbury Road headed out of the village, we took in the quiet. "It's a fine evening," Michael murmured. "When we get home, why don't we sit in the garden for a while?"

It was a habit we'd formed quickly — relaxing in the back garden for a bird quiz. I'd let Michael page through my old copy of *The Observer's Book of British Birds* as I asked, "What's that now?" of a movement in the shrubbery or a call on the wing. He would begin to rattle off his guesses — dunnock, linnet, redwing, blue tit, pied wagtail, blackcap, chaffinch.

Michael hadn't known a great deal about birds two years earlier, when he had taken on the post as Rupert's personal assistant and producer of his BBC Two television program *A Bird in the Hand*. My dad — the Indiana Jones of ornithology — was popular with all ages and used his charisma for good, to enlist followers as citizen scientists, teaching them how to care about the world around them. Rupert had taken a chance on Michael, because he'd needed to replace his previous assistant, aka me, rather quickly, but his gamble had paid off in spades. Michael, with a background in public relations, was a fantastic idea man.

Now, as we paused on the pavement with the evening sun turning everything gold, we basked in an atmosphere of intimacy, longing, and promise. The garden would be the perfect place to talk. I drew close to Michael until we were standing nose-to-nose.

"Yes," I whispered, my lips grazing his. "The garden."

I glanced over his shoulder and down the road toward the cottage door and saw a woman sitting on our doorstep, face buried in her phone. With her black hair pulled up into a ragged bun, and her legs stretched out across the pavement, she was surrounded by plastic grocery-shopping bags and had a rucksack in her lap.

Michael caught the direction of my gaze and turned to look. "Pammy?" he muttered.

As if possessed of super hearing, her head snapped up from her phone and she looked toward us. She broke into a smile and clambered up, tugging on the hem of her microskirt, dropping her rucksack, and tripping on one of the shopping bags before righting herself. She held out her arms and said, "Surprise!"

CHAPTER 2

Pammy, Michael's sister. We gave her hugs, and she and Michael stood looking eye-to-eye, although Pammy — all arms and legs — always seemed a bit taller. She shared the Sedgwick family characteristics of dark hair, blue eyes, a mouth that turned up at the corners. But on Pammy, the usual traits had been squeezed onto a face too long and narrow for them to settle well, giving her the appearance of constant apprehension. Still, that smile made up for a lot.

"What a surprise," I said, although that wasn't the word I was thinking.

"Do you know," Pammy began, "I realized I'd never seen this adorable cottage you go on and on about, Julia? And really, Michael, you've been quite mum about the village and how charming it is."

She stooped to disentangle her heel from one of the plastic bags before continuing with a tinny laugh. "You two live the perfect life, don't you? And so, a weekend in the country, well, it sounded wonderful, and I thought, why not now?" She examined her hands and scratched at a cuticle. "It was just a wild idea, but as I had no other plans . . ."

Running out of steam at last, for one moment she looked at us blankly. Then her face crumpled and fat tears cascaded from her blue eyes, plopped onto her chest, and were soaked up by her tight, low-cut T-shirt, which read: *I'm Yours!* in bold pink writing, with a little heart at the bottom of the exclamation point.

"Ah, Pammy, don't," Michael protested and waved his arms weakly. "What's wrong?" He threw me a pleading look. The sight of a woman in tears can make the strongest man crumble.

"Come on, let's go inside," I urged, reaching round her and unlocking the door.

No one would guess that Pammy, at forty-two, was actually a year older than her brother Michael, because, when in crisis — a frequent occurrence — she turned to him, not their older brother, Miles. Of the four Sedgwick siblings, Pammy set my teeth on edge even more than Miles, and that was saying a great deal.

She continued to weep loudly as she stepped empty-handed into the cottage ahead of us. Michael and I picked up her bags and rucksack and followed, nudging her aside and stacking everything behind the door. Pammy had taken three steps, which put her in the kitchen, before stopping. She sniffed sharply and turned off the tears as she glanced round.

"Oh, how sweet," she said. "Is this it?"

"Pammy, what's happened?" Michael asked as I pushed past to switch the kettle on.

She stuck out her bottom lip. "I've left him. I just couldn't take it any longer. I deserve to be treated properly."

Of course that was it — she'd broken up with her boyfriend. What was his name? I couldn't recall. He was the fourth or fifth since Michael and I had met just over two years ago. Each of Pammy's breakups had been the end of the world, and none of them had been her fault.

I crossed my arms tightly and leaned against the kitchen counter. "Did he go back to his wife?"

Michael cut his eyes at me as Pammy scrunched up her face again and wailed, "He *promised* me he was getting a *divorce*!" One tear leaked out the corner of an eye, and she cocked her head at Michael to make sure he saw it. "I didn't know where else to go. Then I remembered you two and how lovely you've always been to me. And I thought, perhaps I could stay with you? Just for tonight? I promise I won't be any trouble — you won't even know I'm here! And I'll leave tomorrow, really I will."

"Could you not go to Pickle's?" Michael asked. I heard the exasperation in his voice, and it echoed in every fiber of my being.

Pickle, a year older than Pammy, and the only easy one of the lot, was stability personified — married with two lovely daughters in secondary school. Patsy Sedgwick, the mother of the four and an oasis of calm in a sea of diverse adult children, lived with Pickle and her family. So had Pammy. At least for a while.

Pammy put her nose in the air and harrumphed. "Mum would be fine, because she would understand. But she's been brainwashed by the Queen of Perfection."

There you are — so much for our evening. But Michael had a soft spot for Pammy — God knows why — and she was family. His family, although, they would become mine, too, wouldn't they, if we . . . ?

"Of course you can stay tonight," I said. "We can manage one night. You won't mind the sofa, will you, because it's all we've got?" Unless she wanted to curl up in the kitchen sink.

"Oh, Julia, you're the best." The kettle switched off. "Are you making tea?"

* * *

Michael took off his coat and tie and put together a salad, and I slipped off my heels and cooked an omelet with shallots and mushrooms for our supper, even though I was still full of wedding cake. We opened the French doors for air, and once or twice or thrice, I glanced longingly out to the back garden.

Pammy sat at the table like a baby bird waiting to be fed, and during the meal filled the conversation with royal gossip and her worry that Prince George had difficulty making friends. After, she retreated to the sofa to stare at her phone, hoping for a reconciliation text, no doubt, while we washed up.

"You know," Pammy said, at last putting her phone down as we finished in the kitchen, "you aren't the easiest people to find. I knew your cottage had a bird name, but I couldn't remember which. Pipit? It's not one I've heard of. So, first, I stopped to ask a fellow I saw on a bicycle." She flung an arm out in a generally northern direction. "He was a friendly sort, but he'd no idea. In fact, no one seemed to know who you were. And so, finally, I had to go in the pub."

"The Stoat and Hare?" Michael asked. Had she been in the pub while we were in the garden at the wedding reception?

Pammy wrinkled her nose. "No, looked a bit posh, that one. I went over to the one the other side of the green. And I thought perhaps you two might pop in, so I decided to have a drink and chat with the barman."

No one at the Royal Oak "chatted" with Hutch, whose conversations consisted of growls and grunts.

"I asked where your cottage was, and you'd've thought I wanted the moon. He said had I tried walking down the high street and looking for myself."

There you are, that's Hutch.

"So, I did. And I saw your Fiat, Michael, and knew I was in the right place. Did you see I've parked behind you? And so, here we are, the three of us — all snug and homely."

I surveyed the scene. As she rattled on, Pammy had dug into her shopping bags in search of her toothbrush, and now a pair of trousers lay draped over the back of the sofa and the floor was littered with tops, three shoes, and several pairs of knickers, making the place look like the reject room from a church jumble sale.

"Well," I said. "Early night, what do you say? I'm shattered, for one."

"Are we not going down the pub?" Pammy asked.

"No, we aren't," Michael replied curtly. "You must be exhausted after all your . . ." He sighed. "Look, do you want to, you know, go up and clean your teeth first?"

"You've only the one loo?" Pammy peered up the steep staircase.

"Yes, only the one. Upstairs, through our bedroom." I could hear him grinding his teeth. "Why don't you go first?"

It took her a few more minutes to locate all she needed before she made the climb. She closed our bedroom door, and I heard her close the bathroom door, too. Michael took my hand and pulled me over to the sofa, shifting a stack of Pammy's *Hello* magazines that had spilled across the cushions. We sat in silence. He played with my fingers, and I stole a look at him. Worry lines had appeared on his forehead, and his blue eyes — remarkable for their ability to reveal his innermost thoughts — had faded to a dull gray.

"I'm sorry," he whispered, frowning.

Our evening had turned to dust and blown away, but I reminded myself that although I was disappointed, what about Michael? He was on the verge of asking the big question, and he'd been thwarted by the appearance of a sibling who drove him round the bend, but to whom he couldn't say no. He was too kindhearted for that. I put my hand on his cheek, leaned close, and whispered, "It's only for one night."

* * *

The rustling of plastic shopping bags at three o'clock in the morning has to be one of the worst forms of torture ever invented. The darkness seemed to amplify the sound as it made its way up the stairs. At last, Pammy switched on a lamp, and the two-inch gap under our door allowed the light to pour in. My tightly-squeezed-shut eyelids were no defense. I sighed and got up.

"Julia," Michael said, reaching for me.

"Hot cocoa," I replied. "You stay, I'll bring you a mug."

I paused for a moment on the landing, adjusting my long T-shirt. Below, I couldn't see a bare spot of floor. Had Pammy's bags started to procreate?

"Oh," she said, looking up at me. She still wore her short skirt and T-shirt, and the dark circles under her eyes were magnified against her pale skin. "You couldn't sleep, either?"

"No," I said, and took three calming breaths before I could continue. "I thought I'd make cocoa. Would you like some?"

"Lovely."

I picked my way to the kitchen and stayed there as I stared at the pan of milk, willing it to defy the laws of nature and come to a simmer quicker than it should, so that I could get back upstairs. Behind me, the bag search finally ceased.

As I stirred in the chocolate and sugar, I said, "Breakups are difficult, I know, Pammy, but I'm sure you realize now — or you will soon — that this fellow probably never had any intention of divorcing his wife. He was playing you."

"I'm never going to trust another man again for as long as I live," she vowed, making her way to the kitchen table. "He said he loved me. He said he was going to buy me a ring. And think of his wife. He lied to her, too."

"You're well shot of him, I'd say."

Pammy collapsed in a chair and watched as I poured up the cocoa into three mugs. "Is Michael coming down?" she asked.

"No, and I can't stay. I hope you don't mind, but I have to work tomorrow. Here, you drink this and go to sleep. All right? Tomorrow, you know. Tomorrow things will look better."

I left her sitting in the kitchen, her feet drawn up on the chair and her chin resting on her knees as she gazed at the steam rising from her mug.

Michael had gone back to sleep. I left his cocoa on the dresser and sat on the floor at the open window, waiting for the dawn chorus to begin.

CHAPTER 3

"Let me help you carry your things to the car," Michael said to Pammy after breakfast. "I'm on my way now. I've got a meeting with Rupert this morning to go over a few things."

An appointment he'd made ten minutes ago in the loo with the door closed, probably begging Rupert to work on his day off. But I couldn't blame Michael for wanting to get away. I was already dressed for work — pencil skirt, white blouse, thin cardigan — and had made an excuse to leave for the TIC straight after breakfast, even though we don't open until noon on Sundays.

"No, I'll be all right, you two go on." Pammy walked away from her breakfast dishes and sank onto the sofa with her second mug of tea. "I'll have a shower and then I've only got to sort through a few of my things here. I left in such a rush yesterday. I felt it was better that way. I know when I'm not wanted."

Michael swallowed. "You've got somewhere to go?"

"I'm going to ring Amy. You remember Amy, Michael? She and Roz have a flat together in Leicester. You remember Roz? I'll give them a ring. Don't worry about me."

"Well, then," I said in my perky tourist manager voice. "Good luck, Pammy. I know things will work out. You'll meet the right fellow, you really will. It's only, this wasn't the one." Michael and I walked backward out the door until we stood on the pavement in the sunshine looking in at Pammy, still on the sofa. "So, there you are then. Let us know how things work out, won't you? And just pull the door closed when you leave."

* * *

At the TIC, I locked the door behind me and switched on the kettle. As I waited for it to come to a boil, my mind filled with an image of plastic shopping bags strewn across the floor of the cottage and Pammy with her legs stretched out on the sofa, phone in one hand and tea in the other. The image disturbed me greatly.

Having nothing that desperately needed doing, I filled my morning with tidying our wall of leaflets and cleaning out the tiny fridge in our work area behind the counter. I ended up washing the floor on my hands and knees.

At last noon arrived. I unlocked the door, turned the sign to *Open*, and pinned my nametag on just as the bell above the door jangled. I began the afternoon with three women — Finnish ramblers spending the summer on the coast nearby and looking for the longest treks about the estate. I sent them off with maps, as well as brochures about our Wednesday farmers market and our well-regarded Smeaton's Summer Supper, now in its third year. A family of four took their place.

The woman wore shorts and hiking boots with a shirt thrown over a tank top and her blond hair pulled back in a ponytail. The man, who had a headful of black hair that curled round his ears and his face, carried a beaten leather satchel, with a fishing rod sticking out like an antenna. The boy, about twelve, and the girl, several years younger, looked smaller versions of the adults. They both had rucksacks slung on their backs.

"Good afternoon," I said, reaching for a map.

"Thanks, but we have one already," the woman said, waving a crumpled specimen. "We were here last weekend, too. You were all quite busy and so we found what we needed and slipped out."

Nothing made me happier as the TIC manager than to see repeat visitors. "Well, we're delighted you've chosen the Fotheringill estate again. As you already know, we've loads to offer. It would take you a summer full of Sundays, and you still wouldn't be tired of us."

"Sundays are family days," the girl said. "That's the rule."

The woman laid her hands on the girl's shoulders and laughed. "Not only a rule, but also we actually enjoy it. And as we rarely see Dad during the week, we plan our weekends carefully, don't we? This one here" — she nodded to the man — "wanted to go south to Margate."

"But we took a vote," the girl said, "and Dad lost."

"Majority rules," the boy said.

"And I know when to give in," Dad said, giving his wife a quick smile, which she returned.

"We thought we'd stop on our way through the village and tell you what a grand day we had last Sunday." The woman smiled at the children. "A picnic by the abbey ruins, and after that a fine nature lesson from a fellow who lives near there. He was ever so helpful, wasn't he?"

The children nodded. The girl drew out a colored-pencil drawing from a pocket of her rucksack and held it up. "He showed me a red squirrel, so I drew this picture for him."

"He told me he'd seen a silver-studded blue," the boy said. At my blank look, he added, "It's a butterfly. They're quite rare. He took Dad off and showed him the best bends in the river for fish — bream and roach, isn't that right?"

As the family praised this fellow, it came to me we should have a person of the month on the estate — calling out a resident who went above and beyond in order to share the village and countryside with visitors. As a prize, we could offer the winner a hamper full of Suffolk ham and cheese and a cake from Nuala and perhaps a voucher for dinner at the Stoat and

Hare. Fantastic publicity. I made a mental note to contact the *Bury Free Press* and the *Sudbury Mercury* — the papers in our two closest towns. I was sure they'd want to cover the story.

I had learned from Michael how to think big about promoting the estate. I'm usually more of a detail person, but once I caught on, I had trouble slowing myself down, and had added several events and programs to the estate's calendar that caught on. I would need to explain this latest idea to Linus before plunging in. He would love it, of course, but he wasn't that keen on my tearing off in new directions with no advance notice. I wondered what we could call this new program.

"Who was this fellow that was so helpful?" I asked, thinking we might have our first candidate for the commendation.

"Bob," the little girl said.

"Bob," the boy echoed.

The parents nodded. "Bob."

Bob? I'd need a bit more than that to award the prize. "Do you remember his second name?"

They looked at each other quizzically until the dad said, "I don't think he told us."

Bob who lives somewhere out by the abbey ruins. I'd look into it. There were a couple of farms out that way and a hamlet, Wickham Parva. which consisted of a handful of cottages and a few pensioners. Or did he work on a farm? Still, shouldn't be too difficult to suss him out.

"A young man, was he?" I asked.

"No, not too young," Mum said. "He looked a bit worn, you know. As if he might've lived rough for a while." She turned to her family. "Right, you lot, perhaps we'll take a look at the churchyard today. He mentioned it, do you remember? Good wildlife habitat."

This Bob knew his stuff when he spoke of the churchyard. Irish yews grown into enormous dark forms provided cover for birds, and thick boundary hedges offered food. Easy spotting for song thrush, bullfinch, wren. Little owls — yes, we've got them, too. The grass was left uncut until late summer, encouraging wildflowers for bees and butterflies.

Apparently, a good colony of early purple orchids grew near one of the seventeenth-century gravestones, which were themselves home for endangered lichen. And outside the far gate, a pond full of frogs. A new leaflet began to write itself in my head — *Life in the Churchyard*. I'd make a few notes later.

"Could we have our picnic there?" the girl asked.

"Hang on, what about my fish?" Dad protested. "We can do the churchyard another time."

They readjusted their packs and looked ready to leave. "Have you signed up for the Fotheringill e-newsletter?" I gestured toward a notepad on the counter. Launched two months' previous, we had only fifty-three subscribers as yet, and most of those from the estate, but I had set myself a goal of two thousand by the end of summer. I was beginning to think I'd been a bit too ambitious. "You may see Bob's name in there soon," I said. "He's in the running for our monthly commendation called the OFE — the Order of the Fotheringill Estate. It's a new program."

"Well, thanks, but—" Dad began.

"We promise not to sell our mailing list," I hurried on. "And the newsletter will let you know of special events you might like to come back for."

"I'll write it down," the girl offered.

"Go on, then," Mum said. "But be firm, so the nice lady can read it."

I took the girl over and presented her with a pen, just as the bell jingled and Willow arrived, followed like a mama duck by seven Girl Guides and their leader. Low-level chaos ensued as the space became a swarming mass of humanity — it didn't take many bodies for that to happen. At last, the TIC emptied, but only after Willow made sure no child got away without several of her activity books in hand.

* * *

Willow had started at the TIC as an intern, and, even though she taught at the local primary school, continued to help out when she could. With Vesta away on her weekend honeymoon, I appreciated the backup.

More visitors arrived and we got busy. It wasn't until late afternoon that we had a chance to catch up, sitting behind the counter in our work area.

"Awfully lucky we have a school half-day Thursday," Willow told me. "I'm going to scout out the best location for our watercolor challenge, Brushes Up for St. Swithun's! I've sorted the categories into under-twelves, teens, adults, and superadults, and the prizes will be awarded on his festival day. Wasn't it incredibly generous of Nuala to offer to bake a cake depicting the church? She can make the most wonderfully amazing creations."

Good old St. Swithun. He was one of those fellows with a story you don't mind telling the little ones, and his tale, as so much else in Britain, was tied to the weather. If it rained on St. Swithun's Day, July 15, forty days of rain would follow. If sun, forty days of sun. Fingers crossed.

Just before five o'clock, Willow straightened the counter and readied to leave.

"Now, Julia," she said to me in her teacher voice, "I'll see you later in the week. Meanwhile, you have a lovely evening and day off tomorrow. I know how much you look forward to it."

True. As much as I enjoyed being manager of the TIC, I blocked off the hours between five o'clock closing on Sunday and opening Tuesday morning to do absolutely nothing. I'd lie in bed Monday morning as Michael trekked off to a meeting or whatever film location they had. I might spend the day reading, sitting out in the back garden, or choose to go up to Bury Saint Edmunds for a spot of shopping or off to Cambridge to visit Beryl or a friend. On my day off, my life was my own.

"Thanks, Willow. Cheers."

I locked the door behind her, went back to our work area, and switched on the kettle. I rummaged in the biscuit tin, coming up with the last two in a packet of malted milks before ringing my sister.

She answered with, "Took you long enough. Well, so?"

"There was a bit of a problem," I replied.

My older sister, Bianca Broom, lived faraway in St. Ives, Cornwall. She was married with four adorable children, aged from twelve down to — what was Estella now, eighteen months? But no matter how far away or how busy her world, Bee kept her finger on the pulse of my life. Naturally, in the days leading up to Vesta and Akash's wedding, she'd been able to winkle out of me my belief that Michael was on the precipice of proposing. She expected news the second it happened.

"He didn't ask?" Her voice rose, sharp and high, and then dropped to a muffled tone. "No, Enid, it's all right. I'm talking with Auntie Jools. Yes, of course, you may — here she is."

Therein followed a brief conversation with my nine-year-old niece about her desperate need for a cat and canvassing support for an appeal to her father. Only after I had promised to put in a good word did she hand the phone back to her mother.

"Michael's sister has come to visit," I said. "Pammy."

"The one with the string of breakups?" Bee asked.

"Yes. She stayed last night. It put everything else on hold, you might say. But she should've left by now."

"Then what are you doing still at the TIC?"

How does she do that? "Work," I said. "I had a few things to catch up on."

"Is that so?" Bee asked, heavy with sarcasm.

"Look, I only wanted to let you know what happened. Or didn't happen. And I will ring as soon as."

I had to raise my voice toward the end, what with the shriek of a toddler in the background and Bee shouting, "Emmy, see to your baby sister, please! Yes, tea is coming, Emmet — can you not wait two minutes?"

"Byee!" I called, but I doubt that she heard.

* * *

When I locked the TIC door, I stood for a moment, unable to move. At last, I looked at myself in the glass door. "Just walk home, will you?"

Pammy's car — a ten-year-old dark blue Ford Fiesta with a dented passenger door — had not budged an inch as far as I could tell. I had feared as much, but hadn't been able to admit it even to myself, as if thinking it would make it so. Michael sat in his own car, parked behind her. He'd switched off his engine, and now gripped the steering wheel, his forehead resting against his hands. I stopped ten feet from the cottage, and his head rose.

He saw me and got out. We met me at the door and looked at each other.

"I rang Pickle," he said. "She won't take her, but she wished us luck."

"Miles?" I asked, key in hand.

"Yeah, I rang him, too. He laughed."

We took deep breaths and opened the door, pushing as it caught on the sofa pillows, which had been piled up on the floor.

An empty plastic bag, caught in the breeze, rose up off the stairs and drifted toward the kitchen as if hitching a ride on the trade winds. Clothes were piled on every available surface and a few skimpy dresses hung from the rails of the staircase. Pammy sat cross-legged on our sofa.

"Back already? The time just flies, doesn't it?" she asked brightly, picking up three empty mugs from the floor beside the sofa and taking them to the kitchen sink where they joined the breakfast dishes. "It's terrible the two of you are forced to work on a Sunday. I just don't know how you put up with it."

"Why are you still here?" Michael asked.

"Why?" Pammy echoed. "Amy. It's only that she asked could I hold off a day or so, you see, and I told her I was sure it would be fine, and isn't it cozy here with the three of us?"

"You said one night."

Pammy's lightheartedness faltered at her brother's words. Her brows rising to a peak in the middle of her forehead. "I didn't think you'd mind. It's all right, isn't it? I'll be gone tomorrow. I promise."

Promises, promises.

"Well, let me just see what I can do for our tea." I moved into the kitchen and checked the cupboard. The last tin of tuna had vanished. I opened the fridge and bent down to take stock. Gone was the packet of Parma ham and the remainders of a spinach pasta salad. My tummy rumbled, and when I spotted an almost empty pot of clotted cream, I had half a mind to grab a spoon and finish it off on the spot. I could just do with a burger from the Stoat and Hare. I turned and gave Michael a baleful look.

"Here now," Pammy said, "why don't we all go down the pub?"

"*No!*" Michael and I shouted in chorus. The last thing we needed was for Pammy to find a new local and make herself at home. More than she already had, that is.

"I'll nip down to the shop," Michael offered, "and get something for our meal. Won't be a minute."

I retreated to the bedroom and changed clothes, going back down only when I heard him return. We made short work of an early dinner, a really lovely cassoulet that I would've preferred to spend more time over. Conversation centered on Pammy's worry that Princess Margaret's grandchildren weren't getting their due — this according to the latest exposé in the *Daily Mail*. After Michael and I washed up, I announced I was going to bed.

"But it's still light," Pammy complained.

True. Outside, dusk had barely fallen. Summer evenings are meant to be enjoyed, and here I was about to be held prisoner in my own bedroom. But if lack of a nightlife was a strike against us, perhaps we could bore Pammy out of our home. It was certainly worth a try.

"Well, we both work," I reminded her.

"But aren't you always going on about Monday being your day off?" Pammy countered.

I'm far too free with information about my personal life. Before I could come up with a better excuse, Michael stepped in.

"Julia's helping us with filming along the Little Ouse in Brandon tomorrow," he said, and I was filled with gratitude for his lie.

"Oh, birds, right," Pammy said. "Tramping along in the rain and mud and all that."

"Yes," I said, "birds, mud, insects, the lot." I stood on the bottom step of the stairs as a thought occurred to me. "Listen, Pammy, what about your job? The one at the . . ." As the words left my mouth, I remembered what her latest job had been — receptionist in the office of a builder. A married builder, now her former boyfriend.

Pammy threw back her shoulders and lifted her chin. "I am currently seeking other employment."

"Well, good luck," I said and continued my climb briskly before she asked what vacancies there might be on the Fotheringill estate.

"I'll be right up," Michael said.

Hope blossomed in my heart. They would have a brother-sister talk. Michael would tell her in no uncertain terms to shove off — that there wasn't enough room for three in our tiny cottage.

I made a show of closing our bedroom door to give them privacy, but still the murmur of voices floated up. I shouldn't eavesdrop, so I created my own masking noise, washing out my uniform blouse in the bathroom sink, rummaging in the wardrobe for an empty hanger. I opened the window by our bed and hung my laundry off the latch to dry. My ears picked up a sharp note from Michael and a warbling response from Pammy. I got in the shower.

When I emerged from the bathroom, pulling on my nightshirt, Michael sat on the edge of the bed, elbows resting on his knees. I stood in front of him, and he rested his head on my stomach, his hands wrapped round my thighs.

"Her life is always in bits," he murmured. "I don't know why that is. They've all given up on her, and it makes me feel as if I'm her last hope. But she knows she needs to move on, get hold of herself. She'll be gone tomorrow — the next day at the latest. And then" — his fingertips danced lightly on the back of my knees — "we can pick up where we left off."

He looked up at me, and I saw his eyes change from gray to clear blue, as if clouds had been swept away. I rested my arms on his shoulders and kissed the corner of his mouth where it tugged up into a smile. His hands traveled up my thighs.

"All right if I come up and use the loo?" Pammy shouted from below.

CHAPTER 4

"You're gone today, right?" Michael asked his sister the next morning as he glanced out the window at the lashing rain.

From the sofa, with a mug of tea on the floor beside her, Pammy waved her phone. "Ringing Amy now."

Michael and I were out the door as quick as hares, but we had to huddle in the next doorway, sheltering from the heavy shower. He grabbed my hand.

"I'll see you there?" he asked.

"Yes. I might stop in Bury first for a bit of shopping." It was, after all, my day off. I left him at his car, pulled the hood up on my mackintosh, and walked to the lockup where my own little Fiat stayed. It was off a lane and behind Nuala's Tea Room, and I could see Ms. Darke herself filling the window display with plates and platters piled high with cakes and scones and flapjacks and fruit tarts. Perhaps I'd come back early, sit at the little table in the far back, and hide behind an enormous slice of Nuala's chocolate cake.

* * *

The rain dampened my shopping spirit, although I still managed to spend an inordinate amount of time trying on clothes in H&M. But I bought nothing, apart from a sandwich at the Debenhams café, before heading for Brandon. When I arrived, I parked near the bridge and walked down to the path along the Little Ouse, where Michael, Dad, assistant producer Basil Blandy, and the crew stood under a tarp, busy watching a nestcam of fledgling Cetti's warblers. I joined in, and then helped out with Dad's script for a voiceover. After that, during a dry spell, he and I sat on the open tailgate of his old green Range Rover drinking tea from dented tin camping cups.

"You and Michael enjoy the wedding?" he asked, looking down into his tea. *Enjoy the wedding?* That wasn't a Dad question. I narrowed my eyes at him in suspicion. I didn't think Rupert had a clue what might've been in the works for Michael and me that day, but I could see my stepmum, Beryl, putting him up to it after Bianca blabbed to her.

"Yes, we're quite happy for Vesta and Akash."

"Michael seems a bit off this morning." Dad's gaze darted at me and away, as if considering a connection between the wedding and Michael's mood.

"We've a houseguest."

He put down his tea. "You don't have room for a houseguest."

"Too right." I told him the tale of Pammy, and afterward heaved a great sigh. "Here she is making herself at home in our Pipit Cottage, and we're being squeezed out to the edges."

Rupert got a faraway look in his eyes. "Cuckoos are brood parasites, you know. A cuckoo hatches in another bird's nest and proceeds to eat all the food and grow and grow and often turfs the other birds out."

Yes, that was it — we had a cuckoo in our nest.

"The thing about cuckoos, Jools, is that they aren't always successful, otherwise we'd have no dunnocks or meadow pipits." He swigged the last of his tea. "And they're on the decline, and no one is quite certain why. One idea is that it's their food source. Adult cuckoos need to eat a great deal before they begin migration. A great deal of their diet consists of Hairy caterpillars. They find them in open fields, verges, and hedgerows — and there's the problem. We're losing these habitats,, because of modern farming practices."

That's the trouble with having an ornithologist for a father — everything you say can be turned into a science lesson.

"One of our organic farmers has a new field that he's left for meadow this season," I replied. "And all the edges to his fields are wild and probably full of leaves those hairy caterpillars feed on. You should do some filming out there."

There you are. I am my father's daughter.

"That would be grand," Rupert replied and then came back to the topic at hand. "She'll be gone soon, won't she. Michael's sister?"

"Yes," I said in a rush. "Today. Tomorrow." Next year. My blood ran cold.

* * *

I left them to it and wandered down the rather quiet high street of the Brandon until I came to a window that held a single plate with half a Victoria sponge, dusted with confectioner's sugar. Minty's Tea Room, the sign overhead read, although much of the green lettering had flaked off, leaving behind only the impression of an apostrophe.

I stepped inside and glanced round the space, empty of customers, as I shed my mack. Décor was in short supply here. Faded red, white, and blue plastic bunting stretched above the windows, and on the wall, framed portraits of Queen Victoria and Queen Elizabeth II. I recognized them as paint-by-number, because we'd had the same as children. To my left were two plastic tables with faded cotton cloths, with a further table on the other side of a set of shelves, which were sparsely stocked with specialty teas, both leaf and bag varieties. To my right, the long glass case held three rather lonely-looking offerings — two-thirds of a walnut-and-coffee cake, an uncut loaf of gingerbread, and five fruit scones.

"Hello, good afternoon." A young woman slid off a stool in the corner behind the case and scurried over to me. She wore a black dress, white apron, and a cap that looked like a doily pinned on her head and she clasped a notepad to her chest. "Are you expecting anyone else?" she asked in a hopeful voice.

"No, I'm alone," I said.

"Oh well, then, sit where you like, and I'll come to you."

I took the table behind the shelves and asked for a slice of gingerbread and tea.

When both arrived, the waitress retired to her stool and I stuck in, finding the fare to be surprisingly good.

Another customer entered, a man who walked straight through the shop, past me, and stopped short only when he arrived at the back wall lined with baking supplies. He had well-cut, thick, salt-and-pepper hair, wiry eyebrows, one of those chiseled faces, and a dark Burberry trench coat with what looked like a tailored suit beneath. He glanced round, ignoring me, and abruptly pivoted, running into the young woman, who had crept up behind him with her notepad.

She gasped and jumped back. "Hello, good afternoon. One?" Her nose twitched.

"Do I look like two?" he asked sharply.

"No, sir, you don't. Please, sit where you like and I'll come to you."

He chose the table just the other side of the shelves from me, trying out and rejecting three plastic chairs as if he were Goldilocks, before finally settling in the fourth, which must've been just right. The young woman edged up to him.

"Now sir," she said. "What would you like?"

"Do you have any plain scones?"

The woman threw a look over her shoulder at the glass case as if another plate might've sneaked in while she was busy elsewhere.

"No, sir. But we have fruit scones."

"Fresh?" She nodded rapidly, setting her doily cap to wobbling. "Right," he said. "Fruit scone. Tea. I want your own blend, and I don't want bags."

"Yes, sir. That is, no, sir. Thank you."

Off she scampered. I peered through the shelves at the fellow's back as he sat motionless, hands folded on the table. *I know your type. Nothing's ever right for you, is it?* Behind the counter, dishes clattered and the water steamer hissed, followed by a familiar mechanical humming.

"Don't use the microwave!" the man shouted.

A small shriek, and a dish crashed to the floor. "Yes, sir. Sorry, sir. Won't be a moment."

When the woman brought out the tray, I could hear the rattle of crockery, and I hoped she wouldn't drop the whole thing.

"Would you like butter, sir?"

"Is it real butter?"

A pause, and then, in a hopeful voice, "It's buttery spread."

"If it isn't real butter, I don't want it. I'll have strawberry jam."

I would've told him where he could put his jam, but the young woman said nothing, only fetched a small pot and beat a hasty retreat after she'd delivered it. I finished, gathered my things, and approached the counter. As I paid, I announced, "I so enjoyed my tea and gingerbread. Are you the baker?"

The woman's eyes lit up. "Yes, I am. That's very kind of you, ma'am."

"You know, I believe I'll take one of your fruit scones away with me — they're my favorite." I made a show of drawing a business card out of my bag. "I'm the manager of the Tourist Information Center in Smeaton-under-Lyme. We're just the other side of Bury on the Fotheringill estate. You've a lovely spot here, and I want you to know I will be recommending Minty's to any of our visitors coming up your way."

"Oh, thank you, ma'am," the young woman gushed.

"I'm happy to do it, because, you see, I understand that a little thoughtfulness goes a long way." I gave the fellow a look out of the corner of my eye as I whirled round and walked out.

* * *

Rupert and Michael had schedules to hash out, including a last-minute opportunity to appear at the Whitby Regatta in August, and so I headed home, wishing I could delay my arrival as long as possible. But before I was entirely prepared, I'd left my car in the lockup, and I was walking toward the cottage.

So, I put my head in Three Bags Full and chatted with Willow's aunt, Lottie Finch. Lottie and I had tossed about the idea of an autumn crafts market, and, in desperation at the thought of what might wait for me at the cottage, I decided now would be the time to talk about it. After that, I bought toothpaste at the chemist and then, ignoring the paradox, stopped at Sugar for My Honey, where I bought a quarter of handmade rhubarb-and-custard boiled sweets. After that, with no more diversions to hand, I marched up to the door of Pipit Cottage, steeled myself, and went in.

"Oh now here you are," Pammy said from the sofa. "Dreadful, Julia, that you were dragged off to work today." I noticed her clothes had migrated back into bags — could this be a start of packing up?

She set an empty mug on the coffee table next to an empty plate, and I picked them up, made my way to the kitchen, and saw a mountain of dishes in the sink.

"Did you not want to go out today, Pammy, take a walk?"

"Nah, it was tipping out there, didn't you notice? And also, I don't have a key to get back in."

Oh God, stepped in that one, didn't I? *There'll be no spare key for you, that's for certain.* "Yes, it was dreadful. I think it's only just let up." I made a show of looking out the window as the cottage door opened and Michael walked in. With the light behind him, his face was in shadow, but there was something about his stance.

"There's the boy home," Pammy announced.

"Cup of tea, anyone?" I asked. "I could certainly use one."

"There's no milk," Pammy replied.

"There's no milk?" Michael asked Pammy, quiet and intense. "There's no milk?" he repeated, his voice rising to fill the room. "Well, I'll tell you what you can do about that. *You can get your arse off that sofa and down to the bloody shop and buy a bloody pint of it!*"

He stomped up the stairs as Pammy's jaw dropped.

"What got your knickers in a twist?" she shouted as her brother slammed the bedroom door. "Little birdies took against you, did they?"

She snatched a plastic bag and turned it out, followed by another and another as she scattered clothes and muttered about the trials and tribulations of having a bossy brother. She found her purse and shook out a few coins onto the coffee table. Forty pence. Pammy glared at the money.

I reached into my own bag for my purse, pulled out two twenty-pound notes, and handed them over. "Here," I said. "And while you're there, find us something for dinner, all right?"

"Yeah," Pammy said glumly. "I don't know what he's on about."

Don't you? "Just a long day, I'm sure," I said.

Pammy left and I went upstairs. Michael stood at the window, his hands stuffed in his trouser pockets, gazing down at the wet, drooping foliage in the back garden. He turned when he heard me. "I'm sorry." He shook his head. "I seem to be saying that a lot lately."

I went over and slipped my arms around his waist, and he buried his face in my neck.

"Is it Pammy?" I asked. "Because, you know she'll be gone soon. Tomorrow. Or the next day."

"Not Pammy. At least, not entirely." He rubbed my back absentmindedly. "It's what Rupert wants — a new segment."

"Not the puffins? Does he want that fellow from the Shetland Islands to host it?"

"No, not puffins. Twitchers. And he wants Gavin Lecky."

CHAPTER 5

That explained Michael's black mood. On top of the tension with Pammy underfoot, now he'd have to work with Gavin Lecky. Michael had taken against Gavin from the start, which I chalked up to the clash of opposing personalities. That, and the one-night stand — actually one-afternoon stand — Gavin and I had had just after I'd signed my divorce papers a few years back. It was an accidental meeting. I'd gone up to Marshy End, the Lanchester family cottage where Dad filmed for *A Bird in the Hand,* and Gavin had come looking for Rupert in his never-ending quest to get a twitcher segment on the program. But that afternoon had been ages before I'd ever laid eyes on Michael. Intellectually, he knew there was nothing to worry about, but when did intellect ever win out over emotion?

No, what really got up Michael's nose was that Gavin could be a bit shiftless — unable to keep a job, a wife, or a girlfriend. Tough life being a twitcher. Gavin's raison d'être remained laying eyes on the rarest birds he could, and he would drop everything to do so. That made it difficult to keep a job. Once, he had walked out of a motorbike shop where he'd started only the day before when word came that a blue rock thrush, a bird seen once a decade in the British Isles, had been spotted in Stow-on-the-Wold.

We kept off the subject of Gavin the rest of the evening, and brother and sister acted as if they'd never said a cross word to each other. Pammy had shopped well — stuffed pasta shells and a salad. She'd even remembered bread for our breakfast toast and had found a cheap but good bottle of wine, something for which I was grateful as she spent most of the meal updating us on Princesses Beatrice and Eugenie's latest Twitter flameouts.

* * *

By Wednesday morning, I was becoming inured to Pammy's presence, seated on her sofa throne and surrounded by her adoring plastic-bag subjects — and that frightened me.

"Are you not having a cup of tea?" she asked as I stood at the door, ready to leave.

Tuesday had passed without note. Michael and I had been out the door before Pammy was fully awake. If we kept this up — arriving later, departing earlier — there would come a time we'd meet ourselves coming and going. Pammy had started to speak of "end of the week at the latest, really and truly" in regards to Amy and the phantom flat in Leicester, and that's what I repeated to Bee when she sent the text *Have you got rid of her?*

Vesta, fresh from her weekend honeymoon, had asked her own not-very-subtle questions about Michael and me. Although I had tried to sidestep the issue of the cuckoo in our nest, I knew that wouldn't fool her. Vesta and my sister were two of a kind. They were always able to glean more from a conversation than I thought I'd offered.

Now, although gasping for a cup of tea, I snatched at the first lie I could. "Wednesday is the farmers market on the green," I said, slipping out the cottage door. "I like to check on things before the TIC opens."

I texted Vesta to tell her where I would be and left opening to her. I headed to the green, breathing the fresh air of freedom. I arrived just as the opening bell rang.

A warm glow of pride filled me on Wednesdays. The farmers market, now in its second year, had been my idea, and popular from the start. Although I usually shopped the market midday, morning was a lovely time, because everything looked so fresh and pristine as the farmers put the finishing touches on their displays. These days, the market practically ran itself, and a committee of vendors kept an eye on things. They checked in with me only as needed.

As I walked through, the calls began.

"Julia! Could we get flooring for the stalls? The mud's sucking my feet down."

"Julia! It was chucking last Wednesday and I've another leak in the tarpaulin."

"Julia! What's become of the food writer you said would review us?"

But the committee wasn't working as well as we'd hoped, leading Linus and me to realize it was time to appoint an actual market manager.

I tossed off my answers, making notes in my phone as I went. "Right," "Got it," and "Would you put that in an email, Rog?" Meanwhile, I followed my nose to the stall for Solly's Sausages, where the grill was already hot.

"Bacon roll, please."

There now, that was more like it. I perused the stalls with my mouth full of greasy, salty pork, crisp at the edges, and wrapped in fluffy warm bread. When I arrived at Pockett's Organic Fruit & Veg, the sight and fragrance from a table of glistening crimson strawberries stopped me dead.

"Guy," I called. "They're gorgeous."

Guy Pockett, who ran our newest accredited organic farm, looked up from setting out butterhead lettuce in a red-and-green checkerboard arrangement. He wasn't a tall man, but he had a substantial head of tawny hair — short on the sides, it rose on top like a yeast bread, adding several inches to his height. He was every part the greengrocer as he wiped his hands on his apron and grinned. "'Marshmello' that one's called." He held out a bowl of strawberries, and I picked a sample. "They've got a fantastic flavor, but they don't keep long."

"Mmm, I doubt that will be a problem," I replied, wiping a drip of juice from the corner of my mouth. I bought two baskets and glanced round for Cossett's Dairy stall. "I'll need double cream next."

"What about that proposal I sent you?"

Guy had within him a bottomless pit of wild schemes to boost interest in the market, many of them spontaneous and the rest poorly thought-out, such as the ill-fated "Famous Carrots in History" competition and the last-minute "Walk Like a Vegetable" race. Both had ended in disaster and crying children. Although he'd apologized, I was the one who had learned a lesson — Guy's rash actions led nowhere. Although long on inspiration, he fell woefully short on follow-through. As I was a detail-oriented person at heart, this set my teeth on edge.

Since the news had circulated about the prospect of a market manager, Guy had made it clear he was hot to fill the role. Foreseeing impending disaster, Linus and I had chosen to put off the decision.

But a fortnight ago, Guy had come up with an idea that had promise — invite the chefs responsible for Smeaton's Summer Supper in August to put on cookery demonstrations at the market. I decided to walk him through the planning.

"Right," I said. "Look, it's been ages since I've been out to see you. Why don't I pop round and we'll chat about it."

"No, don't. Hang on a tick," he said as an older woman sauntered forward and eyed the table. She had her hair secured under a head scarf, and wore a plaid coat buttoned up to her chin. An empty shopping bag dangling from one arm as she inspected Guy's display.

"A good day to you now, Mrs. Thomason," he said. "I can see you have strawberries on your mind this morning. Here now, what do you say to this?" He held out the sample bowl with a smile and a twinkle in his eye. "There's your afternoon tea sorted."

"Lovely, Guy," she said. "But you promised me early peas this week. Where are they?"

"Next week for sure," Guy responded. "But in the meantime, have you taken a look at these tiny courgettes — flowers still attached, mind you. The fairies left them for us on the doorstep overnight. Toss these in a hot skillet with a knob of butter, and you'll have that man of yours begging for more."

Mrs. Thomason blushed, but laughed. "Oh go on, then, give us a few." She turned to me and said, "He's a bit cheeky, but I don't mind. Guy makes shopping at the market such fun."

Bagging up her purchase and taking her money, Guy said, "Let me come to you, Julia. Saturday all right?"

Saturday we drowned in visitors at the TIC. "First thing Friday morning?"

"Friday," he confirmed, and turned his charms on another customer.

I continued my shopping — asparagus, salad, smoked salmon, eggs, wholemeal bread, and a chicken-and-ham pie for the evening meal. I had paused to admire a bundle of pencil-thin carrots, when I heard a man's voice from two stalls away at Cherie's flower stand.

"You call yourself a florist and you have no hybrid teas?"

"I call myself a flower grower, sir, and I don't do hybrid tea roses, because I find them a bit too fussy and not nearly as beautiful as the old-fashioned shrub roses. That antique pink is quite fragrant."

"Where are the dahlias?" he asked.

That voice — ill-concealed superiority combined with impatience — I knew it from somewhere. Minty's teashop in Brandon! I peeked round the wall of the marquee, but could not see him.

"No dahlias until August," Cherie replied calmly. "I've these June bouquets picked just this morning from the best of what's blooming."

"What's in this one?"

"Cow parsley, tickseed, and the blue comes from cupid's dart."

"Cupid's dart?"

"Yes, it's the one with—"

"I'll take that bunch."

I watched him walk off— Burberry coat flapping behind and holding the massive bouquet as if he were carrying a staff. I crept up to Cherie's stall.

"Not the best way to begin your morning, is it?" I asked.

She shook her head. "And people wonder why I spend so much time with my flowers."

* * *

Michael texted me just before I closed up Wednesday to say he wouldn't be back until past seven. I considered my options — two hours on my own listening to the trials and tribulations of Pippa Middleton, according to a blog called Royal Relatives Reveal or . . . what?

I headed up the high street, skirting quickly past the cottage door, and at the corner, I saw a woman peering up Westbury Road. She wore a garnet-toned tailored suit, and her chestnut hair fell in waves to curls that rested on the shoulders.

"Hello," I said. "Can I help you find something?"

She turned to me, took note of my uniform and nametag, and flashed a brilliant smile. Pert nose, milky skin, and an expert hand at eyeliner that I could only dream of.

"I certainly hope so," she said. "I was sent this way to the chemist. I'm in desperate need of solution for my contact lenses."

I nodded down the road. "Just there on the left."

"Of course," she said and laughed, "right under my nose."

"Is this your first visit to Smeaton?"

"Not my first visit." She reached in her bag and handed over a card. *Deena Downey, Sales, VidMetronics*, followed by a phone number and email address. Along the bottom of the card, the words *Control Your World* shimmered in green.

"VidMetronics," I sounded out the word.

"Our company provides video-sharing software systems that help businesses—" She stopped and laughed. "But not to worry, I'm not trying to make a sale. Suffolk isn't my patch. No, it's your lovely village that's brought me here. I'm on the road constantly. I work out of our office in Stoke-on-Trent, east to Lincolnshire and Norfolk. But I've needed a place for a midweek break that had nothing to do with my clients. Smeaton is perfect. Well, thanks, now for the directions. Perhaps I'll see you again."

We parted and I carried on, considering the allure of the midweek break. Did I need to take Wednesdays off? I laughed aloud at the idea as I reached Nuala's Tea Room, and took note of a dark green Morgan Roadster parked at the curb. It looked as if it had come straight out of a Jeeves and Wooster story.

Nuala, wearing her customary full skirt and ballet slipper shoes with her short, curly black hair sprinkled with gray stood with hands clasped in front of her, smiling at a customer who sat at the table in the corner with his back to me.

"Oh, I do have a young woman in to help me here and at the café at the Hall," she was saying. "Gone are the days when I could run two places all on my own."

"But still, Nuala," the man said, "it's your expertise that keeps the standards high." Although he had his back to me, I could hear the smile in his voice, a warm, friendly, and almost intimate tone.

"Julia!" Nuala exclaimed as she came forward. "I'm delighted you stopped. What will you have now? No chocolate cake until Friday, I'm afraid, but what do you think — rhubarb ginger? A scone?" Nuala gestured toward the next room where the bakery cases held her fare and I glanced that way to see, in pride of place atop the counter, a massive bouquet of cow parsley, tickseed, and cupid's dart.

At that moment Nuala's customer rose and turned round, drawing my attention. There he stood, The Man-Who-Could-Not-Be-Pleased from Minty's on Monday and the flower stand that very morning.

"Oh, hello," he said casually.

Nuala looked from him to me. "Do you two know each other?"

"No," I said.

"I saw you in the tea room in Brandon on Monday," the man said. "In fact, you're the reason I'm here. I heard you mention Smeaton."

All my fault, was it?

"Anthony Brightbill," he said and extended his hand. "Tony."

"Julia Lanchester," I said, shaking his hand and smiling. "Lovely to meet you. Welcome to our village." *And why are you so charming now yet tried the bite the head off that frightened young woman at Minty's?*

"Are you on holiday?" I asked.

"A bit of holiday, a bit of work. A bit of personal business." He smiled at me, a charming, engaging smile. "I'm afraid Nuala has had to put up with me both yesterday and today. I've found a piece of heaven here, as I'm sure you're aware."

"Oh, now, Tony, that's going a bit far." Nuala laughed in a breathless sort of way.

The glass door rattled open and Nuala's laughter petered out as Linus walked in, tucking his bicycle trouser clip into his jacket pocket and smoothing over the flap.

"Good afternoon," he said, taking in the three of us. "Julia, good to see you. Nuala, I stopped for only a moment. Hello." He extended a hand to Brightbill. "Linus Fotheringill, how do you do?"

"Lord Fotheringill, pleased to meet you. Anthony Brightbill. Tony." The men shook — two firm pumps — and I sized them up. Brightbill had a couple of inches on Linus and no facial hair, although Linus's pencil-thin mustache barely counted. Both men dressed well. Both had good manners, except I knew that Linus's good manners were not the exception.

"You're spoilt for choice here at Nuala's," Linus said, "but let me say, I can highly recommend the Battenberg cake. It's certainly my favorite, as Nuala can attest."

"I'll keep that in mind," Brightbill said. "But I've just had one of the best scones I've ever tasted."

"With real butter?" I enquired. He cut his eyes at me.

"Are you staying locally or only passing through?" Linus asked. "If the latter, I do hope you'll keep us in mind for a return visit."

"Oh, I'm already on a return visit. The first of many, I hope," Tony replied, his eyes on Nuala. Two red spots appeared on her cheeks.

Linus's smile faltered. He recovered quickly, and the others took no notice, but it didn't escape me. I studied the threesome in front of me — Brightbill's easy charm, Nuala's red cheeks, and Linus's momentary loss of good cheer — and I understood.

Over the past couple of years, Linus had continually found ways to be in Nuala's presence, whether discussing the café she ran at Hoggin Hall or asking her to stay to dinner after a long workday. Of course, those social occasions were never just the two of them, but usually a jolly group of friends. And therein lay the problem.

I could see that being part of a group had masked Linus's true feelings and his real intentions, which I was certain were on the romantic side. But past affairs of the heart hadn't gone well for him, and, as much as he may care for Nuala, I sensed a great reluctance in him to try again.

Of course, it wasn't any of my business, and so I'd never broached the subject with either of them. Nuala enjoyed Linus's company, I could see that, but she was on the shy side herself. If he wouldn't make a move, I doubted she would make it for him. And now, in waltzes this debonair and appealing Anthony Brightbill "Tony," and I didn't like the way he looked at her. Someone needed to make a move.

"Linus, are you staying?" I asked.

"No, I'm sorry I can't. I've only . . . well, Mr. Brightbill. Tony," Linus corrected himself when Brightbill held up a hand, "I do hope we'll see you again. A good afternoon to you all."

"I, too, should be on my way." Brightbill smiled at Nuala. "Very nice to meet you," he said to me.

"Your motor?" Linus asked, nodding to the Morgan.

The two men left discussing cars. Nuala frowned faintly at Linus's retreating figure, and I arched an eyebrow at Brightbill's back.

"Well," Nuala said weakly, "I'd better start cleaning up. Did you want tea, Julia?"

"No, thanks. I've just realized I left my shopping at the TIC."

My shopping had little to do with wanting to leave — I needed to get out on the pavement and insert myself into the men's conversation to make it clear to Brightbill that Linus and Nuala were . . . well, they were something, and he'd better just keep moving on to the next tea room.

But the men stood at the front of the Roadster in deep conversation. I heard something about "torque" and a "cyclone engine." Fascinating.

I gave them both a wave as I passed. *I'll let you off for now, Mr. Tony Brightbill, but if you continue to loiter in our village, just know I've got my eye on you.*

CHAPTER 6

I stood outside the cottage, juggling my trove from the farmers market as I dipped one hand into my bag and felt round for the key. My hand lit upon a small paper bag, and without thinking I took hold and the object within crumbled. Oh yes, my fruit scone from Minty's on Monday. First sighting of Mr. Anthony Brightbill.

A voice behind me asked, "Here now, can I help?"

"Gavin!"

Gavin Lecky had found his style and stuck with it — cropped black hair, stubbly beard, black leather, and that single earring, a hovering kestrel. He wore it well.

"Hiya, Julia," he said with a smile. Although tough on the outside, I'd seen past Gavin's shell and now when I looked at him, I saw an eager fellow who loved birds, but had no anchor in his life. I felt a wee bit sorry for him.

"So, Gavin, twitchers on the telly," I said by way of congratulations.

He grinned even wider. "Yeah, wore Rupert down at last, didn't I? How's Sedgwick taking it?"

"He'll produce a fantastic segment, you know he will. You won't wind him up, will you?"

"I don't know what you mean." Innocence didn't play well on Gavin — he loved to annoy Michael.

The cottage door opened as Pammy, with one hand on a hip, said, "You know I can hear you talking, why don't you just . . . oh."

Pammy looked at Gavin. She shifted her weight to one leg and dropped her arms to her side, where her fingertips reached past the hem of her skirt. She wore a tight T-shirt sprinkled with sequins that read *Isn't Love Grand?*

Gavin stared at Pammy. His grin warmed, taking on a sultry quality, and with a voice he saved for women, he asked, "Julia, aren't you going to introduce us?"

I did. Gavin cocked his head.

"Sedgwick?"

"Yes," I said. "Pammy is Michael's older sister."

"Barely older," Pammy corrected. "So, Mr. Gavin Lecky, are you a . . . an orthnio . . . ornili . . ."

"I'm not," Gavin said, rescuing her. "I'm self-taught when it comes to birds. I learned everything in the field — out on the tors, perched on bluffs. I nearly died once. Julia can tell you about that."

Yes, nearly died once — in a pig hut.

"Gavin, were you looking for Michael? Because here he is now." I nodded to Michael's Fiat as it pulled up behind Pammy's Fiesta.

Gavin lost a bit of swagger, but held his position on the pavement as Michael slammed his car door. "Lecky?"

Pammy remained in the doorway, paying no attention to her brother. I thought better of inviting Gavin in for tea.

"Sedgwick." Gavin straightened up. "I've some ideas for the segment, and we'll need a meeting about—"

"Yes, we will." Michael kept his voice even and businesslike. "Where are you living these days?"

Gavin colored slightly. "I'll give you my mobile number and we can arrange something," he said, which told me he was probably kipping on a friend's sofa, as he was wont to do.

"Wouldn't—" Pammy began.

"Thanks," Michael said. "We won't keep you."

"Yeah," Gavin replied. "Be seeing you, Julia." He looked at Pammy. "And you."

Pammy giggled. "Bye now, Gavin."

* * *

Thursday held such promise. Time was running out for Pammy. She'd sworn to be gone by the end of the week, and I chose to believe her. Michael and I had made it our mantra — *end of the week, end of the week*. We'd celebrated that morning by spending a few intimate yet ultimately frustrating moments upstairs saying goodbye before Pammy requested permission to enter for her shower. Michael left for work.

Lighthearted, magnanimous, and too early to open the TIC, I opened wide the French doors to a glorious day and refilled the feeders in the back garden. I sat on the terrace with my cup of tea and called out to Pammy my sightings as she kept to the kitchen, huddled over her phone.

"Ah, look at that. Fledgling blue tits. Fluffy messes of blue and yellow. Adorable, aren't they?"

I heard a noncommittal grunt.

"The goldfinch has settled in on the feeder now," I continued. "He's mad about those sunflower seed hearts. He'll be there for a while."

Another grunt.

My tea finished, I returned indoors, made myself ready for the day, and had almost walked out the door before I couldn't take it any longer.

"Any word from Amy?" I kept my voice light, but my heart was in my throat.

"She's fair swamped with work today." Pammy looked up from her phone. "I'll text her later."

"What does she do — her work?"

"Windows."

"Windows," I repeated. "Computers?"

Pammy set her phone on the coffee table. "Shop windows — she decorates them. And does costumes for a local dramatic society. Doesn't get paid much for it, though, and they barely give her a budget. I helped her out last year when they did *The Lion King* — I dressed the entire cast for under fifty quid."

Overwhelmed by the amount of information Pammy offered about her own life, I could only answer, "Well done, I'd say."

Pammy shrugged. "People underestimate charity shops."

* * *

The new leaflet *Life in the Churchyard* needed photos to accompany the text I'd written.

"I can talk Dad out of a few from his vast image library," I said to Vesta as we settled at the table in our work area.

"The church guild might have some you could use," she replied.

"Salmon and cucumber or chicken and stuffing?" I asked, holding up a sandwich packet in each hand. Vesta took the salmon, and I tore opened the other. "They might do. I'll ask. And I'll snap a few myself while I'm there this afternoon. Willow's asked me up to see how it's going — her watercolor competition, you know. Everyone's to paint the same scene, and she wants to show me which one she's chosen. And something about kneelers."

"That's the needlepoint kneeler project." As organist at St. Swithun's, Vesta had a better idea of what went on inside the church than I did. "New kneelers depicting life on the estate. I'm doing one of that enormous old mulberry tree in the garden at the Hall."

"Yes, of course — and Lottie's taken on Suffolk sheep, flax, and spinning. I'll snap a few shots of kneelers, as well, for the next newsletter."

"I see we've reached sixty-one subscribers," Vesta said.

"Time to up our game — I'll go round to each vendor at next week's market and leave sign-up sheets."

* * *

"Good afternoon," I called to three women who sat with needlepoint in their laps as they kept an eye on the church's gift shop, which occupied an alcove in the far corner. The flower guild sold bookmarks with St. Swithun's image, a booklet telling the short history of him and his church in Smeaton-under-Lyme, and various church-related but non-specific tea towels, aprons, and mugs. There was also a secondhand bookshelf, which allowed parishioners to unburden themselves of their old James Patterson paperbacks guilt-free.

I approached and looked over shoulders admiring the women's work and commented on each. "Ah, the Fotheringill coat of arms. English bluebells, lovely. And, there's our Alfie," I said about a stitched profile of our locally famous rook. At last, I asked after Willow.

"Oh, she's around," one of the ladies said. "Gone out for a final look at the view of the church from the other side of the pond before she posts the competition rules."

"Well, I'll walk out and find her, then," I said.

But there was no need, for at that moment one of the huge oak doors creaked opened to reveal Willow, both hands pushing on it before she stumbled in and, with an anguished cry, collapsed.

"Willow!"

I reached her first, the other women not far behind. Whether she'd merely swooned or completely fainted, she recovered enough to push herself upright, panting, her face flushed and her eyes wild. She'd lost a sandal just as she had entered, and her feet were muddy and grass-stained — as were the knees of her lilac leggings. I grabbed hold of her shoulders to steady her.

"Willow, what is it?" I asked.

"Give her air, girls," one of the women ordered her companions, holding an arm out to bar their way. "Are you sick, dear? Annie, bring the bin over for her."

"No," Willow whispered. "It isn't me — it's . . ." she grabbed hold of my forearm and squeezed, pointing to the opposite wall of the church.

My head whipped round in the direction she indicated, and I thought about what lay outside the wall.

"The churchyard? You've seen something in the churchyard?" Had a funeral been scheduled and she'd been spooked by the casket?

Willow shook her head frantically. "The pond."

This was as frustrating as a game of charades, but Willow didn't seem to be able to say more than two words at a time. I took a moment to smooth the shift she wore, a busy floral print, and only then did I see the dark, rusty smear on her chest, accompanied by more mud.

"Willow, you're hurt!"

"No," she gasped. "Not me — *him*."

"You've seen someone at the pond. Is he hurt?"

"I didn't see him." She grasped my wrist with a muddy hand. "I wasn't looking down, and then I . . . fell over him." With an anguished look at the dark red smear on her chest, she added, "He didn't move. And then I noticed . . . the *flies*."

The women leaned in closer to hear. I glanced over my shoulder to see that Annie had indeed brought the rubbish bin over, just in case.

I whispered, "You mean, he's dead?"

"Quite."

CHAPTER 7

"Ms. Wynn-Finch, you'd better show us the way."

I had phoned the police before anyone moved, and reached Detective Inspector Tess Callow at the Sudbury constabulary. When I gave her the scant information I had, she instructed us to stay in the church until they arrived. One of the ladies had posted herself at the door while the rest of us fell back to the shop alcove, where Willow sank onto a chair and Annie switched the kettle on. Just as the tea was ready, the lookout reported, "Two Battenberg cars" — she referred to the police cars' yellow-and-blue livery — "and a black Volvo."

Willow took a sip of sugary tea and coughed as DI Callow and Detective Sergeant Natty Glossop trooped in. I had met them before, but was struck again by what a study in contrasts they were. Callow was tall, with muscle but no bulk, her prematurely gray hair short and swept back in a severe manner. Her detached efficiency stood in sharp contrast to her sergeant, who was ginger-haired and quick to smile, although just as quick to drop it in an effort to rein in his enthusiasm. They were accompanied by Moira Flynn, who had been in uniform last time we'd met as a police constable, but had since. been promoted to detective constable.

She wore a dark suit that set off her thick red curls, and led the way for several uniformed PCs.

"All right, Ms. Wynn-Finch," Callow said, "show us what you've found."

The rest of us followed them out the door and round the corner to the other side of the church, and stopped. We stood at the edge of the oldest part of the churchyard with lichen-covered headstones slightly askew and almost illegible. The pond, in a slight depression, lay out the back gate of the churchyard and at the end of a path through tall green grass. With the needlepoint women clustered behind us, Willow told her story of how she'd walked out to take in the view. Her voice trembled, and she stuck close to me, her hand shaking as she indicated the path she'd trod. She'd seen no one else.

"You don't really see the pond from the road," I said, taking Willow's hand, which was cold and clammy. She'd wiped most of the mud off onto her dress. "There's a stand of hazel along the verge. And it's closer to the next field than the church."

"How was it you noticed the body?" Callow asked.

Willow shuddered. "I didn't see him. But there was an odd smell. At first, I thought it was the smell of the pond and the green growth — until I fell over him. And then, the flies rose up. I'd disturbed them, and they swarmed round my head," she said, her voice uneven and low. She swatted the air. What little color she had regained now drained from her face, making her freckles stand out. "Oh dear." She shut her mouth tightly and gave me a pleading look.

"Excuse us."

I rushed Willow to the nearby yew hedge where first she was sick, and then, she began to cry. "Oh, Julia, it was awful. That poor man. Do I have to look again?"

"Certainly not." We walked back to the police. "Willow needs to sit down. I'll take you out to the pond," I said. Callow stared at me for a moment, followed by a single nod.

The needlepoint ladies escorted Willow back into the church, and the rest of us walked the path, the police ahead of me, fanning out from left to right, eyes to the ground as they went, swatting at the grass with batons, looking for God knows what.

"I think she was on the far side," I told them as they came up to the water, and we circled round, giving the pond's edge a wide berth. It wasn't an enormous expanse of water — perhaps thirty feet across and a bit wider, irregularly shaped and with occasional clumps of willow and red-twig dogwood. Moorhens nested on the tiny islet in the middle.

"Why was she out here?" Callow asked as the uniforms crept closer to the pond.

"We're running a watercolor competition for St. Swithun's Day," I said. "The fifteenth of July. It was Willow's idea. Everyone will have to paint the same view. She'd chosen this one, I think." And it was a lovely view — the pond in the foreground, the wild graveyard nestled up against the medieval church with its tall, square Norman tower. At this time of day, the afternoon light hit the scene perfectly, the cattails rising in clumps along the edge and a mallard paddling along lazily.

"Boss," the sergeant called. Callow joined him near the water. I stayed where I was, but forced myself to look at what they'd found.

A man's body, face down with arms and legs splayed out. Grass and reeds and the brown color of his clothes acted as camouflage. Willow had been admiring the view of the church, so it was no wonder she hadn't noticed a corpse at her feet.

He'd fallen just at the edge of the pond, and his face was in the shallows — more mud than water. His trousers and jacket looked rumpled, and the bottoms of his shoes had holes. Even from my position, a good fifteen feet away, I could see the back of his head was dark and the hair matted.

And yes, now I saw the flies, but I also spotted something out the corner of my eye that Willow might not have seen — a carrion crow flying off. I took a step back and shifted my gaze to the yellow flag iris growing further along.

Callow and Glossop donned blue evidence gloves and bent over the body, doing what they could without disturbing the scene. The uniforms, stock-still in the grass, waited. The DI stood and began to give orders, pointing at the body, sweeping her arms across to take in the field, and nodding toward the churchyard. Blue-and-white police tape appeared from someone's pocket, and soon the entire pond was circled in what looked like bunting for a fête. Callow made two quick phone calls and then motioned her DC over.

"Flynn, drive Ms. Wynn-Finch to Hoggin Hall, and I'll join her there." The DI nodded to me. "And take Ms. Lanchester with you."

* * *

"There now, love, this'll do you good."

Sheila Bugg, housekeeper-cook at Hoggin Hall, set a cup of tea in front of Willow, who stared into the steaming brew as if trying to identify it before murmuring "Thank you" and obediently taking a sip.

We'd been greeted at the door of the Hall by Thorne, the butler, who had taken the call from the DI. He was, as always, impeccably dressed in a dark suit that contrasted well with his white, cotton-ball hair. He'd recently started wearing glasses and their silver rims completed his look. Thorne reported that neither Linus, who was on his way home from a meeting in Diss nor the young master, en route from a day conference in Aberdeen and not expected to return until that evening, had been informed of events as yet.

"Cecil is the 'young master,'" I explained to DC Flynn. Cecil, thirty-something years old, carried the official title of Lord Palgrave, although he preferred to be called Mr. Fotheringill in estate business. But to Thorne, he would always be a child of the Hall.

Sheila had been ready for us in the kitchen with tea, and we — Flynn, Willow, and I — had settled at the table and awaited the arrival of DI Callow. It didn't seem the time for small talk, so none of us spoke, apart from me congratulating Moira on her promotion.

When Callow arrived, she declined tea and began her interview standing over us until I nudged an empty chair with my foot. Its squeak caught her attention, and she took a seat and continued. The DI went over Willow's story again, her questions prodding here and there. A few queries came my way. Who frequented the area? How busy was the path? When was the last time we were out there?

Willow responded clearly, taking a swig of her tea after each answer. She explained she'd wanted to take a final look at her choice for the watercolor competition, and that it had been a week since she'd stood on the same spot. "That poor man," she murmured.

The DI reported that no identification had been found on the body. Did we know of anyone locally who had been reported missing? We shook our heads.

"I'll need to talk with the vicar," Callow said.

"Reverend Eccles is away," Sheila told her. "He and his wife left after the wedding on Saturday for a fishing holiday in the Highlands."

"I can get you the verger," I offered. "She'll be able to get in touch with him."

Callow wrapped up the session by saying, "When we get the body cleaned up, Ms. Wynn-Finch, we'll need you and Ms. Lanchester to take a look" — Willow's cup clattered into its saucer, and Callow caught herself. "At a photo," she added. "We're finished for the present."

The housekeeper, who had added the occasional commiserative tongue click during the proceedings, set another pot of tea on the table and took away the first. "There now," she said, "that's fresh. Help yourself." She nodded to the plate of shortbread that no one had touched, although I'd been giving it the eye.

As Sheila put an arm round Willow and led her out of the kitchen, Callow said, "Ms. Wynn-Finch, we'll need your clothes and your shoes. Mrs. Bugg, DC Flynn will go with the two of you and provide a bag."

"Yes, of course," Sheila said, and turned to Willow. "You can have a bath here. I'll ring Lottie and explain."

As Flynn followed them out and the door swung closed, Willow looked up at the housekeeper and said, "Flies, Sheila. There were flies — so many of them, buzzing . . ."

After they'd gone, I slumped in my chair, put my elbows on the table and dropped my chin into my hand. DI Callow stood at the door as if listening for approaching footsteps, and, hearing none, she unbuttoned her jacket and sat. She picked up the teapot and nodded to my empty cup. I pushed it across the table toward her and sighed deeply.

"Do you need to get back?" she asked as she poured.

"No, Vesta is all right. I texted her. I didn't tell her why, just said I was delayed."

"So, the newlyweds have returned. How was the wedding?"

As I poured milk into my tea, I thought how Detective Inspector Callow had taught me you could never judge a book by its cover, or a person by her manner while on the job. Since meeting her under unpleasant circumstances a year ago the previous autumn, we'd become friends. Tess's girlfriend worked in London and was home only on weekends, and Michael was often in another part of the country with Dad during the week, and so the DI and I would occasionally knock about together, sometimes meeting for a drink and a meal at The Den, a roadside pub in Foxearth — a place where she felt comfortable being a civilian.

"The wedding was lovely," I replied, biting off half a shortbread finger.

"It's only that I thought you might text me with news," she replied, snapping her shortbread in two.

My sister, Vesta, Beryl, and now Tess. I kept my secret quite poorly, it seemed — the idea that Michael and I might have an announcement of our own. But the warm and exciting anticipation of sharing big news had faded, and it felt as if what I had expected to happen had been five years ago, not five days. An unpleasant thought had crept its way into my brain. Perhaps I'd invented the entire thing. Perhaps Michael hadn't intended to propose at all, but had wanted to talk about — I don't know, buying new curtains.

"Nothing to text you about," I confessed. Knowing it was no good to lie to the police, I told the story of Pammy. "But really, she's to be gone the end of the week."

"When I was growing up," Tess said, "we had an uncle — my mother's brother — who came for a week and stayed for three years. That made eight of us in a two-up, two-down. He had to kip on the sofa. Turned out his wife had run off with the dustman and taken all their savings. Mum felt sorry for him."

Here was a rare glimpse into Tess Callow the girl, and I was torn between being fascinated and seized with fear that Pammy might try the same trick. "How many brothers and sisters did you have?"

"Too many."

Her phone rang and she stood to answer, buttoning her jacket as she did so. After only a few words, she ended the call.

"FME," she said, and I blinked. "Forensic medical examiner. We've got one booked. Body is on its way to her."

"Do you know how he died? And when, because it didn't look . . . you know, fresh." Poor Willow.

"I'd say he'd been there a good few days, but we won't know for certain until — well, here it is Thursday. Might be Monday before we have any results."

"That Inspector Francesca would have the report by the end of today."

Tess arched an eyebrow. "We are not a television program — and neither do we have the budget of one."

Police detective shows on the telly — it was a bit of a joke between us, although I thought Tess had a secret crush on this Inspector Francesca, because she never missed an episode.

"We'll have to wait for manner of death as well," she said. "The head injury was obvious, although that had been exacerbated by—"

"Yes, fine, thanks — I get the picture." I waved my hand to dispel the words. "Could he have done that himself? Fallen and hit his head?"

"On what?" Tess asked. "And it would have to be quite a fall to receive such an injury. No, not an accident."

"He was murdered?" I whispered. "There, outside the churchyard? Why?"

"Who was he?" she countered. "What was he doing out there? Was he local, and if not, what brought him to the estate? We've a great many questions to answer. Have you noticed many new people in the village lately?"

"More than last year, not as many as we'd like. Remember, that's my job — luring strangers to the estate. Our visitors."

"Has His Lordship installed CCTV anywhere yet?"

I shook my head. "You know how Linus feels about that. He doesn't want his tenants to feel he's spying on them. Shopkeepers are welcome to install cameras in their own businesses, but I'm not sure any have."

Tess took our cups and saucers to the sink. "I'm returning to the scene. We've recovered footprints in the mud, although they look fresh, and so they're most likely Willow's. The rain on Monday probably washed away anything useful." She looked round the kitchen walls, a subtle tone of maize. "Is this is new paint job?"

Sheila had taken the project upon herself in the autumn. Lovely of the DI to notice, but it only served to remind me that another suspicious death had brought the police back to our village.

CHAPTER 8

Detective Inspector Callow offered to have an officer drive me back to the TIC, but I preferred not to show up in a police car, and so I walked back into the village from Hoggin Hall, taking my old shortcut down to the road. I looked back up toward the church, and could see at least one Battenberg car still parked. I wished I had worn my trainers, as my spike heels sank into the soft verge, but when I reached the low bridge over the brook, the pavement began and I made better time.

Who was this poor dead fellow by our pond? From the state of him, as much as I was willing to take in, it looked as if he might have been down on his luck. Caught in a violent encounter? The thing is, the pond isn't really on the way to anywhere and far enough off the road so that you'd have to be looking to see anyone there. It lay between the church and a field, and on the other side of the field sat a few fine houses that had been built for the fourth earl's in-laws in the late eighteenth century. Now, one house was a pensioners' home and the others were let to families. Perhaps the police were already knocking on their doors.

I paused in front of Nuala's Tea Room at the sight of a dark green Morgan Roadster parked at the curb, and my thoughts shifted from a body at the pond to Mr. Anthony Brightbill, who had apparently set up at Nuala's as his second home. Vesta had said she'd close up, and so I didn't think twice about taking action. I pulled open the door of the tea room so violently that the bell jangled off its hook and fell to the floor with a *clank*.

Two girls sitting at the window table gasped, and Nuala looked in from the room next door that held the bakery cases. Brightbill, occupying the same table as before, had a pencil in hand and a newspaper turned to the crossword. He glanced up, eyebrows raised.

"Sorry," I said in a stage whisper, picking up the bell and standing on tiptoe to reattach it.

"Here, let me."

"No, thank you, Mr. Brightbill, I've got it."

"Please, it's Tony."

I turned, straightening my blouse and tugging on my skirt. He smiled at me — that winning, debonair smile. I smiled back, but said nothing.

"Everything all right, Julia?" Nuala asked.

I inhaled deeply, taking in the scents of sugar and butter and chocolate and spices to clear my head. "Fine, yes. I've only stopped to ask . . . what you've decided to take to the church's cake stall on Saturday." I congratulated myself on my quick thinking. One Saturday afternoon a month, the church had a cake stall with tea, all proceeds going to Conserve Our Choristers. I had absolutely nothing to do with the event, but it made a fine excuse, because everyone knew I was naturally inquisitive about cake.

The girls paid and left and Nuala hovered in the doorway, always looking as if she might rise *en pointe* at any second. "I've a cherry-and-almond traybake and a chocolate sponge with an orange glaze. Next month, I'll do a Victoria sponge with peaches instead of strawberries. Do you think?"

I momentarily lost my irritation at Brightwell's presence as a vision of a peach sponge cake rose before me. "Oh, I'd say it'll do quite well."

"Tony," Nuala said, "we've some fine bakers in the church. You should drop by the cake stall on Saturday."

"Ah, Nuala, it's tempting, but sadly, I'm not able to. Weekends are difficult."

"Linus is on his way back from Diss," I said, apropos of nothing except I wanted Nuala to keep him in mind.

She nodded. "The quarterly meeting for Suffolk Estates Association."

"Of course, *you* would know that," I said, laying a hand on Nuala's arm. "The way you and Linus keep up." *Well, there you are, sir — Nuala and Linus closer than you thought.* My work here was done. "So good to see you again, Mr. Brightbill."

"And you." He cut his eyes at Nuala and back to me. "See you next time."

* * *

Muttering curses on Anthony Brightbill's head, I clattered down the pavement, seeing nothing but red and walking straight past our cottage and all the way to Three Bags Full, before I remembered I didn't need to return to the TIC. I stopped and peered in Lottie's wool-shop window now closed, as it was gone six o'clock. But the shop brought me up short, reminding me of the afternoon's tragedy. Perhaps Lottie had gone out to the Hall to fetch Willow. I'd check on her tomorrow to make sure she'd recovered from her ordeal.

I turned and went back to the cottage, walking straight past both Pammy's Fiesta and Michael's Fiat. The gang's all here, I thought bitterly. The door of Pipit Cottage opened just as I got to it, and Michael started out.

"Hiya," I said.

"Where's Pammy?"

I gasped. "Is she gone?"

"No. At least, not for good." He went back in, and I followed. Pammy's loyal subjects, the plastic bags, had been shoved to the side, and so there was at least a clear path to walk. Two drained mugs on the coffee table along with the wrapper from a packet of custard creams as well as a sink full of dirty dishes stood as evidence of her presence in the not-too-distant past.

"I don't suppose she could be out for a walk?" I asked.

"Pammy doesn't like the outdoors, haven't you noticed?" Michael sighed, took out his phone, and sent a text. "I should be glad, but it's odd."

"Yeah," I said, dropping my bag on the floor along with my spirits. Shouldn't we be happy to be alone?

Michael tossed his phone on the sofa and came to me. "You shouldn't have to put up with my family business," he said as he kneaded my upper arms, rubbing away the tension I hadn't noticed was there.

"No, I should put up with it, because she's . . . she's your sister and I . . . should."

I looked down at the floor to avoid his gaze, but he put a finger under my chin and tilted my head and I saw a few stars in those deep blue eyes. I met him halfway in a soft, lingering kiss, interrupted by his phone vibrating.

Pammy's reply. *Out for a drink, home soon.*

"*Home?*" My voice tightened.

"A figure of speech. She didn't mean anything by it," Michael said. "Come on, we've a couple of minutes to ourselves. Let's sit in the garden. What do you say?"

He poured us wine and we settled on the terrace, chairs shoved together, his arm round me and my hand on his thigh. This was how it had been before Pammy — the two of us chatting about the minutiae of our days. But this day held bigger news. I told him about that poor man Willow had found.

"They've no idea who he is?" Michael asked.

I shook my head. "And Tess wouldn't say for sure before the medical examiner takes a look, but it appears that he was killed with a blow to the back of his head."

"Perhaps an argument with someone that got out of hand."

"Left there for days. And we none of us knew it."

"But it's nothing to do with you," Michael said firmly.

"It certainly isn't," I agreed. "Let the police take care of it."

"Good."

Willow's wan face, spotted with freckles, rose before me. "Except, I hope Willow's all right."

Michael and I grew quiet, enjoying the evening light and each other. I heard a drumming against wood somewhere nearby, and I squinted into the dense growth beyond the back garden wall. Had my peanut feeder finally attracted a great spotted woodpecker?

"Rupert told me today he wants to do a piece on cuckoos," Michael said. "Talk about their decline and what we can do. Said he'd use the old rhyme about the bird."

"*The cuckoo comes in April and sings its song in May*," I recited.

"I need to look for file footage to cover those months."

"*In June it changes tune*," I continued.

"We'll pick it up there and talk about the importance of verges, fields, and their edges. Those hairy caterpillars, you know. Migration."

"*And July it flies away*," I concluded, but then added, "Or so it goes, although fledglings can stay on much longer."

Michael took my hand. "Rupert told me where he'd picked up the idea. Don't worry. She won't stay long."

"I didn't mean anything by it." My face warmed. "It's only—"

"You don't need to apologize. It isn't fair for her to do this, and you've been a saint to put up with her. But it'll all be over now. End of the week."

"It hasn't been so bad." Always easier to say these things when they were nearly finished. "And I'm sorry she's had such a time with boyfriends."

"Finding Pammy on our doorstep last Saturday," Michael said, "well, I blamed her for spoiling things. I wanted the moment to be perfect. But" — he sat up — "why does it have to be perfect? What about now? Here we are, the two of us alone. We don't have to wait." He put our wine glasses on the stone terrace and took my hands.

He was going to do it — propose! My heart fluttered inside my chest like two song thrushes mating. Wait, two doves. Turtledoves. No, too large — like two little wrens beating their tiny wings.

"Julia—"

"Yes, Michael?" I breathed.

Bam, bam, bam!

The sound of the beating on the door bounced off buildings on the high street, echoing throughout the village.

"Wakey, wakey!"

Pammy's voice defied the science of sound by shooting straight up in the air, flying over the terrace of cottages and dropping down into the back garden and onto us like a pail of cold water. *Splash.*

"I know you're home!"

"*Bloody hell!*" Michael shouted. He shot off his chair, dropped my hands, and stomped into the cottage, cursing his way to the front door. I followed, the fluttering of my heart turning to thuds.

"Well, I've been out here for ages," Pammy snapped at her brother when he'd flung open the door and told her to be quiet. "I knocked and knocked, but couldn't raise you. What else was I supposed to do, kip on the doorstep for the night?"

Michael held his breath and his face turned scarlet, so I jumped into the breach.

"Right, well, what took you to the pub, Pammy?" I moved into the kitchen and thought about a meal. By some miracle, I found the remains of the chicken-and-ham pie and a wedge of cheese.

"Your friend came by," she said, settling onto her usual place, slipping off her shoes and stretching out her legs. "But the two of you weren't home yet, and I said I didn't know when I'd see you. So, he invited me for a drink. He's very sweet. It's thee best time I've had in ages."

"What friend?" Michael asked.

The stillness in his voice set off an alarm in my head. I looked up from the fridge.

Pammy grinned. "Gavin — the fellow you're putting on the telly."

Michael gripped the back of a kitchen chair until his knuckles were white. "I don't want you seeing him."

"You what?" Pammy asked with incredulity.

"You heard me. You're not to see him again."

"You're not Dad, you know. You can't tell me what to do — *little brother*."

This had "disaster" written all over it. Gavin couldn't hold onto a girlfriend or a wife for the life of him the way he either dragged them off on twitcher escapades or deserted them at a moment's notice, and Pammy's record was none too clean. But giving her an ultimatum would only make Gavin more appealing. Couldn't Michael see that?

"Look, what he means" — I made my voice silky soft and full of reason — "is that a drink is fine, but you don't want to read anything into it."

"Why?" Pammy asked. "What's wrong with him?"

"Nothing's wrong with Gavin." I heard a choking sound from Michael. "It's only that you're quite vulnerable right now."

Pammy dismissed us as she took up her phone. "I don't know what you're on about. It was only a pint and a plate of chips. He didn't bloody well *propose* to me."

Michael kicked the chair, and I caught it just before it went over.

CHAPTER 9

During the meal, brother and sister reached détente, and he and I were treated to a Pammy-sided discussion about the latest rumor that the Duchess of Cambridge eats a Wimpy burger every day for her tea, a habit she must hide from her children. At last, I wrested the conversation away and filled the remainder of the time with stories from the TIC and the village. I avoided the tale of That Poor Man — with Pammy's penchant for gossip, no telling what she might do with such a bit of news. By the time she retreated to her lair, I had landed on the problem of Nuala's would-be suitor.

"There's a fellow hanging round the tea room," I said. "He's good-looking, suave, about Nuala's age. I believe he's making a move on her, and I don't like it."

"Are you sure he isn't after her cakes?" Michael asked as he cleared the table.

"It's more than her baked goods. He's too friendly, and I don't want him stepping on Linus's toes."

"Ah, Linus and Nuala." The corner of Michael's mouth tugged up into a smile. "Are they or aren't they?"

"See," I said with triumph, "you've noticed, too, haven't you? That he's interested in her."

"Then why hasn't he made his move?" Michael asked. "What's he waiting for?"

"He's shy," I replied. "But I do think he cares about her. And now here's this fellow at the tea room every afternoon this week saying how much he enjoys her scones and acting all cozy."

"Are you sure that's what he's on about?" Michael asked, as if I would ever read something into a situation that wasn't there. "Do you want me to go meet him?"

"He won't be round until next week. He says his weekends are too busy."

Pammy's head shot up from her phone. "He won't see her on weekends? You know what that means, don't you?"

I hadn't realized she'd been following the conversation from the sofa. "No, what?"

"He's married." I stared at her, and she continued. "Yeah. Typical — he's all over you during the week, but when the weekend comes, it's back to the wife."

There's the voice of experience. Rage erupted inside of me.

"*He's married?* He drives over here every day from who knows where, chatting up Nuala, and *he's married?* Well, someone needs to warn her. And say something to Linus."

"Why doesn't *someone* leave the matter alone?" Michael asked. "And let the three of them work it out?"

Little chance of that, and he knew it. But I'd let it drop for now.

"Well, Pammy," I said making a show of scanning the sitting room. "Off tomorrow?"

"Sorry?" she asked.

"Friday," Michael said. "End of the week. You'll be off to Amy's."

Pammy went back to her phone. "I thought Saturday was the end of the week."

* * *

Friday morning on my way to the TIC, I tapped on the window at Nuala's and gave her a wave. The tea room wasn't actually on my way — it was in the opposite direction. However, that made no matter.

"Oooh, rock cakes," I said, nodding to the fresh rack of free-form treats studded with dried fruit and sprinkled chunky sugar crystals. "Perfect for our elevenses today." As Nuala made up a box for me, I introduced my topic in an oblique way. "You'll be out at the Hall this afternoon, won't you? Running the café?"

"I will," Nuala replied. "But don't worry, I'll leave you a slice of chocolate cake here in the shop before I go."

"No," I said, "that isn't what I . . . oh, well, yes, thanks. I'll stop in for it later. But what I meant was that I have been thinking how much Linus loves his afternoon cuppa sitting with you in the kitchen at Hoggin Hall after the café closes."

A smile flitted across her face, gone before it could ever take hold. "Yes, well, he likes to check that everything is running smoothly."

"Now, Nuala, I'm sure you know better than that. Linus uses business to disguise the real reason he spends time with you."

A frown appeared and stayed. "Perhaps it may have crossed my mind that he might . . . but, really, Julia, I don't think I should read anything into it. And I haven't seen him at all this week, except on Wednesday when you were here. When he met Tony."

As she said his name, she smiled and the smile stuck.

"Yes, Mr. Brightbill," I said. "Nuala, is he . . . are you . . . that is, has he . . ." This was not the sort of conversation I'd ever had with a woman old enough to be my mother, and I couldn't quite find the right words to use without embarrassing us both. "You know what I mean." A lame finish.

Nuala giggled, which I took as a bad sign.

"No," she said, "at least, I don't know. But Tony has asked would I have dinner with him one evening next week."

"But Nuala," I whinged. "Linus. Has he never said anything?"

Nuala's face and neck reddened. "Only about my Battenberg."

* * *

Linus was the one I needed to talk with. He needed to up his game, unless he used "Battenberg" in some covert sexual sense that no one had caught onto yet. Really, shyness is one thing, being wary because of your past experience, yes, I can see that. But he had better step it up or he'd find himself left behind in the dusty verge watching Nuala motor off in a forest-green Morgan Roadster.

As I approached the TIC I espied Cecil and, the way he paced up and down in front of the window he looked as if he might be trying to wear a path in the pavement.

When he saw me, he pulled himself up to his six-foot height and looked down his patrician nose. "Julia." It was a statement — an accusation even. Certainly not a greeting.

"Cecil, come in."

I handed him the box of rock cakes and unlocked the door. He followed me through, set the box on the table, and hovered while I filled the kettle and switched it on. Then, he stuck his hands in the pockets of his green canvas jacket and posed as if beginning an oration.

"I'm quite concerned about what's gone on right here under our noses on the estate. If this event is in any way connected to the number of non-tenants that pass through on a regular basis, well, I'm afraid we will have to revisit our policy on tourism." He ended his ultimatum with a huff.

"Sit down, Cecil."

He remained standing, and arched an eyebrow.

"*Sit down!*" I pointed to a chair. "Please."

He held on for another moment before he sat, folding his tall frame into the chair, then sinking further as his shoulders drooped.

"I'm worried about Willow," he said, keeping his hands in his pockets and scowling at the table.

Here's the thing I had learned about Cecil — he had spent a lifetime perfecting his lord-of-the-manor airs, but they were a ruse, a way he'd hidden his fears and insecurities for his entire life. He'd come to terms with several important issues only in the last year or so, but habits of a lifetime can't be undone in a day. So, I chose to look past the occasional upper-crust moments, because when those were swept away, he was quite a likable fellow.

"It's terrible what happened. How is she?"

He ran his hand through his blond hair. "She's upset, as you can well imagine. Finding that man dead, it seems to have affected her in strange ways. She's fixated on the oddest things."

"Flies," I said. "Yes, well, that's probably the shock."

The kettle switched off, and Cecil drummed his fingers on the table while I poured up the tea.

"Police at the Hall," he fumed. "Again."

"Not to worry. They behaved themselves."

That got the hint of a smile out of him. He leaned forward, elbows on the table. "I want to take her away for a few days," he said. "To help clear her head. Don't you think?"

"But, Cecil, what about her class, the children?"

Cecil sighed. "Yes. She insisted on going in even today."

"And I believe the police may want to see her again. They'll need to talk with all of us. They don't even know who the man is. Why don't you wait a few days and see how it goes, all right?"

After a most reluctant nod, he said, "Yes, of course. I'm awfully glad you were there with her. And, I didn't really mean that about the tourists."

Vesta arrived, and Cecil went on his way. I remembered Guy Pockett, and as the morning wore on, wondered if he'd lost interest in his latest scheme. I wouldn't let him off the hook on this one, however, and so I began to search for his phone number just as he burst in. Under one arm, he carried a worn brown leather portfolio stuffed with papers.

"Running a bit late," he said, out of breath. "Sorry."

Vesta tended the counter while the farmer and I sat in the back and hashed over his idea of cookery demonstrations at the Wednesday market. Before long, the small worktable was awash with paper, mostly Guy's scribbled notes, along with his incomplete lists and figures, all splotched with mud stains, as if he'd composed his proposal while out in the fields.

If I could keep Guy to this scheme, it just might work, bringing in more customers to the market who would get ideas for how to use the freshest ingredients and be able to buy them on the spot. And it would all lead to Smeaton's Summer Supper, and more attendees meant more recognition for the estate.

At last, reaching over to switch on the kettle again, I said, "We can do only so much today, but this is a fine start."

"The sooner we launch the demos, the faster our numbers will pick up," Guy said. "We don't want to lose time."

"I'd think you've your hands full with taking on that extra field, Guy — as you're on your own now." Fran, Guy's business and personal partner, was now his ex-partner, having relocated permanently to a Christian retreat on Iona, off the western coast of Scotland. I had heard no further details. "How are you doing?"

"Grand, yeah, everything's fine," Guy said, tilting his chair until it rocked on the back two legs. "I've a couple of lads lending a hand. No problem. It's all under control."

"Good. I wouldn't want anything to happen to those gooseberries coming ripe. And will you have that purple cauliflower this year? It was quite the eye-catcher."

"Flew off the stand last season, I can tell you. So, we're set for the demos?"

"This all depends on the chefs and how much time they're willing to give," I replied. "Perhaps we could ask Fred at the Stoat and Hare to be first — the most local chef, after all. And, of course, I need to sort through the electrics, hand-washing facilities. I'll need to get Health and Safety out for a look. Right, go through the season with me again, week by week, so I can get this straight. Where did my list go?"

We shifted through papers, pushing them here and there. Guy set a stack over next to the computer, but they slipped off and papers when sailing onto the floor. He bent over to gather them up. "Sorry," he said with a laugh, "I'm better organized when it comes to lining out the carrots."

The bell above the door jingled. I gave the latest visitor half a look, then did a double take as I identified not a tourist to the estate, but Detective Sergeant Natty Glossop with a tidy black portfolio in one hand and a clear plastic bag with Willow's sandals and clothes in the other. He would have news, of course, about That Poor Man.

"Good morning, Detective Sergeant," Vesta greeted him.

"Sergeant?" Guy asked echoed in a low voice.

"Yes, Sudbury police," I explained. "There was an incident yesterday, and he's just stopping in for an update."

"I won't take any more of your time, then," Guy said, standing, scooping up papers, and cramming them back into his portfolio.

"We haven't settled on the chefs I'm to contact," I said, but Guy didn't stop. He nodded to Vesta and the DS and disappeared out the door. Right, there's another project deftly moved off his plate and onto mine.

"Good morning, Sergeant Glossop," I said.

"Good morning, Ms. Lanchester."

The kettle switched off, and I saw the sergeant's eyebrows lift.

"Tea?" I asked.

"Ah" — he made a show of looking at his watch and straightening his jacket — "well, if you've got a pot going."

And a rock cake. I shifted the rest of the papers and set them on top of the computer, and the three of us settled just as the bell jingled. I made Vesta stay seated as I gave a woman directions to Birdbrook, a village to the west of the estate. She may not have been lingering on Fotheringill turf, but I did score her email address for the newsletter. Eighty-three,

I noted. We were well onto a new page of the notepad. I'd get the sergeant to sign up, too.

"We won't have a photo of the victim until Monday," the DS told me. "Hard to tell much about his facial features until the FME cleans him up. These things take time, you know, and we always seem to be down an officer or two. Although, the boss doesn't make any friends when she makes demands, I can tell you that."

I'd heard about Tess's frustration with staffing often enough and was relieved not to be on the receiving end of one of her "requests."

"Yes, but look at Moira Flynn. She went from a uniform to a detective constable," I pointed out.

Natty grinned. "Yeah, she's that sharp, she is." He coughed the grin away and got back to business. "I thought I'd look in on Ms. Wynn-Finch. I've her clothes and shoes to return. We've matched her prints to the ones in the mud, but of course, they were fresh. The body'd been out there so long, with the rain on Monday, we're unlikely to get anything else."

"Willow will be at school now," Vesta said. "She teaches year three, the seven- and eight-year-olds."

"I'll go round and see her aunt at lunch," I said. "Shall I return them for you and you can catch her up when you have the photo?"

The DS handed over the bag with Willow's sandals as Vesta asked, "You've no idea who he is?"

"Not a clue," Glossop replied. "Mispers has turned up no match."

Missing Persons, I mouthed to Vesta. Police-ese, my second language.

The sergeant shook his head. "It's a struggle, I'll admit. We haven't even been able to sort out much of a timeline, what with the condition of the body and no witnesses. Who was this man and where was he going? Who did he meet and why? Someone's not talking."

That someone certainly wasn't DS Glossop, who seemed to catch himself as he let his frustration seep out.

"But not for long," he said, perking up. "We'll get it sorted. We found an old bicycle left outside the churchyard in the shrubbery and have checked for prints. They're his — the victim's. And another set, too, but we've no match on file. Could they be the perpetrator's?" Glossop asked, and I drew forward, hoping for an answer or at the very least a guess, but the sergeant exhaled in a huff, blowing all speculation aside. "And so, job one, once we have the photo, is to talk with everyone here on the estate."

"You can ask at the Stoat and Hare," I said. "They let rooms. Really lovely place, you know, although, I suppose it wasn't really his sort of place."

"We'll leave no stone unturned."

"You might try the holiday campsites on the estate," Vesta offered. "We've two designated, although I dare say there's the odd tent put up here and there in good weather, regardless."

"There are caravans in the field past the drive to the Hall," I added. "No one uses them as yet — they still need a refurb. But it wouldn't be difficult to pry a door open. I'll mention it to Linus if you like and—"

"No, Ms. Lanchester," Glossop interrupted, pulling a notebook out of his jacket pocket. "We'll take it from here."

I raised an eyebrow at that. In days past Natty Glossop might've given me a bit of slack, but apparently he'd learned from his boss that the public shouldn't be putting a nose into police business. Fine, let them carry on.

"Here now" — Vesta popped up and pulled a foldout map from the wall rack — "we can at least mark these places for you."

I cleared crumbs off the table, and we set about directing the DS to the holiday sites that could hold a clue to the identity of That Poor Man.

"I can show you one thing we do have," Glossop said, as he reached for his portfolio and pulled out a paper.

I flinched, already forgetting there was no photo of the body as yet, and glanced down out of half-closed eyes. I saw a photo of an old, rusted red-and-black OXO tin. A pencil laid next to it gave it perspective. It looked to be a small one, not even four inches long and about an inch wide. It must've once held a few beef-stock cubes, but now it was what they call "vintage" — something you'd find in a collectibles shop. A second photo showed the tin open, and inside, nestled amid cotton wool, were pieces of a bird's egg of a dull blue with brown spots.

"It was in his trouser pocket," the sergeant told us.

No identification, no photos, no money — only a keepsake, something a little boy might have. Perhaps it belonged to his son, I thought, and my eyes pricked with tears.

"I don't suppose," the sergeant said, and waited as Vesta offered me a tissue and I blew my nose, "you know what sort of a bird that came from?"

"Mmm, I'm afraid I'm not that good at eggs. My dad would know. Would you like me to—"

"No, thank you, Ms. Lanchester. I'll send this off to Rupert."

I pursed my lips at him in annoyance at not being allowed to at least act as messenger. Regardless, I would need to ring my dad before Natty got hold of him in case Rupert jumped to the conclusion this murder investigation involved me, which it did not.

The sergeant shook his head with regret. "Sorry, Ms. Lanchester, it's only that the boss has started this investigation already a bit cheesed off, and I don't want to get in her way. A problem with the FME's schedule has popped up."

I couldn't fault him for not wanting to step wide of the line when Tess was on the case.

Glossop reached for the photo, and hesitated.

"But I don't see why you can't make a copy of this thing," he conceded. "You could show it round. And see here, we may need to circulate a photo of the body, too. Shall I drop one by?"

"Yes, that's fine. But, we won't have to put it in the window, will we?"

CHAPTER 10

I ate half my sandwich at lunch, and then grabbed the plastic bag with Willow's clothes and sandals. As few visitors perused the wall of leaflets and maps on their own, I told Vesta, "I'll just nip down to Lottie's shop. I won't be long."

At Three Bags Full, Lottie and another woman had their heads together at the counter.

"Shall I come back?" I asked.

"No, stay," Lottie said, "it's fine. I'm only placing an order. Will you wait?"

I nodded, and the women continued their business while I admired the shop. Skeins of richly colored wool were socked away in floor-to-ceiling cubbyholes, making me feel as if I were tucked up in a cozy bed. A wall of jewel tones gradually gave way to earthy hues followed by soft baby pastels, then into undyed creams and browns and black. Displays of shawls and collars and cardigans begged me to slip one on. I couldn't knit a stitch, but that didn't mean I didn't admire the work of others.

I glanced over at Lottie, a woman who carried her own sense of style, untempered by her age. Late fifties, I guessed. Today, she wore a thin knit poncho in a gentian blue — it draped languidly off one shoulder bare but for a spaghetti strap. The full skirt that fell just below her knees was in a red, yellow, and green print showing parrots and other exotic birds. Perched on her head atop her short salt-and-pepper curls was one of those pillbox-style hats, but made of fabric — blue, trimmed in yellow ribbon. Those in the know said that Willow took after her aunt much more than her parents, whom I'd never laid eyes on.

"Bye, now," Lottie called to her supplier. She slipped off her readers — black framed and studded with polished colored glass — and said, "Well, Julia, and how are you today?"

"I'm all right. Oh, Lottie, I'm so sorry Willow had to be the one to find That Poor Man. Did she tell you what happened?"

"She told me about the flies," Lottie replied and nodded to the back of the shop. "Come on, now. I'll put the kettle on."

We sat on low stools behind the counter, mugs of tea in hand.

"Willow insisted on going in to school today," Lottie said.

"That's good. Staying busy may be the best thing for her."

"She was reluctant to leave off her latest project. Her class is creating a three-dimensional timeline of the Fotheringill estate dating back before the Romans. It's quite an undertaking and made from a variety of materials. Willow is quite creative that way — using scraps of fabric, bits of wool, drawings, painting, dried plants, salt-and-flour relief."

I glanced round the shop. "I can see where she came by such creativity."

Lottie smiled. "Willow is a gentle soul. So unlike her parents, although my sister and her husband are quite suited to each other. And they love her, of course, but they see the world in black and white. I should've spent more time with her when she was younger, but I was always away living in Paris or Amsterdam. I sometimes wonder should I have taken her with me on my travels, but I'm not sure that sort of nomadic life would've suited her any more than her real home did."

"I'd no idea you'd lived all over. Did you run a wool shop in Paris, too?"

Lottie's laughter bubbled up like a fountain. "No, but I did pose in the middle of the Place de la Concorde wearing nothing but a shawl knitted from spun raw wool. A bit of performance art, you might say. It's what brought me to my love of natural materials." She shivered. "That was a cold April day, I can tell you."

Well, there you have it — never make assumptions about a person. I had shoved Lottie into the cubbyhole of little knit-shop lady, and as it turned out, she didn't belong in a cubbyhole at all.

"But eventually," she continued, "I grew tired of that sort of existence and decided that a smaller life can be all the richer. I came back to England, looked round, and landed here. So did you, and we're all quite happy about that."

I blushed, but it may have been because of the image that had lodged in my mind of a nearly naked Lottie in the middle of Paris. "Mine was an impulse move," I said, "but the best thing I've ever done."

We finished our tea, and Lottie set the mugs on the windowsill. "I suggested Willow stay at the Hall for a few days. Cecil will look out for her. You know, I never would've put the pair of them together, but look how well that's turned out. They're good for each other, and that makes all the difference."

* * *

Saturday morning, Michael slung his workbag over his shoulder, preparing to leave for Hickling Broad in Norfolk for a bit of early scouting on a winter feature about marsh harriers. But he hesitated, fingers drumming on his thighs and eyes darting round the static scene in the cottage. I held my breath. Pammy didn't seem to be aware of the tension in the room ensconced on the sofa and engrossed in her phone as she was. I gave Michael's back a rub and said, "It's all right. You go on."

But it wasn't all right. It was Saturday, the end of the week even by Pammy's calendar. And yet, she showed no signs of shifting herself or her baggage. I sighed, slid my feet into my heels, and left for the TIC, hoping for a stream of tourists that would keep Vesta and me without a moment to think of anything else.

At the end of the workday, I stayed late to put the counter and wall of leaflets to rights and then dragged myself back to the cottage, my steps getting slower and slower until I saw what I had hoped I wouldn't — Pammy's Ford Fiesta gathering dust at the curb. Michael arrived behind me, slammed his car door, and took my elbow.

"Right, let's get this over with," he said through clenched teeth.

He threw open the door. It banged off the oak post against the wall and rebounded toward us. Pammy leapt off the sofa, her phone falling to the floor.

"It's Amy," she blurted out, and swallowed hard.

At least she had the good sense to know her game was up.

"What about Amy?" Michael demanded.

It was sad news. Amy and Roz had given up their flat in Leicester. Roz had reconciled with her ex-husband, and Amy had moved into a bed-sit, which afforded absolutely no room for a guest, as it had only the one bed, a sofa, and a tiny kitchen. Sounded awfully familiar to me.

"You can't stay here," Michael told his sister. "Not any longer. You can go to Pickle's. I'll ring her now while you" — he waved at the plastic shopping bags, piled up into a pyramid in the corner — "get your things together."

"I can't go to Pickle's," Pammy cried. "It's too far away."

"Too far away from what?" Michael's voice rose in challenge.

"*Stop!*" I shouted. "Please, just . . ." I heaved a great sigh. "It's all right, Pammy. You can stay."

"No," Michael said, grabbing my hand. "It isn't fair."

I don't know what made me do it. I was nearing forty years old and getting soft, I suppose. But here was Pammy older than I was with a string of bad relationships and not a sibling who would take her in. I wouldn't want it known I could be so coldhearted.

"We can't turn her out," I said to Michael. "She's family." It took a great deal of effort to say it, but my reward was the look in his eyes — turned that twilight blue I loved — and the smile that tugged at the corner of his mouth. He put his hand at the back of my neck, drew me close, and kissed me softly.

"Thank you, thank you, Julia." Pammy clasped her hands to her heart. "It won't be for much longer, really it won't. Because . . . because . . ." She hesitated for a split second and then held up her index finger. "Tomorrow, I'm going to look at a flat."

"A flat?" Michael repeated. "Why didn't you say so?"

Pammy put a hand on her hip and stuck her nose in the air, re-establishing her big-sister status. "Well, you didn't give me the chance, did you?"

I thought there had been a bit more to Pammy's split second of hesitation, but I kept quiet about it, because at that moment, I desperately needed hope, false or otherwise.

* * *

Sunday morning at Pipit Cottage, I continued to cling to that hope, if only by a thread. Michael was off again on Rupert business, and I finished my tea and stood ready to leave for work only three hours earlier than our twelve o'clock opening time. But how often did I get the opportunity to clean the TIC loo and clear out our tiny fridge?

"So, where is this flat?" I asked, hand on the door.

Pammy didn't meet my eye as she replied, "Oh, over near the . . . er . . . I'll be back by tea time."

As she unzipped her rucksack and began rummaging through its contents, I caught a glimpse of what looked very much like a pair of binoculars. I studied her attire — tight-fitting denims instead of her usual microskirt, a light jacket waiting on the arm of the sofa, and on her feet, sturdy trainers.

The outfit did not indicate flat-shopping to me, but instead pointed in an entirely different direction, down a path that might possibly lead to a day outdoors with. I resolutely looked the other way.

"Good luck," I muttered, and left.

* * *

Sundays on my own at the TIC were exhausting, and it wasn't until just before closing time that I had a chance to sit down for a cup of tea. The kettle went off just as the bell above the door jingled. I stood, prepared for a last-minute visitor, but instead found Willow carrying a box of what I took for rubbish.

"It's for our Fotheringill timeline," she informed me.

"Do you have Alfie collecting for you now?" I asked as I looked in the box and found a handful of shiny buttons, twigs encrusted with lichen, and various lengths of yarn. Alfie the rook was an avid collector, and always had an eye out for a new treasure.

"Julia, I've made up my mind about something, and I want to tell you about it."

Willow unwound a turquoise scarf so light and airy it looked as if it had been spun from clouds, set it aside, and drifted into one of the chairs, straightening her shift and putting her hands on her knees. The dark circles under her eyes, her furrowed brow, and mouth in a straight line spoke volumes with uncharacteristic gravity. Since I'd known her, I could count on one hand the number of times I'd seen Willow completely devoid of good humor and I would still have a finger or two left over.

"Cecil isn't terribly happy with my decision," she began. "He says it isn't really my concern and I should leave it for others, but he says that because he's worried about me. But I knew I could tell you, Julia, because you would understand that I must take action."

I understood nothing. "Is this about That Poor Man?"

"Look now," she said, tears filling her eyes. "That's all we can call him. He deserves a name, doesn't he? He deserves to be acknowledged for his life. And that's why I am going to do something about it. Find out who he is, what happened to him."

"But, Willow, that's a job for the police."

"You of all people know that isn't always enough — that we must occasionally take action ourselves. You are my role model, Julia."

"No, don't say that. This is an entirely different situation," I said in feeble defense of my previous and unwelcome butting into police enquiries.

Willow leaned toward me, her eyes wide and trusting. "I must do this. It's That Poor Man — he wants me to help him. It's as if he's waiting just behind me. Waiting for me to act."

The bell above the door jingled and I jumped, half-expecting to see the murder victim walk in for a consultation on his case. Fortunately, it was only Cecil in conversation with two men who held Suffolk guidebooks. Willow clutched my arm and whispered furtively, "I haven't told Cecil that last part. You won't—"

"Hello, you two," Cecil said, a jovial, if awkward, smile plastered on his face. His eyes darted from Willow to me and back. I returned a pleasant smile, praying we didn't look as if we'd been talking about a dead body. "Julia, these gentleman are searching for a pub that pulls a good pint."

I leapt up, happy to launch into my usual discourse about how the Stoat and Hare and the Royal Oak are two of the finest alehouses in East Anglia, but allowing my mind to run along on another track, as I wondered if Willow had started to lose her grip on reality.

But when the visitors left and I turned back, she appeared her normal self. Gathering her treasures and returning them to the box, she smiled at Cecil, the small gap between her front teeth always guaranteeing a prompt smile in return.

"All ready, my dear," she told him. "Yes, Julia, our timeline is coming along nicely."

Oh, is that what we had been talking about?

Brushing her hands off, Willow asked, "Julia, have you seen any of those incredibly cute little robin's pincushions about?"

"Sorry?"

"It's a gall on rose stems. Harmless to the plant, but it makes such a lovely mossy ball. I want to use them on the timeline to represent the grasslands on the estate in the seventeenth century. Auntie says she's seen them on dog roses near the abbey ruins. I might nip up there tomorrow afternoon when school is finished. They're awfully sweet."

"We heard a cuckoo up that way last year," I said. "Near the brook by the ruins. Didn't see him, though."

"I don't think I would know a cuckoo if I met one," Willow said.

"He's about the size of a dove," I replied. "And he's got a barred chest, sort of like a sparrowhawk, but cuckoos rest their wing tips below their body. It's a good ID feature."

I saw an imperceptible nod of approval from Cecil. Anything, I'm sure he thought, to take her away from the subject of That Poor Man. And so I carried on.

"Rupert is doing a piece on them, and he'll need footage. I tell you what, as tomorrow is my day off, perhaps I'll go out and take a look for him. I may see you there. Do you know the cuckoo's rhyme?

"The cuckoo comes in April
And sings its song in May
In June it changes tune
And July it flies away"

"That's lovely," Willow said. "I must remember it for our wildlife unit. The children enjoy rhymes, and it helps them remember what we've covered. Last week we all memorized the lines for St. Swithun." She straightened up as if reciting to her class.

"St. Swithun's Day if thou dost rain
For forty days it will remain
St. Swithun's Day if thou be fair
For forty days 'twill rain nae mair

"We did that one so I could tell them about the watercolor competition . . ." Her voice drifted off, and she cocked her head as if listening to a voice no one else could hear.

"Willow, love." Cecil picked up her box. "We'd better leave Julia to close up."

Willow came back to us. "Yes, of course. Now, where's my scarf?"

She twisted one way and the other before she spotted it next to the computer. She retrieved it, uncovering the pile of papers left from Friday morning. They were my notes from meeting with Guy about the chefs' demos at the market along with — I'd discovered too late — a few of Guy's own papers that he'd left behind. But another sheet lay next to the stack. It was the photo of the OXO tin and its contents. Willow picked it up.

"What's this?" she asked.

"Sergeant Glossop brought that by," I said. "It's a photo of the only thing police found in That Poor Man's pockets. They're hoping it might help identify him." For my explanation, I received a black look from Cecil at bringing the conversation back round to where it shouldn't be.

Willow made no mention of That Poor Man. Instead, she tapped a finger on the photo of the OXO tin and murmured, "Is it now?"

CHAPTER 11

I arrived at the cottage to find Pammy waiting on the doorstep. She had a sly smile and a pleased air about her. Both vanished when I asked about the flat.

"Gone," she said with sorrow, and followed me in. We stood for a moment of silent mourning, until she added brightly, "But there might be another one tomorrow." When Michael walked in a minute later, she repeated this news before he could even ask. He cut his eyes at me, and I shrugged.

As an act of appeasement, Pammy offered up a paper shopping bag and declared she had been down to the shop and had bought a pint of milk, a ready-to-bake pizza Akash made up himself, and a bottle of wine. She stood beside the sink while she told us this, so we would notice that it was — for the first time in a week — devoid of dirty dishes.

I should've been happy with this burst of responsibility, but it only proved to plunge me back into despair. Now she's sharing the food costs and cleaning up after herself, as if she really lived here.

Over our meal, Michael attempted to lift my mood and avoid another Royal Report by making small talk, beginning with the nesting habits of blackbirds.

At this, Pammy looked up from her plate and said, "Do you know what amazes me? Swallows, that's what. Those little birds soaring round in the sky" — she waved her fork in the air, drawing a spiral overhead — "and never coming down but for the nesting thing."

Apparently, Pammy took our stunned silence as agreement, for she continued. "And migration. Well, don't get me started on that. Off to Africa in the autumn? That those birds can find their way thousands and thousands of miles there and back again — well, puts us with our satnavs to shame, doesn't it?"

"Yes, amazing," I agreed, glancing at Michael, who took a slug of his wine. I dare not ask where she had come by her newfound information. I believe I knew where, and I was afraid Michael knew, too.

* * *

Monday morning, the three of us stood at the door, ready for our days. For Michael, it was a class in feather identification — one of Rupert's favorite topics. My schedule included confirming lunches with Akash for an upcoming minibus tour and returning Guy Pockett's farm paperwork. I needed to drop in to see Linus and talk with Tess about "that other matter" — Michael and I continued to keep quiet in front of Pammy about the murder of That Poor Man. "And in the afternoon," I finished up, "I'll be at the abbey ruins to listen out for that cuckoo for Dad."

"Some day off," Pammy commented, then noticed that Michael and I stood watching her. "Yeah, right," she said. "A flat."

* * *

"Is Detective Inspector Callow available?"

"Is there something I can help you with, ma'am?" the desk sergeant at the Sudbury police station asked. "Do you have a crime to report? Or is it a complaint against a neighbor? If so, I've a form you could start with—"

This fellow was new. I didn't recognize him, and he hadn't recognized me. "Sergeant Glossop?" I tried. "Or DC Flynn?"

I had learned that asking the police for information face-to-face got me further than a phone call or a text, and if Tess wasn't available, I would go down the list on her team. But the desk sergeant was having none of it.

"I'm sorry, ma'am. Would you like to speak to a family liaison officer?"

"No, thank you. This isn't about me, it's about — I tell you what, I'll wait until one of them is free."

Before he could tell me otherwise, I marched over and sat in one of the chairs that lined the far wall, pulled out my phone, and sent a text to Tess. *in lobby. any news?*

Two minutes later, DI Callow came out from behind a locked door and walked over.

"You've a fine guard dog there," I said.

"Did you tell him your name?" she asked.

"No," I said crossly. I would not ask for special treatment if the result was the desk sergeant recognizing my name from a previous incident or two.

"Come through." I followed the DI from the public area into the depths of the station. As we walked down the corridor, she asked, "Tea?"

"You must be joking." I well remembered the quality of tea at the station. "I'll pop into Winch & Blatch later." The local department store had a lovely café upstairs, and I remembered their Bakewell tart with fondness.

"Nice for some," Tess replied. I reminded her it was my day off.

She took me to an interview room and left me for a minute or two. I perched on a hard chair, and glanced at my surroundings. The place gave me the creeps, as it had on previous visits — sterile, with a band of high windows providing the only natural light, and that big mirror, which wasn't a mirror at all, but a way for people to watch you. I had nothing to hide, and yet it made me nervous. I couldn't imagine what it would be like for a person laden with guilt.

Tess returned with a file folder and sat across from me.

"Do you have any more information for us?" she asked.

I shook my head. "But Willow's quite concerned — more than that, she's rather fixated on the victim."

The DI raised her eyebrows. "Does she need to talk with someone? I could make arrangements."

"No, no, she'll be all right. Do you know how he died?"

"The autopsy report isn't complete, but it's blunt force trauma. A blow to the back of his head that bashed his skull in. He was probably dead before he hit the ground. There were splinters in the wound and bits of moss. The weapon might've been a piece of wood just lying about. We'll send out a team again to have another look at the area, but I don't hold out much hope. The murderer probably took it off and chucked in the nearest stand of trees. This speaks to a moment of passion or rage rather than a planned murder."

She presented these details in her usual cool manner.

"What about the OXO tin with the eggshells?" I asked.

My intention had been to ring Rupert on Friday before DS Glossop got to him with that photo, but it had gone completely out of my head. The result of that had been Dad ringing me. I'd assured him police were taking care of the investigation and it had nothing to do with me, but that wasn't entirely true, because now thoughts of Willow weighed me down.

"Rupert says dunnock, although he had an idea it could be a cuckoo's good attempt at egg imitation."

"So the bird might be identified, but not the person. Could someone have robbed That Poor Man and stolen his money and his identification?"

"I'm not sure he would've been keeping money or ID," Callow replied. "His pockets were so full of holes, it's a wonder that OXO tin hadn't fallen out. His general appearance was one of living rough, I'd say."

"Do you have the photo now? Hasn't your medical examiner had the time to—"

"She got a better deal," the DI snapped.

I recoiled at the white-hot anger that rolled off Tess. She hadn't moved a muscle, and she hadn't needed to — the tension in her jaw, the sharp crystal gaze, and the mere suggestion of high color on her cheeks came together with great effect. A truly guilty person would have no chance against her.

"A what? Does the medical examiner work for the highest bidder?"

"Let's just say she had to take on an autopsy at another station for an investigator with more influence. She's promised results to us by the end of today, and we will at last be able to release a photo."

* * *

I left the station with Tess in an extremely bad mood, headed down the road, and across Market Hill to Winch & Blatch. When I pulled open one door to enter, the other was being pushed out by someone leaving.

"Ms. Lanchester. It's a surprise to see you here."

We both stopped with doors half open. "Mr. Brightbill," I replied, hearing the accusatory tone in my voice. *Are you married?* "Do you live in Sudbury?"

"No, I don't. I only stopped into the café."

"Here? Are you making a survey of the tea rooms in East Anglia?" Had he scared the wits out of the women servers here, too?

He tried out one of his warm smiles on me. "You've no tourist activities to attend to?" he asked.

I bristled. "It's my day off."

"Well, do enjoy your tea. I can recommend the Bakewell tart."

I stood on the pavement, scowling at his retreating figure. Just before he turned down the passageway that led to the city car park, he stopped and glanced in my direction. Caught spying, I jumped back and knocked into the door, causing the glass to vibrate and a clerk to rush up and ask if I was all right. My face blazing, I stomped up the stairs to the tea room, perused the offerings and chose a slice of blackberry sponge just to show Brightbill I was no pushover for his suggestions.

The cake was good, but I'd rather have had the Bakewell tart. See what he made me do? Who was this fellow, anyway, and where did he come from and why was he skulking about our corner of Suffolk? Then, as if cold water had been thrown in my face, I realized those were the same questions we kept asking about That Poor Man.

* * *

I pulled into the gravel forecourt of Hoggin Hall, and my mood lifted as I looked upon its brick edifice, replete with turrets marking the north and south wings. I'd lived in the Hall for a few months when my Pipit Cottage was undergoing repairs, and I felt quite comfortable there, whether in the kitchen, the library with its vast fireplace, or the grand dining room that ran the width of the building at the back. It had been my idea for the Hall to open to the public three afternoons a week — a program now managed for me by Akash. I had pushed for Nuala to run a café on site, and it had become a popular stop for tourists on those open days. It was all part of an influx of new life sorely needed on the estate, and although some in Linus's circle of titled friends thought it a drastic upheaval, he had taken it in stride.

I circled round the building and came in through the kitchen, where I found Sheila Bugg at the sink. She invited me to sit and visit, but I explained my mission, concerning Nuala and Linus and the interloper.

"The thing is, Sheila," I said, dropping my voice even though we were alone, "I think this Brightbill might be married."

The look that came over her face — well, if I had any trouble dealing with Mr. Anthony Brightbill myself, I'd just let Sheila loose on him.

"Someone needs to light a fire under His Lordship."

I raised my hand. "That would be me."

* * *

With a twinge of apprehension, I knocked lightly on the door of Linus's study. We were friends, but would he appreciate my opening a discussion into his love life — or lack thereof?

I looked into the study. The heavy curtains, open to allow the sunlight to stream through the tall windows, fell to the floor in burgundy puddles, and the dark, polished wood bookshelves glowed. Linus had his laptop open on the oak desk, but rose when he saw me.

"Julia, good morning," he said, coming round his vast desk to greet me. "Shall I ask Sheila for tea?"

"Already done," the housekeeper said, pushing the door open with the tray she carried. "I'll set it just here."

Sheila left us, and Linus and I sat on the leather chesterfield sofa. I poured both cups and reached for a biscuit. "Bourbon creams," I said, "your favorite. Are you sure you can spare one?"

"Have at it. It's a pleasure to see you, of course, but it is your day off."

"Yes, well, I have something I want to talk with you about."

"You aren't here to explain that you've embarked upon a new tourism program without telling me?" He said it with a twinkle in his eye, but also with a bit of apprehension.

"Linus, I would never do that." We both laughed "No, not to worry, I have not started anything new." And then the letters OFE rose to the surface of my mind. "Well, actually there is something. It occurred to me that we could have some sort of commendation in each month's newsletter, focusing on a tenant who has shared his or her love of the estate with visitors. We could call it the OFE — Order of the Fotheringill Estate. And we'd offer a hamper full of food and drink and do an interview. We should probably have a sash or a medal hanging on a ribbon. And we need an instantly recognizable logo. Could we base it on the family's coat of arms?"

Linus reached for a biscuit and gazed at it, deep in thought. Had I gone too far?

"I haven't done a thing yet," I added. "Really I haven't. Not without your approval."

He tipped his Bourbon cream toward me. "Well, you've got it. It sounds like a splendid idea, but, we'll discuss each month's winner before the selection is announced?"

"Of course." I dunked my biscuit into my tea and took a bite. "So, I'll tell you where the idea for the commendation came from. We had a young family in a week ago, and they went on and on about a man they'd met out near the abbey ruins. He knew all about the birds and wildlife and was ever so helpful to them. I think he might be one of the pensioners out in Wickham Parva. I don't know them all personally, but I'll find out, because he would make an outstanding first choice for the OFE."

In my mind, I heard an echo from the mother of the family. *Looked as if he might've lived rough.*

"Bob," I murmured. "They said his name is Bob."

"Could it be Bob Treen?" Linus asked. "Although, perhaps he's too young."

And then I saw That Poor Man, face down by the pond, holes in his shoes and in his pockets. A pricking sensation crept up my arms, and it was as if Linus's words came to me in a time delay. I stared at him for several seconds before I could respond. "No, not young," I whispered at last. "This Bob . . . he might have been living rough. Linus, what if he is the man who was killed?"

True, Willow had come upon That Poor Man near St. Swithun's, and the family had met him out by the abbey ruins, but hadn't he mentioned the churchyard to them? Yes, he had.

Linus sat forward and placed his cup and saucer on the table. "Is that right? Have the police identified him at last? I think it will go a long way to settling Willow's mind, you know. She's taken this all too personally."

I shook my head. "No, the police have no identification. Yet. This might help them. It's only, the family didn't know his surname."

Of course it was him — I felt it to be true, but I had no proof, and that pushed the confirmation of my discovery just out of reach. The family might be able to identify a photo of the murder victim, but would we ever see them again in the TIC?

"Wait now!" I leapt up. "They signed up for the newsletter, and so we have their email address. Oh, Linus, I need to ring Tess — DI Callow — and tell her. This could be a break in the case."

CHAPTER 12

First things first. I needed to find the family's email address, and then I would ring Tess — no sense in getting her hopes up. At the TIC, I locked the door behind me, dashed to the counter, and grabbed the sign-up pad for our newsletter.

A dozen or so names filled half the sheet, but these had been written starting just the previous Friday, and the family had been in a week earlier. We must've filled up a sheet since then — perhaps even more than one. When a page was full, we tore it off, and when we had the time, added the names to our database. I whipped behind the counter and rifled through the papers near the computer and making a mess. No sign-up sheets, but I did come across the farm papers Guy Pockett had left behind. I stuffed them in my bag.

So, if the sign-up sheets were gone, it meant Vesta had already put the names in the computer. I booted up the machine and automatically reached over to switch on the kettle. But when the kettle clicked off, I didn't bother with tea. Instead I worked my way into our newsletter list, searching the names by date. But the database wasn't playing fair. Its display of subscribers showed me that the last names were added more than a week ago. What had happened to the names we'd gathered between then and now?

I had seen the little girl write the email address down. Where had that sheet gone> Where were those addresses? Not in the computer, not on a sign-up sheet. Vanished.

My excitement drained away. Our ability to reach this family was critical, I was sure of it. They are the only ones who could identify That Poor Man as Bob. But did I have their email address — the one vital piece of information? No, I had nothing. I sat in the darkened TIC and stewed about the lost opportunity.

I should ring Vesta and ask if she remembered seeing a sign-up sheet with a young girl's handwriting. But the second I reached for my phone, I thought better of it. Vesta already took on more than she should at the TIC, worked far more hours — I wouldn't drag her in yet another day. Unless, of course, she had nothing else going on.

And who would know that better than Akash? I dashed up to his shop, because after all, I needed to confirm the boxed lunches for an upcoming small tour group. While I was there, I would ask what Vesta might be up to.

Gwen was running the till and gave me my answer. "A day out," she reported. "They've gone off to the air museum at Duxford and are meeting an old friend of Akash's. Lovely, isn't it?"

"Lovely," I agreed, silently promising myself that Vesta and I would turn the TIC over the following morning in search of our stray sign-up sheet, and praying it hadn't gone out in last Thursday's recycling.

"How are you and Michael?" Gwen asked. I sidestepped the answer with a vague "oh grand." No need to bring up the cuckoo in our nest. I confirmed the twelve lunches, and bought myself a ham sandwich and a bottle of fizzy water flavored with elderflower and pomegranate.

"How is Tennyson? I see so little of her these days." Gwen's daughter, twelve years old, had started out in Smeaton as a bit of a loner, with only a rook as a friend. "And the village's favorite bird, Alfie?"

"Tennyson's started a nature club at school with two of her friends. And Alfie, well, it's a difficult time of year for him."

"Of course, June. He's started to molt, has he?"

"And making a grand mess of it, too. Feathers everywhere. He prefers to keep himself to himself right now."

"Who could blame him?"

* * *

I drove out to the abbey ruins looking forward to a bit of quiet time on my own, just me and a sandwich and a lot of tumbled-down stone walls.

Sitting in my car, I rang Guy Pockett. "You left paperwork behind for the farm — invoices and the like. I'm up that way now, so I can run them by."

"Hang on, no," Guy replied. "Let me come in and get them."

"But I'm already at the abbey, and you aren't that much further."

"Yeah, but you see, I'm in Bury at the moment. I won't be able to get back to meet you."

"Then I'll leave them at your cottage. I'll tuck them under the mat or something," I offered.

"No, I'd rather you didn't. They would be just the thing for one of the geese to get hold of. I'll come into the village tomorrow and collect them."

His insistence puzzled me until I remembered that he'd been on his own now for about six months, and the cottage might not be as presentable as it had been when he had a partner. "Yes, all right. See you tomorrow."

* * *

The abbey wasn't the most-visited part of the estate, and I believed it that was because it suffered from an identity crisis. The thirteenth-century complex of buildings had been abandoned during Henry VIII's dissolution of the monasteries, after which it had become a school for illegitimate sons of titled gentry, and after that possibly the dwelling for the first Earl Fotheringill before falling into disrepair. The ruins lay off the main road and down a narrow lane through fields. Visitors arrived first at the car park, which was really nothing more than a graveled space for five or six vehicles and where an aged wooden sign directed them along a footpath. No other signage indicated the importance of the site or its history.

Taking my lunch and a blanket along with me, I traipsed up the footpath until what remained of the abbey came into view. There, I paused. In the stillness of the summer afternoon, an atmosphere of melancholy arose from the ruins, as if the buildings couldn't understand how the centuries had passed them by so quickly.

Most of the walls rose only a few feet now — the stones having been carted off over the centuries to build much-needed cottages and barns on the estate. Seen from above, what remained would looked like a connect-the-dot puzzle that only whispered of abbey's former glory with the towering church, living quarters, and work areas for the monks.

Only the undercroft remained standing. Most of it, at least. Monks had used the undercroft — a long room with a low, vaulted stone ceilings that made you want to hunch your shoulders as you walked through — for storing mead, wine, and beer. All the essentials. According to an old and rather drab-looking abbey leaflet, there were smaller storerooms below ground, but they had been blocked off ages ago. Health and Safety, no doubt, but before my time. The undercroft's vast, empty expanse could be a favorite of children. I imagined them spending rainy visits racing up and down the length of the place, their screams of delight echoing off the walls.

I determined then and there to write a new leaflet. The old one gave precious little information, and it lacked the story element I preferred to offer visitors. There was great potential in the place, I could see it now. Better signage would pique people's curiosity. And artwork would bring the place to life, showing monks in the herb garden, at prayer, that sort of thing. A touch of Brother Cadfael. Tales of religious seclusion and intrigue.

I squinted, and the buildings seemed to rise to their previous stature before my eyes. We could stage a reenactment. We could put on a Medieval Day at the Abbey, and tourists would flock to the place. People in period dress would demonstrate crafts, and we'd even offer the proper sorts of food. What did the monks eat? Something palatable, I hoped.

Perhaps we could get Health and Safety approval to use the undercroft for banquets. And, we could organize evening ghost tours. Nothing like a dead monk to create some excitement.

Plans flooded my mind, and I had to shake my head to get them out. My day off, after all. I headed to the far side of the complex and round the back of a broken wall where lay a secret patch perfect for a quiet picnic. Michael and I knew the place well. I spread my blanket and got out my phone, jotting down a few notes about the Abbey Day to work off of later.

The air was pleasant and still. I could smell the green of the grass and something sweet — honeysuckle from the nearby hedgerow, perhaps. A smattering of red poppies bloomed in the field amid a sea of daisies, and I could hear the high, whistling call of a yellowhammer. I glanced round until I saw him at the top of a rowan. He reminded me I needed to go in search of the cuckoo, which we'd heard not far from this spot last year.

I allowed myself one more bit of work. I stood and began a panoramic view of the abbey grounds. It would be just the thing for an updated leaflet, both online and in print. As I held my phone out and slowly turned, I caught Willow walking up from the nearby hedgerow. I waved and called and she waved back, stopping to unwind a purple gossamer scarf from her neck, leaving a paisley-print tunic and her purple leggings.

"I didn't expect you to be here already," I said.

"The head teacher took my last two hours today. Wasn't that nice of her?"

The head teacher could see as well as I could the dark smudges under Willow's eyes and the absence of her usual buoyancy.

"Of course, the children and I had to check our toad house first," Willow said, going to her bicycle, almost hidden on the other side of an outer wall, and rummaging in her rucksack. "Terence Toad had gone walkabout yesterday, but all was well today. And so after that, with the extra time, I cycled out early. Although, it was a longer journey than I realized."

Linus had been delighted when his daughter-in-law-to-be took up cycling round the estate, as it was his favorite mode of transport.

"I've a cool drink here," I offered, "and a sandwich to share. What do you think?"

She came over and settled on the blanket, and I asked about school and the timeline. Willow answered readily, but a Willow sentence that contained fewer than three adverbs was telling. At last, she sighed.

"I don't want to worry you, Julia, but I feel I should tell you that I've decided to directly seek answers to the questions we all have."

"Yes, Willow," I said with relief, "that's for the best, isn't it? Such a dreadful thing to have happen to you. DI Callow told me that the police have someone you can talk with. Someone who will help you sort through your feelings about what happened."

"Oh no, I didn't mean the police. I'm going to ask *him*."

Him?

Willow stood abruptly and brushed herself off. "Well now, I'd better get to my collecting mossy galls. I've had a nose round on the other side of that hedgerow and spotted a good number, and I just came back for my collecting box."

"Do you need help?" I called after her.

"No, I'm fine," she replied as she waved scissors and a shoebox.

I should go with her and have a serious chat about asking the dead for help, but the warm sun made my eyelids feel as if they had lead weights attached. I would talk with Willow, but for the moment, I kicked off my shoes and wiggled my toes. I rested my head on the stone behind me, and closed my eyes, finding I couldn't concentrate on anything except the sun on my face and the call of an insistent robin, singing his heart out as he defended his territory. I yawned. Perhaps he was chastising Willow for stealing his pincushions.

A shadow fell over me and I opened one eye.

"Here you are, now," Michael said.

I squinted and gazed up at him. "I hope I'm not dreaming."

He dropped down beside me and cupped my face, giving me a long, slow kiss from which I did not wish to emerge. "Mmm," he said, his lips against my temple, "you're warm."

"I am warm," I said and kissed him back. "This is lovely. How ever did you find me?"

"You're right where you said you'd be." His arm circled my waist, and he pulled me closer, and I went willingly. "I finished early and came straight here. I thought we could at least have a few minutes to ourselves with no one about." His lips were on my throat, soft, seeking, while a hand slid under my shirt.

"That's the very best idea I've heard in forever." I kicked the empty sandwich box off the blanket with my bare foot.

"Had a picnic without me?" He pulled back, his eyes half-closed and the corner of his mouth tugged up into a smile. One hand went to my waistband.

"Did I?" I asked, breathless and barely able to think of anything except his hands. "Oh, yes, I . . . gave Willow half my sandwich."

Michael's hands ceased their exploration. "Willow?"

"Julia!" Willow called from the other side of the hedgerow. "I've found the most absolutely wonderful collection of robin's pincushions. There'll be enough for all the children."

Her voice grew louder as she approached. "Such funny little mossy galls they are. Oh, look, it's Michael!"

I had leapt up and off the blanket by the time Willow came round the edge of the hedgerow. Michael remained seated.

"Yes, look, here he is," I said. "Willow is collecting mossy galls, Michael."

"Mossy what?"

I felt my color rise. "Galls. Mossy galls. Show him, Willow. They're for school. The children need them for the Fotheringill estate timeline. They're to represent the grasslands. The mossy galls, that is." I rubbed my forehead and wished I would stop talking.

Willow presented a shoebox for Michael's perusal.

"Ah," he said, "there they are, the little mossy buggers."

I snorted.

"Well," Willow said, going round to the other side of the wall and her bicycle, "I'll leave you two to enjoy the afternoon. I'm all finished here."

"Willow, won't you stay?" I asked, and Michael threw me a look.

"No, thank you," she said, packing pincushions into her rucksack and wheeling her bicycle toward the path. "I have that other thing to do. Bye now," she called over her shoulder.

I stared after her.

Michael stood and took my hand. "What's wrong?"

I could feel my face draw up in worry.

"That other thing to do. She says she's going to talk to *him*," I said under my breath. "That Poor Man — the murder victim. She thinks she can ask him questions."

"She what?" Michael's head spun round to watch Willow's retreating figure.

"I'm afraid she wants to go to the pond."

He looked back at me and reached up with his thumb to smooth out the wrinkles on my forehead. "Well, then, we'd better go after her."

"Thank you." I gave him a quick kiss, turned, and called, "Willow!"

CHAPTER 13

Michael folded down the rear seat in his little Fiat and was able to get most of Willow's bicycle in, pulling down the lid of the boot and securing it with a bungee cord. I suggested we stop at the Hall instead of St. Swithun's — too near the pond, I thought — and was relieved when Willow agreed.

As she and I climbed into my car, I asked, "Have you explained to Cecil how concerned you are about That Poor Man?"

"No," Willow replied, frowning, which drew her freckles up into new formations. "I'm not sure how to begin it. And I don't want to worry him further."

"I'd say he'd much rather know than imagine. Why don't you have a chat with him before you . . . you know, do that other thing."

"Well, I might." As we passed an empty layby in the lane, she brightened. "Oh, they're gone now. Did you see them when you came up?"

"Who?"

"When I cycled by earlier, there was a couple with binoculars, looking out in the field and talking and laughing. I stopped and said hello."

"Did you know them?"

"No, but you do. It was Michael's sister and her friend — the fellow with the earring in the shape of a bird."

"Gavin?"

"Yes, that's him. Pammy told me they were watching a chiffchaff feeding on the fly. She said she'd never seen such a thing before."

Willow must've entered a parallel universe as she pedaled out — a place where Pammy enjoyed the outdoors and Gavin sought the ordinary. No, not possible — my brain would not accept this as reality. Gavin didn't do everyday birds. If it wasn't a hooded merganser from America sitting in a pond in Wiltshire, then it was nothing.

* * *

Michael made the left into the drive at Hoggin Hall ahead of us. As I slowed to follow, a green Morgan Roadster pulled round, heading into the village. I narrowed my eyes at it.

When we'd reached the yard, Willow popped out of the car. "Thank you for the lift, Julia, and for bringing my bicycle, Michael." She took her bike. "You're both so kind. Julia, the children and I are going to the market on Wednesday afternoon to buy ingredients for making pease porridge the next day. It's part of our maths unit, weights and measures." She smiled at both of us, and did not move.

"I wonder is Sheila busy?" I asked, looking over Willow's shoulder toward the kitchen and hoping to wrangle an invitation for tea and, at the same time, keep Willow at the Hall.

"Monday," Willow said. "I believe it's her day to run up to the big shops in Bury."

Darn, so it was.

"Well," Willow said, "bye now."

"Yes, bye."

As we watched her push the bicycle round the corner of the Hall, I said to Michael, "I suppose we'd better be off, then. I'll leave my car in the lockup and see you at home."

"Is she all right, do you think?"

"Hard to say, but I'm sure she'll be better when this is all settled. Tess told me they'll have a photo of the fellow tomorrow, and they'd start circulating it."

"Difficult to believe no one knows who he is."

* * *

After shutting my Fiat away, I gave the padlock a sharp yank, wishing I could do the same to Mr. Tony Brightbill's nose. I walked round the corner, past the green Morgan Roadster, and straight into Nuala's Tea Room, where I said hello to an elderly couple who sat at the window, idly stirring the dregs in their cups. Nuala called out a greeting from the next room, and Brightbill, settled at the corner table, legs crossed and with folded-out newspaper, looked over the tops of his reading glasses, and gave me one of his engaging and friendly smiles.

"We seem to be of one mind," he remarked.

"I doubt that," I snapped, and the elderly couple gave me a sideways look. I cleared my throat and smiled. "Good afternoon, Mr. Brightbill. I mean to say, you haven't chosen the chocolate cake, have you? Because, of course, that's what I'm having."

"No, but I've had the Victoria sponge, and it went down a treat. I'm thinking next time I'll choose the Battenberg."

My fingernails dug into the palms of my hands.

"Will you join me, Ms. Lanchester?" Brightbill gestured to a chair.

I will not. "Why, yes, thank you." I plopped down across from him.

"So, Mr. Brightbill, you seem to have made our little village your second home. Have you set up a camping cot in the backroom?"

"I believe in thorough research before making my next move," Brightbill replied as he slipped the newspaper into a leather bag at his feet.

What was that supposed to mean — next stop, Nuala's bed?

"Are you married?" I asked.

The question shot out of my mouth before I could or wanted to stop it, and it caught both of us by surprise. Make that three. Nuala had arrived carrying a small tray with my wedge of chocolate cake and pot of tea. She froze halfway to the table. There was a moment of silence for which the word "awkward" was an inadequate description. Brightbill's face revealed nothing, but I could feel mine warm, and I saw Nuala's cheeks redden.

"It's just that," I hurried on in a rescue attempt, "if you are, wouldn't this be a lovely place to bring your wife?"

The elderly couple stood, gathering up hats and bags. The man leaned over and said, "It is that."

Nuala retreated to settle the bill with the couple, and I stuck a fork in my cake, starting at the end with the most icing, and poured tea while I chewed.

"Where is it that you live, Mr. Brightbill?" Just a casual enquiry, my tone of voice said.

"In the north."

The north — what's that supposed to mean — Norfolk? Scotland? The Arctic?

"Well, you come a long way every day for tea. Are there no tea rooms where you live?"

That was a joke, apparently, because Brightbill chuckled. "Oh, there are a few."

"Have you been to Bettys?" I asked. "Up in Yorkshire? It's one of my favorites when I'm not here in Smeaton. Nothing like a Yorkshire fat rascal from Bettys."

"Bettys aren't the only game in town," Brightbill replied, sounding like a Chicago gangster in a movie. Blighter.

I did not give Nuala's chocolate cake the attention it deserved, although of course, I did finish it. But when my phone rang and I saw it was Linus, I said hurried goodbyes, left Nuala a tenner to put on my account, and answered out on the pavement.

"Hello, Linus. I'm so glad you rang, because I really do need to speak with you. I'm sorry I rushed off earlier."

"Is it about Willow?"

"No. Why?"

"Well, you had an idea about the man who was killed. And Willow, you know, is quite concerned."

Obsessed would be a better word. "Is she still talking about him?"

"She isn't here. Cecil is away until tomorrow, you see, and Sheila isn't back from shopping yet, but Thorne and I expected Willow by now. I rang Lottie at the shop, and she's not been there."

I peered up the high street. Although I was unable to see as far as St. Swithun's or the pond beyond, I could well imagine the sight.

"All right, Linus," I said as I began jogging. "I believe I know where she is, and I'm on my way there now. I'll ring you back."

As the church came into view, so did the police car parked at the side of the road with its blue lights flashing. And then I spotted Willow, inside the wrapping of police tape around the pond and with a uniformed PC on either side of her, their arms stretched out to corral her as if she were a skittish lamb trying to make a break for it. Willow stood in place and swatted at them, as if they were the flies she couldn't stop talking about. I heard the police offer calming phrases. "It's all right, miss." "Will you step away, please?" "Can we ring someone for you?" When I trotted up, one of them called out, "Stop right there, please!"

"Hello, officers," I panted. "I'm Julia Lanchester, manager of the Tourist Information Center here in the village. Is there a problem? This is Ms. Wynn-Finch. Willow, did you introduce yourself? I'm sure you know that Willow is the one who came upon the body of That Poor Man. And you understand what an effect that can have, don't you? And she's come back to . . . acknowledge his passing, haven't you, Willow?"

"I've come back because I need to ask—"

"Willow!"

"But, Julia, it's only that—"

"And now we'll be on our way, won't we, Willow?"

She dropped her arms, standing like a wilted flower, and murmured, "Yes, all right."

The uniforms exchanged glances, followed by one of them talking quietly into the radio clipped onto her shoulder strap.

"Yes, good," I said. "Are you making a call to Detective Inspector Callow? Or Detective Sergeant Glossop? I'm sure they'll explain who we are and that it's fine if — well, not fine, of course, that we are loitering out here. We understand that and we'll—"

A male voice came back over the radio, followed by a woman's voice. I sighed with relief when I recognized it as Tess's. My relief was tempered when my phone rang and the PC nodded to it. "Detective Inspector Callow would like to have a word, Ms. Lanchester."

CHAPTER 14

"You can understand, Willow, can't you, how it would be worrisome to everyone?" I asked as we walked down the high street toward Three Bags Full.

"That I want to talk with a dead man?" Willow asked. I cut my eyes at her, and she had the good sense to offer a chagrined smile. "I can't let it be, Julia. At first, it was incredibly upsetting. The state of the body, you know, and the . . ."

"Flies, yes."

"But over the next few days, it became more than that. And after talking with you yesterday, I feel so strongly there's something I'm supposed to know — something that would be of great help. But I can't think of what it is. It occurred to me, if I stood in the same place as last Thursday, it might help me remember. That he might send me a message."

Willow's explanation had started out quite sensibly, I decided not to push the matter.

Tess had asked me several crisp questions about what Willow thought she would gain by trespassing and possibly compromising a site that may still yield clues. And then the DI had assigned me the task to keep Willow well away from the murder scene, or next time the police would do more than wave their arms round. "Ring if you need me," she had added.

After that, she had radioed the uniforms to release us. I gave Linus and Lottie quick phone calls, followed by a brief text to Michael while Willow and I stood under the lych gate at the end of the church walk.

Now, as we walked past Nuala's, I breathed a sigh of relief to see that the curb in front was absent of a green Morgan Roadster. "Well," I said, "I think a cup of tea with Lottie will sort us out for now. Perhaps whatever that thing is will come back to you when you least expect it. Your aunt, by the way" — time for a chance of topic — "has had quite a colorful life so far."

Willow smiled, and my heart grew lighter. "Oh, God, yes," she said. "Lottie has always been a bit of a scandal in the family. She left home quite young — I think she was sixteen — and ended up living with Fernandes the artist, and traveled the world for years."

And posed almost starkers in the Place de la Concorde. The image was so alive in my mind, it was as if I stood there with her, the traffic whooshing by and horns blaring. I could almost feel a cold April wind nip at my bare bottom.

"I hope that shawl was big enough," I said.

"Not quite." Willow giggled. "I've seen the photos. Of course, that was Auntie's idea, not her partner's. Fernandes created installation art. Do you remember the Brolly Bridge in London?"

"That was a good few years ago, wasn't it? I remember seeing photos of colorful umbrellas covering the footbridge across the Thames. A ceiling of brollies. It made quite a splash."

"Fernandes. The bridge installation that brought them back to England, and Auntie says that's when she realized she wanted to stay in her own home country for good. Moving to Smeaton hasn't slowed her down, of course, it's only changed her focus. Do you know, she wove an enormous tapestry of a

Suffolk winter landscape entirely from natural white, cream, brown, and black wool? It's hanging in the Tate Britain."

* * *

We arrived at the shop, and Lottie took us upstairs to her flat after locking the front door and hanging a "Please ring the bell" sign. She lived in a rambling space with a couple of bedrooms and an expansive sitting room that felt like an extension of the shop below — abundantly colorful, stacked with extra containers of twisted skeins of yarn, and with a loom in one corner. She had poured small glasses of a Spanish sherry and offered a plate of savory tarts made with Manchego cheese and topped with a strip of sweet pepper.

Lottie gave her niece a hug, but wisely didn't ask for details of the recent escapade. Willow appeared entirely, incredibly, and truly her old self by the time I left, although, at the door, she did take my arm and give me a significant look. I responded with a promise to let her know whatever I learned from the police.

At my Pipit Cottage, I stopped on the pavement and counted vehicles — three. Not only were Pammy's Ford Fiesta and Michael's Fiat parked at the curb, but also a well-used red hatchback I recognized as Gavin's.

Having managed to avoid Willow being arrested for interfering in a murder investigation, I opened the cottage door on a prelude to a brawl.

"She's a grown woman, if you haven't noticed," Gavin growled, "and she can make her own decisions."

Michael stuck a finger in Gavin's face. "Don't you talk about my sister that way."

"Hello, all," I chirped, standing in the doorway, because the men blocked my path to either the kitchen or the sofa. Pammy perched on the third step up the stairs, her arms wrapped tightly across her chest.

"Julia," Gavin said coolly, sticking his hands in the pockets of his leather jacket. "As I hadn't heard any details yet"

— he glared at Michael — "I stopped to talk with Sedgwick about the segment for Rupert's show."

"Well, that's nice of you, Gavin, to save Michael having to track you down. Isn't it?" I smiled sweetly at Michael until his eyes, dark as night, lightened to cobalt.

"Yeah," he muttered. "Great."

"So, look" — I scooted past Michael, planting a kiss on his neck as I went — "the two of you can sit at the table here and get this all settled. Pammy and I will . . ."

"Why don't you go on to the pub?" Michael asked.

"No," Pammy said from above. "We'll stay here. Won't we, Julia?"

I caught the worry in the glance she threw me, and I had to admit, I agreed. "Good idea. I tell you what, we'll sit in the garden and have a glass of wine." I grabbed the last of a bottle on the counter, Pammy scooped up two glasses, and we escaped to sit on the stone terrace, keeping the French doors behind us open.

"Do you think they'll behave?" Pammy asked as we sat and I poured.

"We can only hope."

Gone six o'clock. We'd piles of daylight left and a good show in front of us. I watched the birds, and Pammy watched her phone. At least, that's what I thought. But after a few minutes, she pointed out to the garden and said, "That's a . . ."

I followed her direction. "Blackbird."

"Yeah, right, that's it. Blackbird." She cut her eyes at me. "Er, Julia, I didn't actually go look at a flat today."

"Or yesterday?"

"Or yesterday."

I can't say the truth didn't hurt. "So, instead, Gavin's taken you out birdwatching?"

That embarrassed-pleased-hesitant look that marked the threshold of a new relationship blossomed on Pammy's face.

"Yeah. He's really sweet," she said. "I don't know anything about all this nature stuff, but Gavin says it's all right, he'll teach me. I've seen a robin, a starling, a sparrow . . ."

she counted them off on her fingers. "And one of those," she added, nodding to the feeder.

"Goldfinch."

"Is it?" she asked. "Shouldn't he be pink?"

"No, he should be gold. Maybe you're thinking of a chaffinch."

"A what?"

Good luck to you, Gavin.

"We've been all over your estate," Pammy said. "I quite enjoyed myself, actually. Funny, that." Her tone was incredulous, as if she had discovered that walking across hot coals barefoot was, in reality, a pleasant experience.

"Normally," I said, "Gavin goes for the more unusual sighting. Dashing off, for example, to see a bird that has flown in from South America for the day."

"Twitching." Pammy nodded. "He told me it's sort of like hunting, but without killing anything, just so you can add a bird to your list. He said it can be quite exciting."

Or not. "I hear you met Willow today."

"Yeah, she was wearing that paisley tunic in shades of lavender. Linen blend, I should think. It had two pearl buttons at the bodice and a crisscross pattern stitched into the neckline. Not something I see much of in the charity shops. Looked lovely on her."

Ah, so Pammy did have powers of observation, only in a narrow band of interest.

"Did you enjoy it, being outdoors all day?"

"Not all day. Gavin took me to lunch."

* * *

Just when I was beginning to think how civilized Michael and Gavin were behaving, their voices rose in volume and heated up in tone. I nodded to Pammy, and we stepped indoors in time to hear Gavin say, "The birds don't book ahead, you know. I can't tell that far in advance."

"I won't have a camera crew on hold just for this." Michael jabbed a finger at the notes in front of him.

"One camera, one person, that's all," Gavin shot back. "Even you could manage that."

"Of course he can," I slipped in. "Michael's done plenty of shooting — there was that fantastic video of a green woodpecker, remember? And the one with the lesser whitethroat?"

Probably shouldn't've brought that one up. He'd come back wet and cold from several hours at Minsmere reserve waiting out the elusive lesser whitethroat, aka "that damned little bird."

Michael drummed his fingers on the table for a moment, and then slammed his pencil down. "Right, but you've got to give me at least two hours notice — and we're not driving to the bloody Lake District just to stand vigil at a farmer's horse trough."

I beamed at them. "So, all settled?"

"None too soon," Gavin said, checking his phone. "I've got to get to work."

And just when I thought the world couldn't get any stranger, Gavin gets a job.

Pammy walked him to the door, and I distinctly heard him whisper to her, "See you Wednesday." Michael, looking out the French doors with his back to them, slowly rotated his head as if his ear sought a better radio signal. I glanced over at the pair and caught Gavin give Pammy a kiss on the cheek. It made me smile.

"Julia," Gavin said, "what's happened to the field and verges out beyond those ruins of yours? They've gone all brown. It's too early for that. Are you letting the farmers spray?"

"No, we are not. At least, I don't think so. I'm not sure, actually. There's no estate agent, and Linus and Cecil are stretched trying to oversee everything. Where did you say it was?"

He gave me vague directions, and I made a mental note to mention it to Linus. Or better yet, I'd ask Guy Pockett. His farm was out that way. He would know.

***

We were treated at supper to a chicken tikka masala Pammy had come across at Akash's shop on the day of its expiry, so it had been marked down. During dinner, I made a vague reference to Willow and Lottie, because we still hadn't brought up the subject of That Poor Man to Pammy, and I wanted to keep it that way. I ended on a pleasant subject.

"Willow's class has built a toad house. Perhaps she'll snap a photo of the resident and send it in for Rupert's Wild About Schools page on the website. Are you interested?" I asked Michael.

"Interested?" Pammy grinned. "He's Toad of Toad Hall, he is. Isn't that right, Michael?"

Michael laughed and blushed. "Come on, Pammy, you're not going to dredge that up, are you?"

Words of invitation to a big sister. Pammy gave him a nudge with her elbow. "Have you not told Julia about the time you took one of Mum's best handbags and put it out in the garden for the toads to live in?"

"I was only four at the time."

"Yeah," she said. "It's your age that got you off."

I laughed with them. Siblings — one second they bicker, the next they laugh. Seeing these two reminded me it had been days since I'd talked with Bianca. I'd send her a text before bed.

"Dad and I built a real toad house after that," Michael said to me.

Pammy turned thoughtful. "Does it matter how big the door is for a toad's house? Because Gavin says that birds are quite particular about the little doors for their houses."

Michael threw his napkin on the table. "That's fine. Are we to be regaled with lessons from Gavin Lecky now? The world's smartest twitcher."

Pammy grabbed her phone in a huff and moved to the sofa. "Other people can know things, too. You aren't the only one."

I reached over and stroked the back of Michael's hand. "The segment on twitchers will be quite good."

He grabbed my hand and gave it a kiss. "Yeah, it will. And then he'll be more insufferable than ever."

I saw Pammy lift her gaze at the challenge. But I wasn't up for continuing the brother-sister battle, and so I veered off in another direction.

"Pammy, I believe you're right about that fellow being married. The one who's after Nuala. It's despicable, it really is." I held my breath for a moment, remembering Pammy had just exited a relationship with a married man.

"Too right," she said. "Have you warned her?"

"Not yet, but I asked him a few pointed questions today, which he deftly sidestepped." I could feel my ire rising, and I needed to vent. "Making himself right at home, he is, and worming his way into Nuala's good graces. Well, I can tell you this — Mr. Anthony Brightbill is not going to get away with it."

Michael frowned. "Tony Brightbill?"

I frowned back. "Yes, Tony Brightbill. Do you know him?"

"Sure, I—"

"But why didn't you tell me?"

"You've only just now said his name," Michael pointed out.

"Oh, right. How do you know him?"

"We had his account. I mean, HMS had it."

HMS, Ltd. — the Sedgwick family's public relations firm Michael had quit when he took up the post as Rupert's personal assistant and producer.

"Brightbill owns three or four tea rooms in the North," Michael continued. "Upscale places. He wants to unseat Bettys, and he's giving good chase, I've got to admit."

I shot out of my chair, my mouth opening and closing like a marionette. At last, I stammered, "Tea rooms? Is that what this is about?"

Michael held out his hands to me. "Look, Julia—"

"Because I can tell you right now, Nuala has no idea it's about her tea rooms. She thinks he's . . . well, we all thought he . . . Wait, *is* he married?"

"Well, Pammy," Michael said, turning to his sister. "Is he?"

She had kept to her phone during our exchange, but now her head snapped up. "It wasn't like that and you know it. Bit of harmless flirting, that's all. I wouldn't have anything to do with the bloke — he's a bloody Dr. Jekyll and Mr. Hyde, that one. All charm one second, and the next, he turns into a monster."

"There's no excuse for how he treated you," Michael said, "but—"

Pammy cut her brother off. "No excuse for how Miles fired his own sister over one little slip." Pammy slammed her phone down on the coffee table, her face flushed.

"One little slip?" Michael repeated, his eyebrows shooting up.

I wiggled a few fingers in their direction. "Am I allowed to hear the whole story?"

Michael gestured to his sister that the floor was all hers.

"I confused a couple of his appointments," Pammy said in a small voice.

"Let me translate for you," Michael said. "First, Pammy wore Miles down until he gave her a job as receptionist."

"Receptionist," Pammy scoffed. "General dogsbody, you mean."

"And when she begged for more responsibility, Miles assigned her the task of typing up and sending out the schedule HMS had created for the best grand opening of Tony's latest tea room. Somewhere along the way, the details went awry — all of them."

"The phone wouldn't stop ringing," Pammy said, tears in her eyes, "and I got mixed up."

"HMS totally bollocksed an important day for him," Michael persisted. "He missed the launch of his shop in Ilkley, so there was no owner to cut the ribbon, which meant he not only stood up the community, but also the local BBC camera crew. All while he spent a good part of the day arriving at three radio stations across the county at the wrong times. Oh, and let's not forget he stood up the food editor from *Yorkshire Life* magazine. He canceled his contract with us on the spot. Walked out."

"My God," I whispered as the horror of it all became clear. "Now I see what he's up to oozing into our village. He's trying to lure Nuala away. Does he think she'd give up her home and her friends to run one of his places?"

"It's just the sort of thing he would think," Pammy said. "Tosser."

Michael only shook his head.

"So, that's what he's been on about all along." I paced a couple of steps to and fro. "Perhaps he wants to set her up as head baker in one of his tea rooms. Or, would he dangle an even larger scone in front of her — director of all menus and creator of recipes for . . . What are they called, his places?"

"Tara's Tea," Pammy said. "That's his wife."

CHAPTER 15

"What time does he arrive at Nuala's?" Michael asked me the next morning, as we dressed upstairs.

"I'm not sure — three o'clock, four maybe. He stays forever, doing his crossword puzzle and chatting up Nuala. He's probably working his way through her menu. Yesterday, he told me he was actually going to try the Battenberg."

"The nerve," Michael murmured.

My fury, quiet over night, had rekindled the next morning, and I trembled as I tried to button my blouse. Finally, Michael brushed my hands away and took over, but we both laughed when we saw that instead of buttoning, he'd unbuttoned — a more common activity.

I sobered up again quick enough. "Battenberg is Linus's favorite. Brightbill's making it look like a direct personal challenge, and he doesn't even mean it. He's toying with us. Them."

"Why don't I meet you at Nuala's at four o'clock?"

"Would you? Thanks. You know him, so you'd be better at sorting it out and sending him packing. I'm afraid I'd just shove his face into a bowl of double cream, and that would be a terrible waste."

As we left the cottage, I waved at Pammy and said, "See you later." Outside on the pavement, I gave a thought to how easily the days had worn me down. What had happened to my former life?

At the TIC, I unlocked the door and Guy Pockett followed in on my heels.

"Tuesday, you know," he said, bouncing a little in place. "With the market tomorrow, I've a great deal to do."

"I would've come out to you," I reminded him, handing him his stack of papers.

"No, s'all right. Thanks." He took them and set them down on the table by the computer while he pulled several other weathered sheets out of his portfolio. "And for you — I don't suppose you'd noticed these had gone missing. I must've picked them up with my stuff the other day."

At first, I thought the papers he handed me were more farm business, speckled with dried mud as they were. But on closer examination, I saw the bold heading on one sheet: JOIN US! SMEATON-UNDER-LYME E-NEWSLETTER SIGN-UP.

I gasped as Guy's brain shot off in another direction. "Have you done a market feature in the newsletter?" he asked. "Shouldn't it be a regular thing? You could feature a different vendor each time. Do you want me to write one up? I'll put something together and send it off to you, all right? And say, you'll let me know when you want to talk about the market manager position? I'm off now."

None of his words registered — none of them mattered. "Cheers," I called mindlessly as he disappeared out the door.

I stared at the paper. Here it was, the missing page of sign-ups. It started with the date of Saturday week, the day before the family came in. My trembling finger slowly went down the list. The email address had been written by a girl not more than nine years old, so surely I would recognize it. "Be firm," her mum had said.

"*This one!*" I raised my arms in victory.

Yes, a nine-year-old girl's handwriting was different — she wrote more carefully than adults. *PEARS_WE4@bt.co.uk* — this had to be the one.

Vesta arrived as I switched on the kettle. "You'll never guess," I said, dancing a jig on the spot. "I might know of someone who met That Poor Man." I started in on the whole story. "It's a long shot, I know, but it could be something."

"So, this family met a fellow, but only know him as 'Bob'?"

I nodded, staring at the kettle as it rattled its way to boil. "Come on, come on" — I glanced at Vesta — "I've had no tea yet, and I'm gasping."

"Running late this morning?"

"Out of milk," I admitted, dropping tea bags into our mugs. "Again."

"Do you have a photo of the victim?"

"Tess promised one today. I'll email this family first thing. They may be able to come out and look at it. Wouldn't it be fantastic if I could say to police, 'Look, I've found an eyewitness for you'?"

"You could turn the email address over to DI Callow," Vesta suggested, popping open the biscuit tin.

Avoiding the knowing gaze of my co-worker, I paused with the milk jug suspended over my mug. "But what if this isn't the family? I wouldn't want to waste police time."

* * *

"Listen and see how this sounds," I said to Vesta as I popped the last bite of a digestive biscuit in my mouth. A visitor had just departed, and it was quiet. I cleared my throat. "Thank you for visiting the Fotheringill estate . . . blah blah blah . . . Have I reached the family that mentioned meeting a man named Bob? If so, I hope you might do us an enormous favor by helping to locate . . ." I frowned. "'Locate,' do you think, Vesta, or 'identify'? I don't want to say he's dead, because we don't know it's him, do we?"

Vesta suggested "tell us more about him," and I went with it. I hit "send," and was about to follow up with a call to Tess, but the door jingled, and I had no more time to think of That Poor Man, as four Girl Guide leaders arrived to arrange an evening owl walk in August. It was twelve o'clock before I checked our email and found a more enthusiastic reply than I had anticipated.

"Remembering our lovely time and would be happy to assist. I'm free today and will drive up to see you. Best, Tommy Pears."

What, now? Breathless, I rang Tess and got her voice mail. "I might know who the victim is. That is, was. Not me, but someone's stopping by. It's the dad of this family who met a man on the estate that might have been That Poor Man. And the dad may be here soon — I don't really know where he's coming from — and we've no photo to show him. And also, well, I suppose you may want to talk with him. So, let me know."

Not terribly coherent, but that's what happens when you anticipate a scolding for acting without police consent.

* * *

Vesta and I sat at the back table over our sandwiches when the bell jingled. I jumped when I saw it was DI Callow, looking as official as ever — not just her neat black trouser suit and sleek black satchel, but also the icy look on her face.

"So," I said with great cheer, "I'd say you got my message. Tea?"

Vesta busied herself dusting the front window as I gave Tess a clearer explanation about the family and the possibility of an ID.

"Not bad, eh?" I asked, eager for teacher's approval.

"You should've phoned me first," Tess said.

"But see, I didn't need to, did I? Tommy Pears is on his way and you're here and you have . . . Do you have a photo?"

Tess took a file folder from her satchel, and pulled out a close-up of a face. I looked away, getting a first impression only in my peripheral vision. Slowly, I dragged my eyes over to the color photo of a man — late fifties, possibly older

— with receding dark hair. His face was pallid and he looked tired, with lines around his eyes and thick eyebrows. One earlobe was all but missing. Oh God, I hope that wasn't done by one of the crows. No mud and certainly no indication of what the back of his head looked like.

He had brown eyes.

"His eyes are open," I said quietly.

"Computer. It's always best to make the body look as alive as possible — doesn't put people off that way."

"Is that" — I swallowed hard and pointed at the missing earlobe — "from being out there for days?"

The DI shook her head. "It's an old scar, perhaps a childhood accident." Tess studied the photo. "The FME has decided it was most likely later on Saturday he died, judging from the deterioration of skin and—"

"Will you circulate the photo?" I broke in, uninterested in the progression of body decomposition. The kettle came to a boil, and I poured the water and took the milk out of the fridge.

"I've shown it to Ms. Wynn-Finch just now at her school. It was the children's break time."

"How did she take it?"

"She didn't know him."

"But was she all right?"

"She was a bit emotional, but there was another teacher there who took her in hand."

I'd need to check on Willow later.

Tess reached for her tea. "We've a pair of uniforms starting here in the village and another pair going to the hamlets you told the sergeant about." As she poured milk, she added, "That was good thinking about the family."

Rather pleased with myself at the compliment, because the DI gave out few of them, I became modest. "Well, just a hunch," I said.

I cleared the table, shifting things to beside the computer, and as I did so I discovered that the papers Guy Pockett had come to retrieve had been left behind. Again.

"Would you look at that?" I asked no one in particular. "I don't see how he keeps anything straight. Well, I'll not be the cause of wrong deliveries of soil or seed or whatever this all is," I muttered, stuffing them in my bag. "I'll run them out this afternoon."

Tess copied down the family's email address as we heard the door, announcing the arrival of a tall woman, mid-thirties, dressed in slim ankle trousers and a thin cardigan. She had her blond hair pulled back in a ponytail.

"Hello," she said to Vesta. "I'm looking for Julia Lanchester. I'm Tommy Pears."

CHAPTER 16

"You are Tommy Pears?" I asked, coming round the counter. "I'm sorry, I thought—"

"It's Thomasina, actually," she said and laughed. "You can see why I go by Tommy. But you thought I was my husband, Noel. It happens a lot. That was our family email address Tilly wrote down, and we can all check it. I hope you don't mind I came out straightaway. It's actually a bit of a break for me."

"We're delighted to see you," I said. "Thank you so much for returning."

DI Callow came from behind me, held out her badge and warrant card, and introduced herself.

"Oh dear," Tommy said, her eyes darting from the inspector to me. "Is there a problem?"

"Ms. Pears, I would like you to come with me to the police station in Sudbury," Callow said.

"Why?" Panic showed on the woman's face, her pupils dilated, her breath rapid. "What's happened?"

"Nothing has happened," the DI rushed to say, "it's only that we hope you can help us with an enquiry."

"Have you come far, Ms. Pears?" I asked.

Her eyes flickered to me. "London. Dagenham."

"Well, there's no need for you to get back in your car again and drive off to Sudbury — you can chat with Inspector Callow here at the back table." Tess threw me a suspicious look, probably accusing me of trying to hijack her investigation, but Tommy's relief was so clear, the DI relented.

Vesta and I formed a solid front at the counter, and so screening the worktable. We kept busy with visitors coming in and out — she chatted about the opening times at the Hall while I painted a glowing picture of our summer supper, noting tickets would go on sale soon. All the while, I kept an ear out for the quiet conversation behind me, but I picked up only snatches of phrases. "yet to identify" and "the man you met" and "we would like you to look at a photo."

In a quiet moment before the bell above the door jingled again, I heard a small cry, followed by, "Yes, that is him. How dreadful!"

Dreadful, yes, but a relief of sorts. Now, That Poor Man had a name, although only one. Bob. My attention was taken by three history buffs, engaging me in a discussion about airfields of the Second World War, but still I tried to listen to the inspector's questions. Exactly where had the family met him? What time of day? Did he mention where he lived, what he did, where he came from, anyone he knew, if he had any family? She received precious few answers in return.

When the TIC emptied of visitors, I switched on the kettle again as Tommy told Tess, "We didn't see him at all the second time we visited." She became teary and said to me, "And now I know why. Dead all that time. It's so sad. I thought this was about the award you wanted to give him. He was such a kind man, and respectful, too, you know. He said what a lovely family we were and how he always liked to see a dad and a mum and the children enjoying their time together."

Vesta came up with a box of tissues as Tommy's tears spilled over. She blotted her face, but continued to weep into her tea.

The DI remained attentive, but I sensed a mental tapping of her toe, as if she would prefer to be away and onto business rather than clustered round a table not quite big enough for four. "You've been very helpful," she said. "Is there someone you would like us to phone for you?"

"No, I'm all right. I don't know why I should be like this. It's just such a tragedy." Tommy sniffed and dabbed her eyes. "I would like to have talked with him again, just to . . . He said we were a lovely family. And we are, you know."

* * *

The detective inspector stared at the door after Tommy Pears left. "Dagenham," she said. "An hour-and-a-half journey one way. It's a long drive on the merits of one 'Bob,' unknown fellow."

"Tommy said it was 'a bit of a break' for her," I said. "I think she's enjoyed he visits here — until now. So, will the first name of 'Bob' help you identify the man?"

I received a noncommittal half shrug. "I'm going to take a look at those abbey ruins. Is it straight out of the village? I'll put it in satnav."

"'Fotheringill abbey ruins' in your satnav will get you nowhere," I said. "Vesta, are you all right the rest of the afternoon? I could lead Inspector Callow to the ruins. I'm going out that way to hand over this paperwork to Guy once and for all."

"Yes, you go along," Vesta said.

I pointed to the photo of Bob. "May we keep a copy of that?"

* * *

Five copies, to start with. I took one with me and offered to circulate another at the farmers market the next day, but once Tess found out there would be a fair-size gathering of locals, she said she would have DS Glossop and DC Flynn out to sweep the green.

I stopped at the ruins with her, walking carefully through the gravel and grass in my heels, and gave her an idea of the layout. "We should add picnic tables," I said, more to myself than her. "Although there are flat stones, and nooks within all the various walls, so loads of places to relax. The brook runs away there" — I pointed beyond — "but there are no facilities and no makeshift campsites that I know of."

Tess stood still and took it all in. "Right, thanks," she said. My dismissal.

"Well, you'll let me know, won't you? Anything?"

The DI raised an eyebrow.

"For Willow," I persisted. "It would help to have some sort of resolution." I had rung Lottie earlier, who said Willow had been in good spirits when she'd left for school, but then the DI had stopped with a photo of the man, and who knows what having seen that might've set off. "She has got it in her head that there's something she should remember, but can't."

That got the inspector's attention. "She needs to come in and sign her statement — perhaps I'll have another chat."

"Right, I'll leave you here," I said, checking the time. "I'm off to Guy Pockett's farm, and then I must meet Michael at Nuala's Tea Room at four. We've a little matter of harassment to deal with."

"You're being harassed?" Tess frowned.

"No, Nuala is. Well, she's not really being harassed, but . . ." And so I told Tess the story of the aggravating Mr. Tony Brightbill.

"It's her decision whether she goes or stays."

"He's making his interest look like something it isn't," I retorted. "He's a specious suitor, to say the least, and someone needs to do something about it."

"Isn't that up to the earl?"

"Linus needs a nudge."

* * *

I continued to Guy Pockett's farm, bouncing along a deeply rutted track and edging up onto the soft, flat verge whenever possible. And so it was that I came slowly upon a scene of devastation that robbed me of breath. A field that should have been green with swaying tall grass, and dotted with purple selfheal and knapweed, plantains and buttercups, orange clusters of fox-and-cubs and copious amounts of daisies was instead a brown expanse of death. Flowers melted into blobs, and tall stalks, bent as if they had been snapped at the neck, rattling in the breeze. When I stopped, I found myself just opposite Guy's cottage.

And here he came, sprinting from his shed to my car. I jumped out before he got to me.

"What's this?" I pointed to the dead field. "That's your new field. What happened?"

He wiped his upper lip. "What do you mean?"

"I'm not blind, Guy. What have you done?"

"Nothing. I've done nothing." His eyes darted round. He was sweating so profusely, I could smell the fear.

"You're certified organic, you sell organic produce." I pointed behind the cottage to his cultivated fields and saw each rimmed with the same brown death. "You've sprayed herbicide," I said in horrified amazement. "Are you mad? After the years it took you—"

"Things got away from me," he said in a rush. "I was behind in my planting and with Fran gone . . . I only wanted to control the weeds, stop them from invading the crops, and then I had that new field, and how was I supposed to get it under cultivation the way it looked. I didn't mean to do so much, only—"

"You could've asked for help! It took you two years to be certified organic. And you know better — you haven't lessened your workload, you've added to it, because all the insects and birds that would eat the pests will now go elsewhere."

The cuckoos. I had told Dad this would be a prime field to film a segment. He could have highlighted the birds that eat the hairy caterpillars that feed off the plantain and other wild plants. It had been a perfect example of how food production for people and habitat for wildlife can coexist. And now it wasn't.

"I'm sorry," Guy said. "I didn't think. Once I started, I just didn't stop. You won't tell anyone, will you?"

"Don't be daft, Guy, of course, I'll have to tell Lord Fotheringill. But you know that's your organic certification gone."

"I thought I could get it plowed before . . . I didn't think anyone would see."

"And that would've make it right?" I reached into my bag and drew out his handful of bills and invoices. "I suppose you might've got away with it, except you can't seem to keep hold of these."

The photo of the corpse had got caught in the papers, and when Guy took the paperwork, he stared down at the face.

"That's Bob," he said. "What are you doing with a snapshot of him? Why does he look so odd?"

The world round us grew still.

"Yes, it's Bob," I said. "Do you know him? What's his surname? Where did he come from? Where did you meet him? Do you know where he lived?"

Guy blinked at my rapid questions. "He's just Bob. Been round for a few months, I suppose, doing odd jobs for me and at a few other farms, too. I pay him a bit. He never asks for much."

"Where did he stay?"

"He's never said. He just shows up and asks if I have anything for him, and he works and I give him a sandwich and a cup of tea, and he talks about trees and animals in the wood and such. He spotted Fran's old bicycle she left in the barn and asked if he could use it." Guy shrugged. "No point in me keeping it, so I let him. But why are you asking all this. Has he done something?"

"He's dead."

Guy dropped his hand to his side, the papers coming loose and landing in a scattered heap. I put my foot on one that the breeze threatened to catch, and Guy bent over to retrieve the others. With his head down, he asked, "Dead? What do you mean?"

"He was found dead by the pond near St. Swithun's. When was the last time you saw him?"

Guy straightened up and turned away from me, as if looking round the yard for any sign of Bob. "I don't know. A few days ago. No, a week or more. A fortnight? I thought he might've moved on — he seemed the sort. How did it happen? Did he just die?"

"No," I said. "He didn't just die."

CHAPTER 17

My thoughts bounced round in my head as I drove away from Guy Pockett's formerly organic farm. One second I was elated that I'd found a witness who may know even more about Bob than Tommy Pears, and the next second fury took hold as I thought about what Guy had done and the consequences he and the estate would suffer.

What would Linus do — remove him from the farm? And here I had been touting our fields as a perfect film spot for Dad. Well, that was off. We'd find no cuckoos on the Fotheringill estate now. Except, of course, for the one in Pipit Cottage.

The nerve of Guy to think that if no one saw what he'd done, he could get away with it. Well, someone had seen, and he must now cope with the repercussion.

Tess. I needed to tell Tess that Guy knew Bob. Why didn't this man Bob have a surname? Perhaps police could tease more details out of Guy. Bob had worked for him, and so he must've dropped details about his life into idle conversation.

I pulled into the abbey ruins car park. No black Volvo, so the DI had gone. I sent her a text: *Estate farmer Guy Pockett knew Bob. Ask about bicycle.* I added Guy's phone number and sent my text on its way. I followed that with an after-school text to Willow. *How are you doing? How are the toads?* I considered telling her about Bob, but when she replied that she was at the Hall having tea with Sheila, I decided to put that off. I ticked "check in with Willow" off my mental list.

Finally, I rang Linus, and told him about Guy.

"It's a damned shame," Linus said, his words short and clipped — the only indication of his anger. "I'm going to pass this to Cecil. He worked with Guy on the certification. You can be sure Guy won't be at the market tomorrow."

"Yes, and he'll be missed. Such a foolish thing." I kept quiet about the recent quasi-identification of Bob, because I had another pressing issue to broach with Linus. I checked the time — almost four o'clock.

"Linus, are you free at the moment?"

"I can break away. Is there something else?"

"Yes. Nuala needs you."

* * *

I explained before I drove away from the ruins. I hadn't wanted to make it sound as if the situation were dire, but I did want Linus, who was known for his skill at calm and sensible discussion in the face of panic, to see the danger. My last comment "Look sharp, Linus" appeared to do the trick, and I was glad. This was no time for diplomacy.

Not that Linus would ever resort to physically attacking Tony Brightbill. Would he? I started the engine of my car and put my foot down. Perhaps I could reach Nuala's before him. Would he cycle in or drive?

On the road, I slowed behind a car that waited to turn right into Church Lane, and lost my train of thought when I glanced over to the Stoat and Hare and noticed a man just exiting. Something about him — that black curly hair — gave me pause. It was Mr. Pears. What did Tommy say her husband's name was? Noel. The traffic cleared, the car in front of me turned right, and I followed suit, pulling up at the curb in front of the pub.

"Hello," I said, taking my foot off the clutch in such a rush, my car lurched forward before dying. "Mr. Pears, is it?" I called out the window.

He looked at me blankly. "Sorry?"

"I'm Julia Lanchester." I leapt from the car and patted my nametag "From the Tourist Information Center. We met last Sunday week."

"Yes," he said, laughing and touching my arm lightly. "Sorry, of course I remember. We had a fine day."

"Lovely, I'm so glad. But I want to explain that I was the one who sent the email this morning asking about the man you'd met on your first visit here. And it was good of your wife to come out to us."

"She's here?" He looked up and down the road.

"She came to look at a photo we had. You did see my email? Did you speak to your wife?"

He shook his head, letting loose a damp curl on his forehead. "Well, the thing is I've been working in Newcastle, and it's a long drive back — sort of dulls the senses, you know. I've not seen Tommy yet. Is she at your tourist office?"

"No, I believe she's gone by now. I'm sorry you both made the journey."

"Not a bother." He exhaled, his eyes continuing to scan the lane. "And so, about the man?"

"Tommy was able to help us." I hesitated for a moment, and then plunged in. "I'm sorry to have to tell you, but Bob — that nice fellow you met — has died, and the police are having a difficult time finding out who he is."

"Police?" His dark eyes homed in on my face, and he frowned. "What have they got to do with it?"

"Well, er . . . suspicious circumstances, you see."

"Oh, I see," Noel said. "It's just that when you said he'd died, I thought . . . I don't know. I remember it looked as if he was living rough, and, well, a person like that can meet with all sorts of accidents."

I shook my head. "Not an accident. I'm sure your wife will explain. The police may want to talk with you as well, just in case you remember something different. Rest assured, we will not stop until we find out what happened to him. We already have a lead." Best to instill confidence about how we handle things on the estate, I thought, deciding to wrap up our conversation on a lighter note. "Did you enjoy the Stoat and Hare?"

Noel glanced over his shoulder at the door of the pub. "I only nipped in to use the gents'."

* * *

Noel Pears was on his phone as I got in my car. Good. I rather thought Tommy Pears needed some loving care, she seemed so affected by Bob's death. I drove the short distance down the high street to Nuala's, noting both the green Morgan Roadster as well as Linus's bicycle parked out front, before turning into the lane to my lockup. When I'd secured the door, I straightened my blouse and cardigan, and marched off.

When I opened the tea room door, a sea of little girls surged out, each wearing a tiara and all in a fit of giggles, followed by two women, acting as herders. I let them flow round me, before stepping indoors to a thick silence.

My entrance, in the wake of the little girls, went unnoticed. Michael leaned forward in his chair, while Tony Brightbill, across from him, sat back with his legs crossed. The table carried the remains of tea and empty plates — the crumbs on Brightbill's spoke of Battenberg. At their table stood Linus, with his back to me. Nuala was nowhere in sight.

"I was impressed immediately, Linus," Brightbill was saying, "and you can't blame me for wanting to take Nuala away from you. She's quite valuable."

Linus's back was rigid. "If you don't mind, Tony, I'd rather you didn't speak of Nuala as a commodity. She's a *friend*."

"Well, I'm only talking in business terms, of course," Brightbill replied. "And you can't deny it's a great opportunity for her."

All three turned their heads at the sputtering sound I made. I cleared my throat, and said, "Hello. What a surprise to see you all here."

Michael rose and came to me, putting an arm round my shoulder — part protection, part restraint. Linus nodded a greeting.

"As I mentioned to Michael," Brightbill continued, "other concerns had brought me to Suffolk but it's because of Ms. Lanchester I came to Smeaton."

"My fault, is it?"

"My gain, I'd say," he replied.

Linus's thin mustache matched the straight line of his mouth. I could see him breathing heavily, stirring himself up to knock the charm out of Brightbill, I hoped. But instead, he exhaled in a rush and said, "It's Nuala's decision, of course, whether or not she accepts an offer from you. Your corporate environment is beyond the realm of this estate, and I will not be one to stand in her way."

A crash of metal in the next room made us jump.

"Nuala?" Linus called. "Excuse me, I'll just see—"

He stepped away, and we all waited in silence. Michael watched me as I kept my eyes on Brightbill, who glanced with feigned concern toward the kitchen. I heard a brief exchange, ending in Nuala's raised voice, "No, thank you. I'm fine."

Linus reappeared quickly, his face an unpleasant mix of hurt and anger. He toyed with the flap on his jacket pocket before pulling out his trouser clip, and saying, "Well, I believe I'll be on my way now. Julia. Tony. Michael."

He'd left before any of us moved. I slipped out of Michael's hold, but took his hand and gave it a squeeze. "You go on ahead. I'll see you at home," I told him.

"I'll wait for you."

"No, it's all right." I smiled. "I only want to see if Nuala has any lemon drizzle left. Goodbye, Mr. Brightbill."

* * *

Behind the counter in the next room, several empty cake pans lay strewn across the floor. There was no sign of Nuala. I walked further back, and turned a corner where the door of the pantry stood ajar and light poured out.

"Nuala?" I asked as I pulled the door open.

Thunk. Nuala had her back to me as she dropped a sack of flour onto a cart, and, pointing with her index finger, made a show of counting how many sacks remained on the shelves. Over her shoulder, she said, "Oh, Julia, can I help you with something?" She fussed with containers of caster sugar, shifting them an inch or two, and picked up a roll of marzipan and put it down again.

"It's a terrible thing what Tony Brightbill did," I said.

Nuala whirled round, and I recoiled at the ghostly pallor of her face and her hair, which had gone completely white. When I saw the front of her navy apron with a similar coating, I looked up to the top shelf and spied a sack of flour that had split, sifting its contents upon her. I also noticed her powdery face was marked with tracks of tears.

"Did you tell Linus to come here?" she demanded.

"I, well, yes. I thought he could—"

"Use me as a bargaining chip in negotiations?" The red of her cheeks glowed through the coating of flour.

"Nuala, you know that isn't what Linus meant."

"I have no idea what he meant." She stalked past me, out of the pantry and into her work area, where she yanked open the fridge, took out a portion of butter as big as a shoebox, and slammed it on the counter. "But I'm coming to realize that perhaps it's time I, too, look at life as one enormous business proposition. I may very well talk with Tony about what he has to offer."

"No, please, it's my fault that—"

"And now, Julia" — she brushed off her apron and a cloud of flour rose — "Did you need something? Because I've a good deal of work to finish up here."

* * *

I couldn't get anything else out of her, apart from the last half loaf of lemon drizzle. Something had gone quite wrong here. I had believed Linus would step up and tell Nuala how he felt about her and from that moment on, all those dinner parties and games of charades in the library at Hoggin Hall would be hosted not by lonely Lord Fotheringill, but by Linus and Nuala, the happy couple. Was that so far-fetched?

The tea room was empty, the cups and plates left on the tables creating a still life in melancholy. When I stepped out onto the pavement, the cause of this entire disaster stood next to his Roadster, and I wasn't about to let an opportunity pass me by.

"Is this how you do business?" I asked. "Swanning around villages across England, lying your way into people's good graces for your own gain? You do realize that Nuala had no idea what you were really after?"

"I never lied," Brightbill snapped back.

"You lied by omission. You lied with your invitation to dinner, with" — I jerked a thumb over my shoulder — "with bouquets of cupid's dart."

"I did not intend to mislead Nuala, and I believe my offer is a legitimate one."

"Your offer is not welcome," I said.

"We'll see about that."

My reply of *I'll see you in hell first* was cut short when a text came in and I looked down at my phone. *Thx re pockett.*

"Police," I muttered.

Brightbill lifted his eyebrows. "I'm not sure they can arrest me on charges of wanting to hire away the baker."

Such a comedian. "This is about a man who died on the estate. He was found by the pond beyond the church."

When Brightbill attempted to get a better look at my phone screen, I moved my hand away, dropping the phone in my bag.

"Who was he?"

"He had no identification on him," I said. "Police are investigating."

"How did he die?"

I wasn't fooled for one minute by this sudden interest in a stranger's death. I knew this was an attempt to divert me from the matter at hand, and I would not succumb. "We are keeping these matters quiet until we learn more about the situation," I said, as if I could flash my DI badge at him. "We — and the police, of course — are following several lines of enquiry. Although, I don't see how this is any business of yours." And with that, I clapped my mouth shut.

CHAPTER 18

Inside Pipit Cottage, Michael clanged pots and pans and searched cupboards while Pammy busied herself laying out clothes on the sofa. Neither spoke, and yet the heat of angry words filled the air.

The door closed behind me with a *snick*. Michael didn't turn, but jerked his head toward his sister. "She was on the doorstep when I arrived."

"I don't have a key," Pammy shot back at him.

He whirled round and shouted, "*You don't need a key!*"

I couldn't breathe. I almost backed out the door and fled. It had been a terribly long workday, but, at that moment the TIC called to me as a haven. I could hide in the back with the lights off and contemplate my laundry list of woes in peace. Willow's worrisome behavior. My responsibility in pushing the nonexistent relationship between Linus and Nuala to the point of oblivion. The despoiling of an organic farm and its repercussions, and a dead man no one knew, except as "Bob." And, of course, let's not forget the loss of my Pipit Cottage to Pammy. But the worst of it all, Michael and I had missed that magic moment when he might've proposed. It was gone now. Vanished. I knew that. With no commitment to each other, we'd probably drift apart, become just another casual relationship that went nowhere. A stabbing pain in my chest caused me to clutch at my cardigan.

"Julia?"

Michael came to me and took hold of my hand, rubbing it until I released my sweater. Pammy held still, poised above her hoard.

"Would you like a cup of tea?" she asked. I didn't know whether to be grateful for her concern or anguished that she acted the hostess.

"No, thanks. I think I'll go and change," I murmured. Michael kissed my temple before I broke away. My chin trembled, and I felt like a fool.

As I took hold of the stair railing to haul myself up one step at a time, I noticed the dark clothes Pammy had been fussing with.

"Waterproofs?" I asked.

Pammy shot a worried look at Michael, who said nothing.

"There's a short-toed eagle been spotted at Lakenheath," she said quietly, "and we're going to take a look tomorrow. And as it might rain, Gavin thought I should have some gear."

"His?"

"No, I found them up in Bury at a charity shop." She held up the jacket for inspection. "Reflective, the woman said, in case we're there after dark."

She'd better hope to God it won't be an eighteen-hour day in the rain. I marveled at how it hadn't taken Gavin long to drag his new girlfriend into his usual activities. I'd give this relationship one more day. Let her see what it's like to spend hours and hours ankle deep in mud with water cascading off the brim of her hood. And yet, I couldn't wish that on her without a last warning.

"The thing is, Pammy, it can be tiring, you know, waiting out a bird. In the rain."

"I don't mind," Pammy said. "It's an adventure."

* * *

Upstairs, I opened the window, leaned out, and took a deep breath to clear my head. Nearing evening, and I caught a whiff of honeysuckle on the air and heard the birds making a show of it before settling in. A scattering of dark forms against the sky told me the rooks were heading to their roost. I undressed in slow motion, until I stood in my bra and knickers, letting the world outside the window do its work to repair my mood.

Plastic shopping bags briefly rustled their way into my consciousness. They quieted, and in a few moments, I heard Michael's footsteps on the stairs and the bedroom door creak open.

"Hiya," he said in a whisper as he wrapped his arms round my waist from behind and rested his lips on my shoulder.

I turned my head and looked at him out of the corner of my eye. "I've made a dog's breakfast of this business between Nuala and Linus."

"Brightbill lets his charm do the work for him when it comes to business. That isn't always fair, and it can backfire. He should've known from the start what was happening here. Still" — Michael's hands slid down to my hips — "it's Linus who needs to speak up."

"But he won't. He wouldn't want to stand in Nuala's way. Such a load of nonsense." I watched a blackbird scurry across the back garden. "I'm not sure I'm doing such a fine job as Willow's minder. Where is she now? Should I ring her on the hour?"

"Willow has Lottie and Cecil — not to mention Linus, Thorne, and Sheila. She'll be fine." Michael turned me round to face him. "So, let's not give them another thought. At least not for a while." He kissed me and, at the same time, executed a deft move and unhooked my bra with one hand. A shiver ran down my spine.

"Pammy," I reminded him.

He dropped my bra on the floor, as his lips caressed my throat. "Pammy's taken herself off to the Royal Oak. I said we'd see her there later, but just in case we don't show up before closing, I gave her my key." He paused and looked at me with apprehension. "Was that all right?"

I stared at him. Was it? At that moment, I would've given Pammy the keys of the kingdom for an hour alone with Michael. I laughed. He watched me, the corner of his mouth curling up. I pulled his shirt off over his head as a delicious breeze drifted in, cooling my skin but not my desire.

* * *

The light faded, and we lay quietly on the bed until Michael rolled onto his side, propped his head in his hand, and began to trace a figure eight on my stomach. "And what else was bothering you before?"

"Us," I said. "We seemed to be . . . interrupted. I'm not blaming Pammy. It's been fine having her here" — at this, Michael paused in his drawing — "Mostly fine. But it's gone on so long, it's hard to imagine getting back to the point where we might . . ."

"Do you think I will let that go?" His eyes were dark as midnight. "I won't. Hang on, I'll ask you right now." He sat up, and for a moment I thought he'd drop to his knee at the side of the bed wearing nothing but a smile.

"No, wait," I said.

"Wait?"

"Yes, wait. But only until we're ourselves again. Until the perfect moment comes back round. It's all right to wait now, I can see that." I pulled him close. "But not a second longer than necessary."

"Right, not a second longer. I love you," he said into my hair.

I responded in kind, and my tummy chimed in with a rumble.

"I'm starving," I said. "I could just do with a plate of haddock and chips."

* * *

"Guy's life is one rash action after another. I'm sorry that Fran left him, because she was always a good, calming influence, but it's impossible to let this go. He actually thought if no one saw what he'd done, he could continue farming, pick up with organic methods where he'd left off and all would be well."

Michael and I strolled up the high street hand-in-hand, taking our time on the way to the Royal Oak. We'd reached the green as I'd wrapped up the story of Guy Pockett's calamity, and Michael slowed to a stop.

"This Bob did the odd job for Guy," he said. "Do you think Bob saw Guy spraying the field?"

"He could've done. Guy must've sprayed the herbicide a fortnight ago or longer. Bob was still alive then, wasn't he? Guy wouldn't've liked someone knowing, I can tell you. He thought he could hide his mistake."

"Did Bob threaten to tell someone what he'd seen?"

A clamoring of swifts screamed as they dived and swirled round the rooftops of the buildings across the green, but I paid them no mind.

"You mean, did Guy — no, he couldn't've."

"An argument that got out of hand."

I scrambled in my bag for my phone. "I've got to ring Tess."

She answered, and in the background I heard loud but indistinct voices, glasses clinking, and the pinging noise of a fruit machine. I thought I could identify her location with no problem. I invited her to shift from The Den in Foxearth to the Royal Oak in Smeaton, where she would hear some amazing news.

When Michael and I walked in, Pammy sat at the bar, nattering on to Hutch about a rumor that the Queen Mum had covered up a UFO crash at Sandringham in 1962. Hutch — rounded shoulders, matted toupee and a prominent brow — appeared less than enthralled. Relief washed over his face when he saw us, and he offered a rare smile that came across as more of a grimace. Pammy doggedly finished her tale while Michael waited to order drinks and I secured a corner table.

At last, brother and sister joined me. "We've a friend dropping by," I said to Pammy, as I had just heard the rumble of a motorbike in the car park and thought Tess's arrival imminent.

"Yeah, that's grand," she said. "I'm just off to the ladies'. Won't be two ticks."

A minute later, Tess walked in wearing her black leather jacket and boots over tight denims. She drew a few admiring looks. Her only concession to her job was the thin black portfolio under her arm. She scanned the room, spotted us, and approached.

"What will you have?" Michael asked and went back to the bar for Tess's pint.

"Pammy's here," I told Tess. "She's just in the loo. Look now." I hurried through the idea Michael and I had come up with about Guy Pockett. "He does things without thinking, you see, and regrets them later. I don't think he would've meant to hurt Bob."

The DI made notes and returned our information with a bit of her own. "Pockett identified the bicycle as belonging to his former partner. The other set of prints are probably hers, but I'd like to confirm that."

"She's moved to Iona," I said, which seemed even more the ends of the earth than my sister in St. Ives.

Tess nodded. "She'll need to take the ferry into Oban for that. Speaking of Scotland, I got hold of the vicar at last. They've no mobile reception where he and his wife are in the Highlands, and he only checked his messages when they went into the nearest village today. I sent him the photo, and he recognized the victim."

"That's fantastic," I said. "He knew him?"

Tess cocked her head as if to qualify my statement. "The vicar said he'd come in the church a few times — cycled up. He'd seemed a mild-mannered fellow who said he was conducting a survey of the flora and fauna in the churchyard and pond. He even saw him outside the church the day of the wedding, but didn't speak to him."

"And then he went out to the pond to count dragonflies or search for natterjack toads or something and he was murdered." I stared into my pint of ale. "Did Reverend Eccles know the man's name?"

"Oh, yes," Tess said. "He said his name was Bob."

Pammy returned and smiled at Tess, leaving me with a conundrum. How was I supposed to introduce these two?

"Pammy, this is Tess Callow." I still thought it better not to feed Pammy's imagination with a story of murder. Let her keep to gossip about the royal family. "Tess, this is Michael's sister, Pammy."

"Hiya, Tess," Pammy said.

"Good to meet you," Tess replied. "How's the visit going?"

I cut my eyes at her.

"Yeah, it's grand," Pammy said, "but I'll be off soon. I wouldn't want to get in Michael and Julia's way."

Michael returned with Tess's pint in time to hear those words. He kept his gaze on the beer, but I saw a tiny muscle spasm under one eye.

"So, Tess, do you live local?" Pammy asked.

"Sudbury," Tess replied. "Not far."

"Do you work with Julia on tourism?"

"No, I don't."

"Birds?" Pammy guessed.

"Birds?"

"Wait now, are you a twitcher?" Pammy said, her eyes shining. "Is that it? Because, you see, I'm learning—"

"No," Tess said in a rush, her cheeks flushed.

I sputtered a laugh to see the DI on the receiving end of a questioning, but I sobered up fast at the look she threw me. I laid a light hand on Pammy's arm.

"Actually, Pammy, Tess is the detective inspector from Sudbury constabulary."

Pammy's eyes grew wide, and she set her phone on the table. "Cor — you aren't. Are you? Police? Well, you hardly look it." She gasped, leaned far over the table, and mouthed, *Are you working undercover?*

Michael and I should've gone to Foxearth and met Tess at The Den, leaving Pammy here to sit at the bar and rabbit on about the Princess Diana experience at Madame Tussauds or some other topic of her choosing. Now, I'd have to start at the beginning of a story I had never intended to tell her.

"No, she isn't," I said, keeping my voice low as Helen from the sweets shop and her boyfriend took a table nearby and gave us a wave. I waved back, and so did Pammy. "DI Callow has only stopped by because there was something I needed to explain to her."

"Is it about the fellow who died up by the church?" Pammy asked Tess. "Do you know who he is yet? Because Hutch thinks he was MI5 and it was about organized crime — you know, one of those gangs from Norwich trying to take over another territory. Gwen says she and Akash hadn't seen him at all and thought he might've taken the bus up to Bury for his shopping. And whatsit at the chemist, she reckons she sold him some plasters."

Gobsmacked, I could only stare at Pammy, while Michael dropped his head in his hand. What happened to her hiding away in the cottage? Without us knowing, she had managed to do more than get a foothold in the village, she had seized possession. As I wondered how we would ever get rid of her now, Tess slid into her professional role.

"When did you arrive in the village, Pammy? Wasn't it Saturday a week ago — the day of the Widdersham-Kumar wedding?"

"Pammy was on our doorstep when we returned," Michael said. "It was about seven o'clock?"

Yes, that lovely evening so long ago when the cuckoo hatched.

"Exact time of death is difficult to pinpoint because of the condition of the body," Tess said. "At the earliest Saturday afternoon. Did you see this man when you arrived in the village?" She reached in the black portfolio, brought out a photo of the corpse, and slid it across the table.

Pammy flinched, but then drew closer, her brows furrowed and her lips pursed in concentration. Slowly, her index finger moved closer and closer until it hovered over the image.

"He wasn't dead when I saw him."

CHAPTER 19

"And here I was thinking he was just a bloke in your village, you know?" Pammy's voice was full of awe, as the three of us walked back to the cottage. "But instead, he's a murder victim, and I might have been the last person to see him alive when I stopped to ask if he knew where you lived." She shook her head sorrowfully. "He'd never heard of you, Julia."

At the Royal Oak, Tess had expertly extracted all of Pammy's information, and instructed her to appear at the Sudbury station the following morning to read and sign her statement.

"Mmmm." Pammy had twisted her mouth one way, then another. "The thing is, Tess, tomorrow isn't good for me. I've got plans. Not that this isn't important, but well, you know how it is — a previous commitment." She cast a quick glance at her brother, missing the hard stare the DI gave her.

"Right," Tess had conceded, "Thursday morning at the latest."

Tess had left before we ordered our meals, and I had accompanied her out to her motorbike to continue speculating about Guy's motive for killing Bob.

But if Guy did it," I had said, "it was in a fit of anger, an accident. He just didn't think it through." Tess had replied that was the case with most murderers and then added that motive was all well and good, but without opportunity the enquiry wouldn't get far, and that she would be back to Guy Pockett about his whereabouts during the window of the murder.

Now, walking back to the cottage, Pammy continued hashing over her story. "Helen said he'd been into her shop, this Bob. He bought a quarter each of humbugs and kola kubes. I've never liked humbugs. Do you remember Granddad loved them, Michael?"

Tess had put the fear of God into Pammy about spreading her story round the village or improvising on what had actually happened when she met Bob. With relish, Pammy swore to tell only the truth and promised she wouldn't breathe a word to anyone. Apparently, she didn't consider the vow applicable to the three of us on our own.

"Must've been a terrible shock for Willow," Pammy said, shaking her head. "To think he'd been lying there for days — can't have been a pretty sight."

With all of Pammy's knowledge about the case coming from everyone except Michael and me, I had feared she would be resentful. Surprisingly, she had not minded.

"Well, why would you say anything?" she asked. "I'm sure you'd rather downplay it. After all" — she pulled a face — "it isn't as if it's the first time you've had such goings-on round here."

Thanks, I needed that reminder.

"Do you think I've broken the case?" Pammy said with a grin. "I mean, no one else said what I told the inspector, isn't that right?"

I'd give her that — Pammy had provided a piece of information that made even the DI sit up and take notice. When asked to tell Tess everything she could remember about her encounter with Bob, Pammy had done herself proud.

She had set the scene on the table using three beer mats for buildings along Church Lane, a line of thin sugar packets for the road, a sprig of parsley borrowed off an empty plate at the next table for the shrubbery along the verge, and a bottle of brown sauce for the church tower. Michael had corrected her arrangement and stopped her from squeezing out a packet of salad cream to stand in for the pond. "You didn't really see the pond, did you?" he reminded her.

"But it's near the church tower, and I saw that," Pammy insisted.

"Everyone in the village can see the church tower," he replied.

As she had related her tale, Pammy continually threw furtive glances round the pub to make sure no one was listening and in doing so, called great attention to herself. She had told her story in a low voice, and we had to cock an ear to listen.

"I stopped just here." She pointed beyond where the pond lay, the far north end of the village. "Or, it could've been here" — closer to the pond — "or . . . well, somewhere along the road. I saw this fellow walking in the field near the edge of some trees. I stopped and said hello, and he said, 'Wouldn't it be grand to see red squirrels in this wood?' and I said, yes, it would, even though, aren't there squirrels everywhere? Well, so, then I said, 'Do you know where Julia Lanchester lives?' and he said, awfully polite like, 'I'm sorry to say, I don't believe I do.' And I said, 'She runs the tourist place in the village,' and he said, 'Isn't the countryside grand, more reliable than people.' That's sort of odd, isn't it? Maybe that wasn't quite it, but it was something like that. And then he said, 'Perhaps she lives the other side of the wool shop.' That didn't really help me much, because I didn't know where the wool shop was, but I said thanks all the same, and then he said, 'If you'll excuse me, I have an appointment to keep.'"

Pammy repeated this encounter with us on the walk back, ending with a more dramatic conclusion than she could afford in the pub with the DI.

"And next thing you know, someone's bashed his skull in. Makes you think, doesn't it?"

* * *

"Did I wake you?" Pammy asked in a stage whisper that could've been heard at the bottom of the garden. She sat at the kitchen table with her feet tucked up on the seat and her chin resting on her knees and a cup of tea steaming in front of her.

"No, you didn't." I reached the bottom of the stairs and edged my way along to the kitchen for my first cup of the day. "Are you all right?"

"Yeah, great." Her eyes widened as her gaze slid past me to the scene through the French doors. I turned and looked, too.

"Periods of heavy rain" the forecast had said, "with possible breaks." No breaks in sight as the rain had been coming down in sheets for the past hour, and the clouds, hanging heavy above us, looked in no hurry to move along. The abrupt change in the weather had taken several degrees off our summer, and there was a chill in the air.

Michael came down and the three of us had our tea, after which he left with a piece of toast in hand and I returned upstairs to dress. When I came back down, Pammy had pulled on her waterproof trousers and jacket. They were a size or two larger than she needed. She stood in the kitchen waiting for Gavin, her long, narrow face glowing a ghostly white from within the dark hood, which she'd already pulled up.

"You don't have to do this, Pammy," I said, tying the laces on my trainers and stashing my heels in my bag. I secured my mack and paused at the door. "You can tell Gavin you'll go another day."

She shook her head. "No, it's all right. It's quite important to him, you see. And he says I get to choose our next day out."

I attempted to envision Gavin spending a day in charity shops. Fat chance, but I could see I would gain no ground on that subject. "Right, well ,I hope you've layered up under your waterproofs. Have a lovely day."

I opened the door to Gavin climbing out of his car. He, too, was suited up, and he gave Pammy a big grin when she emerged.

"Look at you now," he said. "Ready for anything. Don't you worry about this rain — it'll let up before we even get there." He continued to chatter as he pulled open the passenger door.

"Gavin," I said as Pammy climbed in. "Are you sure this is the best day to take her out twitching?"

His face was eager and his manner free of his usual tough pretense. "Don't you see, Julia, I'm doing what you told me to do."

"I didn't tell you to date Pammy — you can't put that on me."

"No, you said to pay more attention to the woman than I do the birds. So, I'm making sure it isn't all twitching — I'll take Pammy out for a meal. And besides" — he shrugged — "I like it. I like *her*."

* * *

I hoped he liked her enough to cut their twitching day short and find a cozy pub. I slogged to the green and heard the bell announce a dismal opening to the farmers market. No customers were about, and vendors huddled with steaming cups of tea under dripping marquees. I got a "thanks" or two for ordering sheets of plywood to use as flooring — at least they wouldn't spend the day standing in quagmires behind their produce.

The lachrymose atmosphere wasn't due only to the rain — when other farmers saw me, they cut their eyes to the large gap where Pockett's Organic Fruit & Veg should be. I heard murmurs as I walked the aisles, bemoaning the loss of Guy and shaking their heads at his actions. Hadn't taken long for that story to circulate. I attempted to shore up both sales and attitudes by buying more than I needed and offering encouragements.

"As soon as it lets up, you'll have the hordes out" and "A slow start, a busy finish" and "Sheila will be down to shop for the Hall. They've a big dinner coming up on Friday." Wasn't there? Yes, a group from Historic England, I recalled. Linus loved entertaining and took any chance to tout the estate's bounty. This would've been just the occasion to show the world he and Nuala were a couple. I must make her see sense and urge Linus to action.

While I shopped and gave my pep talk, I asked the farmers about That Poor Man who finally had a name. "Did you know Bob?" A few of them had met him and were saddened at his death, but could offer no more. "Nice fellow." "Cleaned out the barn for me." "Wove a bee skep from willow for my little girl." A creative side of Bob — it grieved me we would never know more of it.

Shopping bags heavy with the first early potatoes, asparagus, sausage rolls, a nosegay of roses, and I couldn't remember what else, I circled back round to the road, and found Guy Pockett huddled against a hawthorn hedge — a forlorn figure, hands stuck in the pockets of a windcheater too small for him. He'd pulled the hood up, and his thick hair pushed back against the restraint. The rain hit him in the face and streamed off his shoulders.

"I'm sorry I sprayed the field," he said to me without a greeting. "It got away from me. I've asked to sell at the market next week."

"Guy, regardless of how sorry you are, you can't just step back into the market — don't you understand that?"

"I'll take down all the organic signs. I've got crops that need picking and selling and eating. What else am I going to do?"

Too bad this didn't occur to him before his wholesale slaughter of a field full of life.

"You'll have to talk it through with Cecil. Right?"

"Yeah." He shook his head, flinging rain off the end of his nose. "That detective inspector has talked to me twice now. I'm to go into the police station today, and they'll be out at my farm."

Had Tess told Guy he was now more than someone who had known the victim — now, he was a suspect? Tess would not grass me up as her source, but on the other hand, I was the most likely person to have told her.

"I'm sure the DI's grateful for any details you have about Bob. It's made it possible to identify him." By one name.

I turned to go, but he reached out and seized my arm.

"Do they think I did it? Do you think I did?"

A cold wave came over me and I tried to pull away, but he squeezed harder, and I dropped one of my bags into a puddle.

"You let go of me, Guy Pockett."

Highly aware that we were alone on the deserted high street in the pouring rain, I remembered that Bob had been killed in broad daylight. I began to tremble.

"You can't let them think that." His fingers dug into my flesh, even through the layer of my mack. "You can't."

Movement caught my eye, and my gaze shot past him. "Sergeant Glossop! DC Flynn!"

Guy released my arm and I ran to meet the police, practically throwing myself in their arms.

"Good morning, Ms. Lanchester," Glossop said, straightening his acid-yellow rain gear. "A damp morning for shopping, isn't it?"

"Well, what's a bit of rain?" I said brightly, although my heart still pounded. "You're here to show Bob's photo round?"

Flynn held out a stiffly laminated sheet as if it were a menu in a takeaway Indian restaurant, except this was a photo of the victim.

"Let me introduce you to Guy Pockett," I said, gesturing behind me, but when I turned to look, Guy Pockett was nowhere to be seen. "Well, no matter. Tess knows him. Good luck to the two of you. I hope you'll do a bit of your own shopping while you're here. Sergeant Glossop, I highly recommend the bacon rolls at Solly's Sausages."

They went on their way, and I rescued my shopping bag from the puddle. The roses were ruined.

* * *

On my walk to the TIC, the June rain seeped into my bones and gave me the shivers. Perhaps it wasn't only the rain. I wanted to believe Guy had nothing to do with Bob's murder, but I could still feel the pressure of his fingers biting into my forearm, a tangible reminder of the strength of his grip.

From across the road, several doors down and through the wall of rain, I could see a woman waiting at the door of the TIC. She stood protected from the elements in wellies, a long yellow raincoat, and wide-brimmed hat, with her back to me as she stared in the window. Still fifteen minutes before opening and I couldn't imagine anyone being so eager to visit the estate on such a dreadful day. But it was no visitor — at least, not of the usual variety. When I got close enough for her to notice me, she looked up and offered a timid smile. Tommy Pears.

CHAPTER 20

"You see, the DI needed me to sign my statement, and so I said I could come up today," Tommy explained as she followed me into the TIC and round the counter, where I set down my shopping, filled the kettle, and switched it on. "The children have early lessons — piano and trumpet — and after-school clubs. After I'd been to the station in Sudbury, I thought, well, I'm so close to the village, and I've the entire day to myself. You don't mind that I stopped?"

"Certainly not, I'm happy you thought of us." We shed our dripping rain gear and hung it on pegs. "What we need is a cup of tea, wouldn't you say? And perhaps some of this chocolate-dipped shortbread?" I reached in my market stash and held up my prize.

Tommy pushed damp hair off her forehead with the back of a hand and sat, rubbing palms on her trousers. "You must think me a bit of a ditz coming back to you. It's only I've been wondering about Bob. I know I should ask the police, but that DI seemed a bit scary, and I remembered how kind you were to me. To all of us — the children and Noel, too."

I didn't think her a ditz. She seemed lovely, although a bit emotional about subjects that weren't exactly personal. Not unlike Willow.

"Did Noel tell you I saw him yesterday?" I asked as I set out mugs and retrieved milk from the fridge. "Did he catch you up?"

Tommy's expression was suspended between surprise and wariness. "Here?"

"Well, up the high street at the Stoat and Hare. I explained that you'd already been in. Did he tell you?"

"It's only that, Noel's gone during the week, working," she said. "He does installation and maintenance for a company that provides video-sharing software systems to businesses that require an integrated process which will adhere to the requirements across the range of projects and development as they grow."

"Wow." I stuffed a few tea bags in the pot as the kettle switched off. "I have no idea what any of that means."

Tommy laughed, and shook her blond ponytail. "I've memorized their mission statement, but I couldn't explain it to you." She glanced round the work space and scanned the wall of leaflets as she said, "Noel's territory is north of here. He's got Norfolk, Lincolnshire, and up to Northumberland. He's on the road a great deal."

"Well, so," I said, after a moment of silence. "You wanted to know about Bob, but I'm afraid I don't have much to add. It was awfully helpful of you to identify him, of course, and there have been a few more confirmed sightings" — I made Bob sound like that short-toed eagle — "but still no one really knows who he is or where he lived or where he came from. It's too bad, isn't it? To think he might have some family somewhere wondering about him?"

Vesta opened the door and shook her umbrella as she came in saying, "We'll be swimming up the high street by the end of the day." She gave away not a hint of surprise at our guest. "It's lovely to see you again, Ms. Pears."

"It's Tommy, please." She shifted in her chair. "I'm sorry to intrude—"

"Not a bit of it," I said. "Vesta, the tea's just ready."

Vesta joined us at the table, and we chatted about the weather and the TIC and drawing in visitors, which led me to show them the first draft of the layout for *Life in the Churchyard*. "I don't know, there's something not right about it. Even with these photos, it lacks appeal. Really, would this be the leaflet you would select from the wall?" I asked them. Vesta tilted her head as she studied it. Tommy tapped the paper with a finger.

"You know, if you shifted the text to the left and wrapped it round the photos, your eye is immediately drawn down from the title. It would flow more easily — visually, I mean. And it might do for the background color to go a shade lighter."

I studied the leaflet. "I'll try, although I confess my layout skills are rudimentary at best."

"Oh, well." Tommy's gaze darted from Vesta to me. "Would you like me to give it a go? I'm a graphic designer. That is, I was before the children."

It took her all of ten minutes at the computer. Vesta printed out the next draft, and we admired it for a moment before Tommy took it, picked up a pencil, and said, "Here now, hang on."

She scribbled something in the lower corner and, with a grin, held it up. "It might add a personal touch, and make tourists realize they can rely on you for good information."

A cartoon dialogue balloon read, *A tip from the TIC — look for wild orchids in May!* The balloon was coming from a sketch of a woman with a chin-length bob. I gasped.

"That's me!" I exclaimed. "It looks just like me. How did you do that so fast?"

Tommy blushed. "Oh, well, I've always been a bit of a doodler."

Vesta took the leaflet, folded it, and slipped it into one of the wall pockets so we could take in its effect. "You've quite an eye and a skilled hand."

Tommy beamed at Vesta's praise.

"This will do the trick," I said, and was proved right only a moment later when a brave couple from Manchester arrived, determined to enjoy their day out whatever the weather. They perused the wall of leaflets carefully before making their selection — *Life in the Churchyard*.

* * *

It was practically lunchtime before Tommy left, because after the churchyard leaflet, she worked magic on a redesign of the poster for Smeaton's Summer Supper, discussed what a new leaflet on the abbey ruins might look like, and just before she left became quite interested in the announcement for Brushes Up for St. Swithun's!

"It's Willow's project," I explained, "and we need to start promoting it, but it's difficult, because . . ." And there we were, back with Bob as I explained Willow's part in the case. "She's a lovely woman, and this has been such a shock. She's taken it rather personally."

Tommy ran her eyes over the flier, and said, "Do you think Willow would mind me helping out? Because I'd really love to. Perhaps I could talk with her. Would that be all right?"

We agreed it would. "Willow teaches at the primary school here, and so won't be free until this afternoon. Shall we give her your phone number?"

"Yes, thanks. And could you let me know when you hear something about Bob?" Tommy asked as she pulled on her raincoat. "I don't know why, but I can't seem to get him out my mind."

* * *

"Are you all right here, Vesta?" I asked as I switched back into my trainers and donned my mack. Tommy had only just left, but I could wait no longer to talk with Linus. There was still time for him to sweep Nuala off her feet before Nuala's feet took her north to become . . . something for Tony Brightbill.

"It'll be one of those dead days," Vesta predicted as she pulled out a tapestry bag from a large plastic shopper and began rummaging in it. She looked up, pink cheeks matching the pink frames of her glasses. "Sorry, but you know what I mean. And I have my needlepoint kneeler here to work on, so I'll be fine."

"Thanks. I'll check in later." My hand on the door, I stopped. "Vesta, has Akash said anything about meeting Pammy?"

"Akash hasn't met her, but Gwen has. They got on all right, although Gwen says she seems a bit of a lost soul."

* * *

I hurried through the rain up the high street. I'd had the good sense to remember my market shopping and stopped to leave it on the way to the lockup. I stood for a moment just inside the door of the cottage, taking in the temporary atmosphere of a Pammy-free home. Not that she was forgotten, of course — her plastic bags waited patiently for the return of their mistress.

No green Morgan Roadster sat parked in front of the tea room, but then it was too early in the day for Tony Brightbill to begin his smarmy pseudo-courtship of Nuala. I *harrumphed* as I reversed my Fiat out of its shelter. I leapt out to close the wooden doors of the lockup, and returned to the driver's seat with rain pouring off me and down to the floorboard, forming a puddle. I shifted into gear, but before I could get any further, my phone rang. My sister, Bianca.

"Everyone's out of the house and Estella is down for a nap. I could just do with a catch-up," she said. "First, Pammy."

I switched off the engine. "Still in residence. And I've just learned she's been making friends with people in the village. All this time, I thought she'd spent her days holed up in the cottage. There'll be no getting rid of her now. We'll have her forever, just like Tess's uncle."

"That's the detective inspector?" Bianca asked.

"The point is, Bee, I feel as if Pammy needs some stability in her life, and at the same time, she drives me crazy. And now this — she's got herself involved with Gavin Lecky."

While Bianca roared with laughter, I switched the engine back on, turned up the defogger for the windscreen and waited. She ended with a last snort and said, "That's priceless, that is. How's Michael taking it?"

"How do you think? I can't see this ending well. It's dumping here today, and Gavin and Pammy are off chasing down a short-toed eagle. Can you imagine?" I afforded a snicker, having been on a similar adventure in the past.

"And you and Michael?" Bianca asked, ticking topics off her list.

"A stolen moment here and there. But it's all right, because we've decided we can wait and when this is all over, then it'll be the perfect time for him to propose."

"When Pammy is gone? I thought you said that would never happen."

* * *

In order to clear my head before talking with Linus and to build up a bit more courage, I drove up to the top of Church Lane and parked near the lych gate. I needed time to gather my wits about me and consider how to approach Linus about the scene the afternoon before at Nuala's. Despite the rain, I found myself getting out of my car and walking round and through the churchyard, hoping I wouldn't look like Willow trying to commune with Bob. I needed a bit of quiet, and the place was deserted. Who knows, perhaps Bob was calling me, too, and I needed to look out on the place by the pond where he had died.

I pushed through the tall grass that surrounded the gravestones, feeling the soggy ground soak through my shoes, and scraped past a scrubby hedge maple that slapped me in the face with wet leaves. At the churchyard gate that led out toward the pond, took in the vista, now unimpeded by blue-and-white police tape, and froze at what I saw.

Tony Brightbill stood at the edge of the pond on the precise spot where Willow had found Bob, dead. I knew it was Tony, because I recognized his dark Burberry raincoat. He wore no hat, and the battering rain had plastered his thick hair to his head.

For one moment, my entire being was devoid of thought or supposition or speculation. And then the questions began.

How had he heard about a dead man at the pond — was it gossip in the tea room? But with a jolt, I realized he'd heard that news from me. Regardless of the source, what did he care? Or was Brightbill one of those people attracted by horrific events, inexplicably drawn to the scene of the crime? A stranger murdered in a strange village.

Of course, it might be that Bob was no stranger to Tony Brightbill, and this was no mere gruesome curiosity. Murderers return to the scene of their crime — hadn't Tess once said that? A thin stream of speculation began to flow.

Yes, that's it. Tony Brightbill must have known Bob. Perhaps Bob had something to do with Tara's Tea. It could've been a business deal gone wrong. No, Bob had been living rough for a while, and he looked nothing like a businessman. I threw that idea out.

Had Bob had an affair with Tony's wife and then given her up and abandoned his former life in a selfless act of a broken heart. But Tony had tracked him down, anyway, to seek revenge? No, couldn't quite see that one, either.

Perhaps Bob had discovered a secret about Tara's Tea and had threatened to tell, and Tony wanted to silence him. Yes, it was business, and Tony Brightbill liked business. I kept hold of this possibility.

I considered opportunity. Pammy had seen Bob late afternoon or early Saturday evening. His murder had taken place after that, but not necessarily in darkness, as there was light in the sky well past ten o'clock. The murder occurred a week and a half ago, which was two or three days before the first confirmed sighting of Tony on the estate, which was his visit to Nuala's on that Tuesday. But who's to say he hadn't been lurking on the edges of Fotheringill land for longer?

Had Tony tracked Bob to the estate? From where? And what was Bob doing here in the first place?

My speculation came to an abrupt halt when Brightbill turned away from the pond and headed straight for the gate where I stood, his head bent against the rain. He would think I had been spying on him, and of course I hadn't been, but regardless, I thought it better not to be seen. I fled — skirting the graves and running alongside the brick wall, hoping the low branches of a copper beech hid my movements. A bare patch of ground had turned to a wide puddle, and when I hit the edge and skidded, I nearly lost my balance. Putting my right foot down hard to catch myself, I sank up to my ankle in mud. It made a sucking sound when I pulled it out, and I stumbled on, making it out the lych gate and to my car in the lane, and noting too late the green Morgan Roadster parked in the shadows of a nearby alley.

* * *

I could've walked to Hoggin Hall quicker than driven, the traffic was so thick on the road. My heart raced as I waited for a break in the traffic and I kept glancing in my rearview mirror, expecting any second to see the Roadster pull up behind me, until I saw my chance, screeched across the road, and through the brick pillars that marked the drive.

By the time I pulled my Fiat up to the front of the Hall and switched off the engine, I'd regained my composure and come to the conclusion that Tony Brightbill had murdered Bob. I hadn't totally lost all sense of reason, of course. I realized this was an accusation with nothing to back it up, and I knew that wouldn't fly with DI Callow, so I would need to find some evidence for her.

But at the moment, I had to set aside the entire topic of Bob and attend to the business of Linus and Nuala. I'd turned the floorboard of my car into a mud pit, but at least

I could leave most of the mess behind and put on a decent pair of shoes. I reached into my bag, searching for my heels, but couldn't feel them. I dragged the bag to my lap, opened it wide, and stuck my head in. Where were they? In a last-ditch effort, I hit the flashlight function on my phone, and only then did I realize that I had no heels. So much for presentation. As the rain continued its relentless onslaught, I squished my way across the forecourt.

The great oak door slowly opened to reveal Thorne, who smiled and greeted me with, "Ms. Lanchester, you are most welcome." He stood aside.

"Messy day, isn't it?" I asked, and we both looked at my trainers encased in mud that had splattered up my tights almost to my knees. "I'm so sorry, Thorne — I had a bit of an accident. I won't wear these in, but would you mind if I left them outside here?"

"Please come in, Ms. Lanchester. These flagstones have seen much worse than mud over the centuries."

I went no further than the hat stand and with some difficulty, kicked off the trainers. Thorne produced a towel from thin air, and I wiped as much of the excess mud of my legs as I could. "The problem is, I forgot my other shoes, and I've nothing to change into."

"I'm sure Mrs. Bugg has something you could wear."

Sheila Bugg's shoes always seemed a bit too matronly even for her. "Perhaps I'll stay in my stocking feet. I've only stopped for a moment to see Linus."

Thorne looked at me, twisted his mouth to the side in thought, and then said, "His Lordship has instructed me to explain to all callers that he has left for Peterborough on business." As the butler said this, he cut his eyes down the corridor beyond the grand staircase, nodding in the same direction. I peered down and saw Linus's study door slightly ajar.

"Ah, yes," I said, tapping my finger on the side of my nose. "He's away. Thank you, Thorne."

"And now if you'll excuse me, Ms. Lanchester," the butler continued, "I must go and prop up the roses — the rain, you know." He dropped his voice and added, "I wish you luck."

Thorne retreated in the direction of the kitchen, and I took a moment to compose myself before crossing the entry and walking round the table that sat under the chandelier hanging from the three-story-high ceiling. On the table, an enormous vase overflowed with summer bounty — stalks of pink hollyhocks shot upward, chartreuse lady's mantle billowed, and a purple clematis wove its way in and out. All local flowers, of course. I passed the grand staircase, glancing to the upper gallery, where portraits of Fotheringill ancestors kept an eye on things. I wonder who had interfered in their love lives.

I tiptoed to the study door, and peeked in. The curtains had been drawn and the room was cloaked in gloom apart from a lawyer's lamp on the desk, which threw a stingy pool of light onto the oak surface. Linus sat huddled over a sheaf of papers, his open laptop off to the side. The glow from its screen threw odd shadows on his face, making him look older than he was.

"Hello," I said, pushing open the door and stepping in.

He looked up. "Julia? I told Thorne to say I was—"

"In Peterborough. Yes, he did as instructed. May I come in?"

"Did we have a meeting scheduled?" He toyed with the pen in his hand and furrowed his brow, the wrinkles in his forehead deepening like folds in the hills.

Playing it like that, are you?

"No, we didn't, but there's something I need to talk with you about."

"Is it about the TIC?"

"You know it isn't," I said. "Will you listen to me?"

He paused a beat. "Would you leave if I said no?"

"What do you think?"

A moment passed, and then another. "All right," he conceded.

He rose and switched off the desk light as I switched on floor lamps. He joined me on the chesterfield, glancing down at my muddy stockinged feet but saying nothing.

"Have you spoken with Nuala?" I asked.

"No, and I believe she'd prefer it that way."

"That isn't true, and you know it."

"I've treated her despicably." He sat forward on the sofa, hands clasped tightly in front of him.

"I don't think that's what she's—"

"And I've acted the fool," he added.

"No, you have not acted the fool, Linus, and that's the problem. You need to. Take a chance, risk putting your heart on the line. You can't rely on Nuala to suspect what you're up to and take it from there. As far as I'm concerned, you're far too cautious — the both of you."

"I'm not sure she'd appreciate my advances, and I will not stand in her way if she wants to leave."

"She doesn't want to leave," I said. "It may take a bit of persuading at this point, because she's had her feelings hurt by both of you. You did it unknowingly, of course, but Tony Brightbill is another matter. Do you know much about him?"

In the lamplight, I could see Linus's face go pink. "Well, I may have done a bit of research online this morning. He's successful with those tea rooms, it seems, and is hoping to expand."

"No personal information? No sour business deals reported in the *FT*?"

Linus shook his head. "Nothing that I saw."

A light knock, and Sheila appeared, a pair of what looked like sturdy nurse's shoes in her hand. She surveyed the scene. "That's better," she said, "although you could do with opening those curtains. This isn't a cinema after all. Here you are now, Julia." She set the shoes at my feet. "Those trainers of yours won't see another day. Now, we've sandwiches going in the kitchen for anyone interested."

* * *

Wednesday afternoons, Hoggin Hall opened to the public, and by the time I'd walked out of Linus's study in my new clodhopper footwear, a thin stream of people wandered the rooms and corridors available to them. Akash was on the door, and volunteers were stationed at every turn, with private areas roped off. I followed Sheila to the kitchen for a sandwich, and after, backtracked to the café. The conversion had worked perfectly — creating a small kitchen for Nuala from an old pantry and the adjoining room made into the café with seven small tables. Three of them were now occupied with visitors whose coats dripped and who hovered gratefully over cups of tea.

Nuala blushed when she saw me, and I thought for one moment she might be about to apologize for her behavior the previous evening. I would have none of that, because it hadn't been her fault at all. I was willing to accept partial blame for pushing into a situation that was not totally my concern, but I laid most of it at Tony Brightbill's feet.

"Hello, Nuala," I said hurriedly before she could start. "I'd love a cup of tea."

"Cake?" Nuala asked.

"No, I think — oh, what's this? Is it new?"

Nuala nodded and smiled. "I soaked the sultanas and currants in tea first. Will you try it?"

"I will, of course."

And so we didn't need to apologize or explain our previous evening's behavior — tea and cake took care of it. As Nuala cleared tables, she glanced at my feet. "My, my. Trying out a new uniform?"

We snickered companionably at the joke, and I felt emboldened to plead. "You won't leave, will you, Nuala?"

"Oh, now," she said, not meeting my eye. "Is Vesta on at the TIC?"

"Mmm." A good reminder. I pulled out my phone and sent my second-in-command a text. *All well?* She replied that she was getting a fair bit done on her church kneeler. I responded *I'll be there to close.*

* * *

It was well after three o'clock when I left Hoggin Hall, although it was difficult to tell what time of day it was, as the afternoon continued as the morning had begun — dull, dark, and very wet. The thought of spending the last two hours of my workday drying out in the TIC appealed to me, but instead, I again parked on Church Lane, walked up to St. Swithun's, and picked my way carefully round the churchyard, surprisingly sure-footed this time. I glanced down at the shoes. Sheila had said they were an old pair and she didn't want them back. She had frowned when she saw them on my feet as if seeing them for the first time.

I couldn't say what I expected to find beyond the churchyard at the pond. Did I believe Tony Brightbill would return and search for the mossy branch of oak he'd used to bash in Bob's skull?

The thought did give me pause. What would Tess say about Brightbill as a suspect then? Motive was secondary if you caught the murderer with the weapon.

It could happen, couldn't it? I seemed to be convincing myself of this possibility and, keeping the brick wall to my left, I crept up to the last large yew near the churchyard gate, my breath coming quick from anticipation. When I parted the branches, I startled a blackbird that had taken cover. It chastised me as it flew out, and I apologized and pulled my hands out of the canopy in case there was a nest. Then, I inched round until I had a clear view of the pond.

And there, at the far edge where Bob had lain, I saw not one person, but two — and neither of them Tony Brightbill. One was tall and dressed in wellies, a long yellow raincoat, and a wide-brimmed hat. The other was short and wore a clear slicker over a floral-print shift, short, thick boots, and held a see-through purple umbrella that protected her curly brown hair. Tommy Pears and Willow.

CHAPTER 21

"Julia!"

I jumped at the voice behind me. When I whirled round, I staggered and fell back into the yew, clutching at branches, and saved from landing on the soggy ground only when Cecil reached out and grabbed me.

"What is this?" he demanded. "Who is that with Willow? What are they doing here? What are you doing? What is going on? You haven't been—"

"Cecil, please." I clambered up, knocking his rain hat askew as I righted myself. Rain splattered my face, and I readjusted my hood as I spluttered, "I've just this minute arrived, and I have no idea."

"Cecil!"

Willow and Tommy were picking their way back toward us, and Cecil left me to dart over and open the gate for them. Willow looked radiant. Tommy hung back, her eyes shifting from one face to another.

"Willow," Cecil began, and I heard a pleading note in his voice. "Didn't we discuss this and you agreed it might not be a good idea to—"

"Cecil, dear, let me introduce Tommy Pears." Willow put her hand on Cecil's arm and tilted her umbrella back to smile up at him.

Cecil automatically put his hand out. "How do you do, Ms. Pears? Cecil Fotheringill, happy to meet you."

"Hello, Mr. Fotheringill," Tommy said. "I'm afraid I'm responsible for this."

"Tommy has been a great help to the police," Willow explained in a rush. "Remember Detective Inspector Callow showed me the photo yesterday?"

"That was a poor decision on the part of the police," Cecil complained. "Disturbing you during your school day."

"Dear Cecil, it was better during my busy day, actually, because I had no time to dwell on it. But this is the truly remarkable part. When I saw the photo, I could only be sad for That Poor Man, but Tommy knew his name. He's Bob. She and her family met him out by the abbey ruins. It was Julia who remembered they'd been into the TIC and mentioned him. Tommy came out today, because she rather feels the same way I do, that we owe it to Bob to acknowledge what's happened and ask if there is some way we can help."

A frown passed over Cecil's face. "Yes, thank you, Ms. Pears, for your assistance in this matter. We are, of course truly sorry for the man's death, and we are doing everything we can to help the police with their enquiry. Thank you too, Julia, for your help."

Poor Cecil — still at sea over Willow's unexplainable attraction to a dead man. "Of course," I said, "we all want an end to the matter. But right now, I don't suppose anyone would like to get out of the rain?"

* * *

We paused in the covered entry to the church as we said our goodbyes. While Cecil engaged Tommy in a brief conversation about the estate, Willow walked me to a bench by the notice board. It held a poster with Tommy's new design for the art competition. In the corner, she had sketched Willow, smiling, holding a paintbrush, and saying, "Brushes up!"

"We're so close, Julia, I can feel it." Her cheeks were pink and her eyes bright. "And I know I can be of assistance."

"Willow, you can't take this on. The police are handling it."

"Yes, yes," she said dismissively, and then tapped the tip of her umbrella on the stone floor. "Still, there's something Bob wants me to remember. I need to clear my mind, and it will come to me."

* * *

The rain continued relentless in its pursuit to drown the Fotheringill estate. I reckoned that Suffolk, known for its low rainfall, might be getting its year's worth all in one day. As Tommy, Willow, and Cecil departed, a text arrived from Michael. *Preparing 4 tomorrow evening with nightjars.*

That was followed by one from Vesta. *On your way back?*

I had stayed away too long. I felt a pang of guilt — here I was, once again taking advantage of Vesta. I must stop. I had brought this up to her before, but her response had been, "And what about you working six days a week? This isn't Charles Dickens' blacking factory, you know." No good pointing out I worked only five and a half days — I knew what she meant. When I had opened the TIC just over two years ago, it had filled a vast hole in my life. But perhaps the time had come to put a bit of space between life and work.

Be right there.

Twenty minutes later I'd secured my Fiat in its lockup and arrived at the TIC to find Vesta sitting behind the counter with cups of tea on the table. Across from her, leaning forward and toying with a folded sheet of paper in his hand, was Tony Brightbill.

* * *

What was Vesta thinking inviting a murderer to tea?

That was my first thought, followed quick on by realizing no one had seen what I had — Tony Brightbill at the scene of a violent crime. Tea rooms, my eye. That had all been a ruse.

Brightbill stood, holding the paper close, and said, "Ms. Lanchester, I hope you don't mind that I—"

"I asked Mr. Brightbill to stay," Vesta cut in. "He'd wanted to speak with you, and I told him you'd be returning soon."

Perhaps Vesta did have her own suspicions. She had thought it better Brightbill meet me here with her as witness rather than have him track me down at the end of a deserted lane.

"Well, you should be on your way now, Vesta," I said. "Thanks so much for staying while I was out."

"I'm in no hurry, Julia. Shall I put the kettle on for a fresh pot?"

"Not at all, we're fine." I sounded as if Tony Brightbill and I were about to discuss the virtues of real butter versus buttery spread. I dug in my bag for my phone. I needed to ring the police. "Would you both excuse me for a moment?" I asked, nodding toward the loo. "Oh, and, DI Callow is on her way."

"Yes, she is," Brightbill said.

Without thinking, I asked, "How do you know?"

"I rang her a quarter of an hour ago."

I was gripped with a thrill of fear. He'd called the police here because he was going to confess, right in front of me. Did he require a witness? Did he feel the murderer's need to be the center of attention? Was he about to lodge a formal complaint that I was harassing him?

"There you are now," I said, a tremor to my voice. "Off you go, Vesta."

She buttoned her raincoat in slow motion, watching me, her eyes drifting down to my matronly shoes. As I had spoiled my trainers spying on Tony Brightbill, I didn't believe this an appropriate moment to explain.

"Sheila's," I said. Vesta nodded.

I watched her walk out, and only after she had disappeared did it occur to me that Brightbill could well have been lying about the police. Was Tess really on her way? I edged past him and stood in front of the counter, closer to the door, still unlocked. "Now, Mr. Brightbill, how may I—"

He unfolded the paper he'd been fingering and held it out. I saw it was the photo of the murder victim, computer-enhanced to have his eyes open and look almost alive.

"Bob," Tony said. "Robert Brightbill. He was my brother."

CHAPTER 22

I laid a hand on the counter to steady myself as I took in Tony's pronouncement. "Bob Brightbill," I breathed. "Your brother?"

Tony sank back into his chair. I looked closer and now saw the effects this news had had on him. That engaging charm, which had taken in Nuala and probably anyone else he'd turn it on, had vanished, replaced by a tired man, his eyes rimmed red, his thick hair hanging lifeless after a morning vigil in the rain. Something else that had been unseen but quite palpable, that strong sense of self, had drained away.

"I'm sorry you felt I misled you here in Smeaton," Tony said. "And I'm sorry I treated Nuala so poorly. I can see that now. I'm afraid that although I looked on my interest in a purely business sense, she might've seen it otherwise."

The power of his news deflated my severe reaction to his wooing of Nuala for non-romantic purposes. His brother was dead. How could I fault this man anything?

"Did you come to the village to meet him?" I asked.

Tony shook his head once and then nodded. "I came here hoping to find him. I was working my way through Suffolk. Bob never liked feeling he was being pursued, so instead, I would get the feel of the place and start making general enquiries in conversation. But it wasn't until yesterday when you mentioned an unidentified man had died on the estate that I realized how close I might've come."

"Was he . . . I mean, did he need to . . ." What was I trying to say? *Was your brother escaping the law?*

"Bob never lived a conventional life. He'd no house, no steady work, no family of his own. He spent the years drifting, taking a job here and there. He's probably seen more of England, Scotland, and Wales than most of us. It was a way of living he preferred, and we had to accept that, and draw comfort from the knowledge he would turn up on the doorstep a couple of times a year. So, at the very least, we would know he was alive."

These brothers' lives couldn't be more different. "But why had you come looking for him?"

"I hadn't seen him since late September when he'd been in Norfolk. 'So then,' he said to me before he left, 'I'd better be getting on with things.'"

The bell jingled and I whirled round.

DI Tess Callow saw my alarm and moved swiftly and smoothly toward me.

"Julia?" she asked.

I looked from her to Brightbill. "Is that why you called the police here? To explain?" I asked. And to Tess, "Did he tell you?"

Callow shook the rain off her hair and held out her warrant card and badge to Tony. "Mr. Brightbill? Detective Inspector Callow."

"I hope it was no trouble you driving to the village," Tony said.

"No trouble," Tess answered. "We've been out on the estate conducting a search at one of the farms."

Searching Guy Pockett's place. What had they found? The DI didn't meet my questioning look, but as a reminder, my forearm throbbed where Guy had held fast.

"It's only I thought Ms. Lanchester deserved to hear first," Tony said. "For all the trouble I've given her."

My face went hot. What trouble had he, a man whose brother had just been murdered, given me that I hadn't given him back tenfold?

"Now then, would you follow me to the station in Sudbury? We'll need you to identify the body, and we can take your statement there."

I saw myself being shut out, and I didn't like it. I could skip the body identification, but I wanted to hear Tony's story — all of it. But I couldn't find a way to insinuate myself into the process and watched with resignation as they readied to leave.

"Mr. Brightbill," I said as they walked out. "I'm awfully sorry." I didn't say for what — his brother, my attitude and suspicions. Did it matter?

I locked up behind them and watched as Tess got in her black Volvo and drove off, followed in a moment by the green Morgan Roadster with its top pulled up against the rain.

I had switched off the lights and turned the sign to *Closed* when my phone rang.

"Julia?" A furtive whisper, followed by a roar of laughter and scattered applause.

"Willow, is that you?"

"Sorry. Hang on a tick." Scuffling, shuffling, and the sound of a door closing. "There now — is that better?"

She still spoke quietly, but at least she had no competition.

"Where are you?" I asked.

"Cecil and I are in Colchester for a reception followed by a lecture followed by a dinner. I hadn't intended to come, but he thought it would be best. You know."

Cecil was doing what he could to keep Willow away from the subject of Bob. He'd enlisted me in that campaign, but my results were spotty. Would it be inappropriate for me to share the news that Bob now had not only a surname, but also a brother?

"Willow, my love." Cecil's voice in the background.

"It's all right, Cecil," Willow said. "It's only Julia."

"Did she ring you?"

Not difficult to hear the accusation in that question. *She did not*, I wanted to say, but Willow said it for me.

"No, I rang. It's that thing I told you about earlier. I know you said wait until tomorrow, but truly, Cecil, dear, it would put my mind totally at rest if only I could tell Julia right now."

I waited through a long pause, envisioning Willow looking up at Cecil, expectantly, smiling, and knowing Cecil's resolve would melt.

"Yes, all right, of course, whatever you think is best. We'll need to get our seats for the lecture soon. You won't be long?"

I heard a *smack* as Willow rewarded him with a kiss before the door closed and she said to me, "I've remembered, Julia. It's incredibly amazing, isn't it? What Bob wanted me to know. Perhaps it was meeting Tommy today, and knowing there was one other person who shared what I felt about Bob. Of course, I realize you care, too, but we feel as if—"

"Willow," I cut in, my heart pounding. "What did you remember?"

"I rang Aunt Lottie first, but she didn't answer, and leaving a message didn't seem right. Julia, the thing Bob has been trying to tell me — it's the OXO tin."

With the addition of the victim's photo and a relative, the OXO tin had slipped out of my mind.

"The one Bob had in his pocket? You saw a photo of it."

"Yes, I saw the photo, but no, not the one Bob had in his pocket. There's another just like it, eggshells and all, in Aunt Lottie's bureau drawer."

* * *

I had the TIC door locked and was halfway to Three Bags Full before I had pulled my mack on, all the while images of OXO tins dancing in my head. I'd caught Willow's excitement, and as unlikely as the connection seemed, when wild speculation waved at me from a distance, I waved back.

Late opening at the wool shop, and Lottie stood chatting with a woman about the spinning qualities of wool from Bluefaced Leicester sheep. She gave me a nod, and, as she finished up, I occupied myself with petting a cubbyhole full of mohair skeins. The moment the customer left, Lottie asked, "Julia, you're soaked. Are you all right? Is Willow all right?"

Did I look that disheveled that her first thought was for bad news?

"Yes, of course. She's in Colchester with Cecil. It's only that, she just this minute rang me, Lottie, and she told me . . . well, she asked me to . . . the thing is . . ." I was sure this wasn't how the police conducted door-to-door interviews. And that thought brought me up short. "Lottie, didn't the police come by yesterday? They were in the village."

"I wasn't here yesterday. It was my closing day, and with Willow staying at the Hall, I went up to London Monday evening. I've a few things in a small textile show at a gallery near Horseferry Road, and didn't get home until yesterday evening. Are the police still asking after that man poor Willow found? It would be such a relief for her to put this all to rest."

Lottie had not seen the photo of Bob, which the police had circulated round the village yesterday and at the market today. I had it in my bag, but I chose to begin with the other photo. I pulled out the paper and straightened the bent corners. "Does this look familiar?"

Lottie hovered over the paper with the images of the OXO tin found in Bob's pocket. One showed the tin closed and the other, opened to the empty pieces of birds' eggs. At first she frowned, and then her face lost color, and I saw her fingers go white as they clutched the edge of the counter.

"Where did you get that?" she whispered and cut her eyes to the back stairs that led to her flat. "It isn't—"

"This tin was found on the man who died. It's all he had in his pocket. The police went door-to-door yesterday with this photo, and a photo of the victim. I have that one, too. Do you want to see it?"

"I wasn't here yesterday," she repeated.

When I pulled out the second photo, Lottie drew away from me. I unfolded it, and set it on the counter, dropping my bag to the floor.

She pressed her lips together and squinted, looking hard at the picture, and then her eyes widened, bright with tears, and her face softened.

"Is it you?" she asked. After a moment, she tapped a finger on one of his earlobes, the one with a piece missing. "There's where you caught yourself in your mother's roses when you jumped off that brick wall. Robin Hood escaping from the sheriff. 'I can do it, Lottie — watch!' you said." She shook her head, and tears spilled over. "My Bob. Where did that boy go? What were you doing here — had you come back for me at last?"

"Lottie." I laid a hand on her arm. "Would you like to sit down? Do you want me to lock up for you and I'll put the kettle on?"

"Bob Brightbill — that's his name. And he never wished anyone harm," she wept, her voice thick. "Who would do this to him?"

"The police are working on it," I said. "You'll talk to them, won't you? About how you know him. Whatever you can tell them might help."

Lottie watched me for a moment, as if she couldn't quite understand why I was there. "I don't know what I could tell the police. It was all so long ago. Oh, Julia." She plunged her hand in a pocket and came up with a wadded tissue. "Here now, let me nip upstairs for a moment. You'll watch the door for me."

She climbed the stairs, and I considered my options. Ring Tess? Ask Willow to return immediately to take care of her aunt? But surely I could hear Lottie's story first. And she looked set to tell it, returning a minute later, her tears dried, with a bottle of whisky under her arm and two glasses in her hand.

"Sit with me," Lottie said. "I packed those memories away long ago, and yet, here they are again fresh as ever. But it's been so long since I've spoken about him, I'm out of practice. I can't imagine the police would care about this."

Tony Brightbill would care. Shouldn't he be told? And if Lottie knew Bob, then she must know his brother. But I said nothing, because I wanted to hear her tale, and I knew things would change so drastically as soon as one of those calls was made.

We sat behind the counter where we'd drunk tea the week before, and she poured us each a tot of whisky, taking a swig of hers before reaching in a pocket and pulling out an old rusted OXO tin, identical to Bob's. She opened it, and inside, nestled by cotton wool, were several pieces of birds' eggs.

"You each had one?"

"A matching pair." Lottie laughed and sniffed. "I grew up in the country near Doncaster. We were neighbors to the Brightbills, although not nearly so well off. Bob was the younger son, and I, the younger daughter. We grew up together, inseparable. We were each of us the wild child in our families, you see. My sister certainly had no interest in climbing trees or collecting frog spawn and hatching out tadpoles, and neither did Bob's brother. And so we were a pair, Bob and I, equal in every way. Although, when all was said and done, I was named the instigator — the cause of all the woe."

I stayed silent, watching the tension of her memories draw up Lottie's face into a grimace. But it dissipated, and she smiled. It made me sad.

"When he was thirteen, Bob had an accident — fell off the limb of a beech tree and hit his head." She frowned at the memory. "He lay there so still. At first, I thought he was having me on, but he wouldn't wake up, and I became frightened, and so, I ran for help. The doctor came, and the ambulance. It must've taken an hour for them to arrive. As they were at last putting him into the ambulance, he woke up. He called my name, and I remember shouting 'Hurrah!' or some such nonsense.

"And he was fine after that, you know — no broken bones. He knew us all, remembered everything, and so the family didn't send him to hospital, only kept him indoors for a week or so. They were like that, the Brightbills, always thinking they could take care of things better than anyone else. It was a miserable time for the two of us, I can tell you that. I'd sit by his bed with a cup of tea and his mum alongside us. She didn't want me there, but Bob insisted, and she would always give in to him."

Lottie swirled the whisky in her glass then finished it off, reminding me to take a sip of mine. I swallowed three drops, suppressed a gasp, and took three drops more.

"Yet, after the accident, although he was all right, still he was different. Something had shifted in him. School was no problem — at least the learning part. But before, he'd give up his adventures when it was dinnertime or bad weather. After the accident, he wasn't that interested in listening to his family's common sense. It was as if he remained an innocent, you know, oblivious to the practicalities of the world."

She poured herself a bit more whisky before continuing.

"That didn't sit well with the Brightbills, and so, they sent him away to school when he was fourteen. It might've been a special school, but no one would tell me. Before he left, we made up these tins and divided up empty eggshells we found on the forest floor. 'That way,' he said, 'you and I will remember the same things. You look for me, Lottie,' he said. 'I'll come back, and we'll have more adventures.' But that never happened."

"His family wouldn't let you see him?"

"They no longer had a say. Bob ran away from the school. I don't recall that his family did much about it, but that can't be right. They must've looked for him, don't you think? But that didn't matter, because I knew he'd come back for me, because he'd promised. I waited, at the ready to join him. But he never came and so in another year, I left home myself."

"And you never went back?" I asked, imagining a teenage Lottie wandering Europe like a Romany.

"Not for a long time. Eight years later, I stopped in for a visit, and after that, I went back when our parents died." Lottie's eyebrows rose. "I missed my sister's wedding, and that didn't go over too well. But I visited not long after Willow was born, and occasionally after that."

No wonder Willow adored her aunt — with each visit Lottie brought back the scent of a wider world, the promise of adventure.

The door of the wool shop rattled open, and I found myself yanked from Lottie's story back to the present.

Tony Brightbill stood next to a display of three miniature sheep, hands in the pockets of his Burberry raincoat, his face gray.

"Hello, Lottie," he said.

She looked at him a moment, and her eyes grew veiled. "Hello, Tony. It's been a great while, hasn't it?"

In the stifling silence that followed, I downed the rest of my whisky, hoping for a bit of courage. A fit of coughing ensued.

"Ms. Lanchester?" Brightbill asked.

"Hello," was all I managed.

"How is Tara?" Lottie asked, her voice polite and even. I held my breath. The wife.

A spasm of pain crossed Tony's face. "She died," he said. "Last year. Cancer."

"Oh," Lottie replied, losing the stiffness. "I am sorry."

"I didn't know you lived here," Tony said. "I only found out yesterday when Nuala mentioned your name. I've been trying to get up the nerve to stop in."

"I didn't know you were in the village. I didn't know Bob was here."

"I came looking for him. I wonder was he here because of you?"

They were quiet, and in my mind, the story became clear. Bob had discovered where Lottie lived, and he'd come for her just as he said he always would. My eyes filled with tears.

"Had you never seen him again?" Lottie asked Tony.

"No, no, we saw hi — he would come home a couple of times a year. Did you not know?"

The warm sympathy vanished from Lottie's face. "And how would I know that?"

Tony heaved a sigh. "No one meant to keep it from you, but you've been away so long . . ."

Lottie remained still, and Tony drew his hands out of his pockets and plunged them back in again.

"I'm sorry for that," he added.

She accepted the apology with a slight nod.

"They weren't real visits he made, only stopping by. He'd ask for a bit of money. He could've had more, he knew that, but he would always say 'That's enough for now.' We hadn't seen him since autumn, and so I started looking. Last known sighting was Thetford. I began there and then Brandon and—"

"And you saw me at Minty's?" I asked.

"I hope you can understand, Ms. Lanchester, that I never intended to disrupt your village life. It seemed an easy way to search for Bob, by carrying out a bit of business. It goes over better than storming into a town and asking 'Have you seen an older fellow with no visible means of support hanging about?' I thought I might hear of him, but my brother wasn't the easiest man to track. Especially when he didn't want to be found."

"But I saw you in Sudbury," I pointed out. "Were you there to ask police to help look for him?"

"I didn't need the police to help me find my brother," Tony replied and I thought that this time he certainly had. "No, I was there for the café at Winch & Blatch."

My phone dinged with a text. "Sorry," I whispered and grabbed for it. A message from Pammy: *r u near cottage?*

It was as good an excuse as any. Let these two catch up, and perhaps I could hear the rest of the story later.

"Lottie, will you phone Detective Inspector Callow?"

"Why?" she asked. "What could I tell them that would help?"

"I don't know, but it seems as if the police should know."

With a swift glance at Tony, Lottie replied, "Yes, I will tell the police."

CHAPTER 23

The day had been interminable, but here at its end, the rain let up, and off to the west, I could see a wood pigeon cut across a clear band of blue just above the horizon. There is life after the storm.

I continued up the high street to Pipit Cottage and saw a dim form waiting outside, but only when a car's headlights reflected off the figure did I realize it was Pammy.

She still had her hood pulled up and stood awkwardly, holding her arms away from her body and feet apart.

"Have you been waiting long?" I asked, in a hurry to unlock the door. "Gosh, that was a long day. I hope it all went well." I had hoped Gavin would abandon the twitching and take her for a good long lunch. As we stepped in the cottage and I switched on a light, I asked, "So now, the short-toed eagle?"

"Gone to Dorset," she said, a quaver in her voice.

"Pammy?"

She pushed off the hood and I gasped. Her black hair, combed up into its untidy bun, lay plastered to her head. Her eyes were dark and her skin pasty.

"Oh no, what happened?" I asked as I helped her out of the jacket. Underneath, her T-shirt — purple with Hello,

Gorgeous! scrawled in gold — looked as if it had been put through the wash but not wrung out. "God, Pammy, you're soaked."

Like a sleepy child at bedtime, she passively allowed me to undress her, putting a hand on my shoulder to steady herself as she stepped out of her waterproof trousers. Her legs were covered in gooseflesh, and her microskirt held water like a soggy bath towel. I took hold of one arm and felt her shiver.

"You're freezing! How could Gavin do this to you. I really thought he'd seen sense, but if this is the way he treats you, then I'm with Michael, you should drop him right now."

"I didn't tell Gavin about my waterproofs leaking." She wiped her nose with the back of a hand. "He was so excited, and it was all right at first. We had sandwiches and a flask of tea and found a dryish place under an oak. But it kept raining. When we finally packed up and left, he ran out of petrol and we had to walk and he was late for work and we had to wait for the bloke from the garage and so I said I'd go on because there was a bus stop not far. But it only took me as far as Harrow Green and then it turned off in the wrong direction for me and so I got off and walked the rest of the way."

She wrapped her arms round herself as she spoke. Her voice became weaker and weaker and her teeth chattered.

"Why didn't you ring me or Michael?" I demanded as I looked round for a place to hang her clothes.

"I didn't want to be a bother."

My head whipped round and for a second our eyes met — Pammy's filled with dark hesitancy.

I sighed. "Don't be daft. Come on, straight upstairs you go and have a nice, hot bath. I'll find something for you to wear."

Wordlessly, Pammy pointed to one of her plastic bags. I grabbed it and herded her toward the stairs. She had enough life left in her to stop at the bottom and notice my shoes.

"New look, is it?" she asked with a faint smile.

"They aren't mine," I replied, kicking them off. "Now, get moving."

I wrung out Pammy's top and skirt and draped them over the radiator, even though it was cold. I considered chucking her waterproofs in the bin, but instead, I rolled them up and stuffed them into one of her empty shopping bags. With Pammy occupied, I got back to my other business, and rang DI Callow.

"Tess, I thought the most awful things about Tony, and now I feel dreadful." I hadn't intended to cry, but when the words came out of my mouth and I thought about a sibling dying in this terrible way and Lottie never seeing her Bob again, the whole story engulfed me with sorrow and the tears flowed. "I thought he might've done it — killed Bob."

"And what makes you think he didn't?" the DI asked.

"But" — my voice broke, and I swept the flood of tears off my cheeks — "his brother."

"That may take Anthony Brightbill off your suspect list, but it puts him on mine. Brother killing brother? That's an old story."

I snuffled loudly and searched my sleeves for a tissue. "Well, I can't imagine it."

"A person can lose all sense of reason in a fit of rage." Hard words, but she offered them in a kind voice.

I blew my nose, and said, "But it was the weekend. Pammy saw Bob late Saturday afternoon. Tony wasn't here over the weekend. Was he?"

"He said he wasn't, and we're checking his alibi."

"It's hard to believe Bob was so close and no one who knew him realized it — not Tony, not Lottie."

"Lottie?" Tess asked.

"Finch. Willow's aunt. She runs the wool shop, Three Bags Full."

"And she knew the victim? How? And how did you know this?"

Tess shifted between caring friend and sharp investigator with such ease I sometimes had trouble following her.

"I only just found out. Willow remembered seeing an OXO tin like the one Bob had in his pocket stuck away in a drawer at Lottie's. Lottie and Bob knew each other as children, and he made up the tins as keepsakes."

"And Lottie Finch neglected to report this to the officers who were canvassing the village?"

"She didn't neglect anything. Yesterday the shop was closed, and she was away."

"DS Glossop and DC Flynn were in the village today."

"But they were at the farmers market, not in the shops."

"Yes" — I could hear such an accusatory tone in Tess's one word — "the farmers market, where they discovered you had already been asking about Bob."

"I was doing my shopping," I pointed out. "And there was no harm in me asking the other farmers if they knew him."

"We can conduct our own investigation, you know."

I ignored the remark. "Lottie and Bob hadn't seen each other in more than forty years, but they had been quite close, and this has really hit her hard. She knew Tony, too, of course. He's the older brother."

"By six years."

"She'd no idea Tony was here," I said, rummaging in the fridge and setting a pan of milk to heat on the hob. "He walked in the shop just as Lottie finished telling me her story."

"The murder victim's brother just visited the murder victim's former girlfriend? That's convenient."

"Yes. I've left them to talk things out — hang on, Tess, you can't be suspicious of the two of them."

"It's my job to be suspicious, Julia."

"What about Guy Pockett? Have you abandoned him?"

"I have not. We've found Bob Brightbill's fingerprints in Pockett's barn, but not the cottage. The thing is, it's difficult to pin down a farmer concerning his whereabouts. 'Out in the asparagus field.' 'Harvesting the courgettes.' It's little help. And neither Pockett nor any of the other farmers has any idea where Brightbill lived. We're searching woods for a campsite."

"Guy's upset about it all coming out — what he did to his own field, that is. I think he partly blames me. He was waiting for me outside the market this morning."

I put my hand on my forearm where Guy had gripped me. "Did he make you feel unsafe?"

"I'm fine."

"Come into the station tomorrow morning. It's time we got a full statement from you. And, Julia, bring Pammy along with you."

* * *

I stirred chocolate in the milk and poured up a mug just as Pammy padded downstairs wearing thick socks and oversized flannel pajamas, her hair hanging in straggly tendrils.

"Warmer now?" I asked, setting a mug on the coffee table for her.

She nodded and sipped her cocoa. "Thanks."

"Gavin should've seen you home," I said. He should've done a lot more than that.

"No, it's all right. He couldn't be late for work. He's not got a good record with jobs, and he'd started this one just the day before we met. He's determined to stick it out." Pammy took her bedding from under the coffee table and shook out a sheet.

"Where is it he works?"

"A pub on the A140 near Dickleburgh. Gavin closes and then cleans. It's one of those big places, and sometimes he's working until three o'clock in the morning. Makes evenings difficult."

That Gavin Lecky would put up with such a situation for more than one day was remarkable. I saw Pammy and her influence in a new light.

"You get comfortable. I'll put a cold supper together for us."

While Pammy drank her cocoa, I set out smoked salmon, cherry tomatoes, farmhouse cheese, a bowl of olives, a baguette, and butter. I opened a bottle of wine and turned to offer a glass, but found Pammy stretched out, covered with a blanket, and snoring lustily.

I transferred the food to a tray, stuck the cork back in the bottle, tucked it under my arm, and hauled it all upstairs. Time for my own bath.

Pulling my cardy and blouse over my head, stepping out of my skirt, and stripping off my tights, I dropped everything in a heap in the corner, and reached over to turn on the hot water. That's when I saw the black-and-blue imprint of Guy Pockett's hand on my arm. I stood gazing at it, considering what a moment of fury can do and Guy's penchant for acting first and regretting later.

* * *

By the time Michael arrived home, I had bathed, changed into a light, loose, long-sleeved nightie and had sampled a bit of everything on the dinner tray.

"Hiya," I said, rising and offering him a glass of wine. "All ready for the nightjars?"

"More than ready — overready. Your dad doesn't do anything by half." Michael nodded toward downstairs. "Pammy didn't stir when I walked in."

"She had a long day. And there was a problem with her waterproofs."

"What problem?"

"They weren't. Plus, the short-toed eagle was nowhere to be found."

"That I've heard," Michael said, washing his hands before he popped an olive in his mouth and kissed me. "Lecky rang. They thought it had gone to Dorset, but instead it's moved somewhere onto the Cambridgeshire Fens, and he wants us to film it tomorrow."

"Good. Isn't that good? You'll get it over with."

"That, indeed, is the good part." Michael poured us wine.

"Here, you get stuck in." I held out a plate for him to fill, and a black-and-blue fingerprint peeked out from my sleeve.

Michael caught my hand and brushed the fabric up to my elbow. "What's this?"

I shook my head. "It's all right. I don't think he meant it."

"He?"

I explained in a clinical manner, concluding with, "Guy's a little upset, that's all. He got carried away."

Michael cupped my elbow and ran his fingers lightly across the bruising — a gentle act that belied the fireworks in his eyes.

"I want Guy Pockett charged." Michael's voice was tight with fury. "Have you told Tess? If he's capable of this, he's capable of murder. And if he thinks that you suspect him, you could be—"

"I'm going in to the station tomorrow. But there's more to tell you."

* * *

We had our picnic on the floor of the bedroom as the evening sun shot a last ray in through the window. It took the entire meal to tell Michael everything, and when we'd poured out the last of the wine, he exhaled slowly.

"I never knew anything about Tony's family," he told me. "Apart from his wife. At Nuala's yesterday, all Tony said to me was that he was here looking into 'other concern.' He didn't say what. So, Bob came looking for Lottie, and Tony came looking for Bob. And Guy Pockett got in the middle of it."

I yawned. "I'll try to squeeze a few more details out of Tess tomorrow. God, this means I'll need to ask Vesta to cover for me again."

He reached over and rubbed my calf. "You shouldn't work so many hours."

"Said pot to kettle." I gave him a kiss.

In the quiet of the next moment, we heard the plastic-bag brigade strike up the band.

Michael sighed. "By the way, whose shoes are by the door?"

CHAPTER 24

A timid knock on the door the next morning might've sounded like thunder the way it brought Pammy's and my conversation to a sudden halt. Michael was upstairs, and this early-morning caller could only be Gavin, ready for another hunt for the short-toed eagle, but this time with Michael. The intense blue Suffolk sky heralded a return to summer — the men would have a better day for twitching than Pammy.

She still wore flannel pajamas and thick socks, and sat on the sofa with her knees pulled up under her chin. I lifted my eyebrows.

"Should I let him in?"

"Yeah, sure."

"Hiya, Julia," Gavin said quietly when I opened the door. He tried to peer round me. "Is Pammy in there? Because I have to talk with her. To apologize, you see, because of what happened yesterday."

"I'm here," Pammy called.

Gavin took a step in and stopped. I nudged him further so I could close the door, and he made it as far as the foot of the sofa.

"Would you like me to leave?" I asked Pammy.

"No, you stay," she said.

Good, because it would've been difficult to eavesdrop from the bedroom. I sat at the table in the kitchen as official observer. Gavin scowled at me, and I smiled back.

He pulled himself up, straightened his leather jacket, and turned to Pammy. "You've every right to be angry with me. I should never have left you alone after the day we had. When you didn't answer any of my texts, well, I knew you'd probably had enough, but I had to give it one more try to tell you how sorry I am about the day and the weather and running out of petrol and not seeing the short-toed eagle and all. So, I'm sorry. I won't let anything like that happen again — I really won't." This sounded like a rehearsed speech, and I wondered had he spent his whole night practicing while he mopped the pub floor and scrubbed out toilets.

Pammy didn't respond, only watched him through the steam rising from her mug of tea.

"You were fantastic yesterday," Gavin persisted, "sticking it out like that. And all for naught."

"We saw that duck," Pammy offered. "The one with the green head."

"Yeah," Gavin said. "Mallard."

"We saw loads of them, didn't we?"

I put my hand over my mouth to cover a smile. Not exactly the rare bird Gavin yearned to add to his list.

Silence again. Pammy drank her tea. Gavin fidgeted, and then said, "And so, it's your turn now."

"Yeah?" Pammy asked.

"That was our deal. You came with me yesterday, and so now you get to decide where we go and what we do next. You remember I've this Saturday off, don't you?" He spread his arms wide. "I'm all yours."

"Saturday?" Pammy asked, as if she'd never heard the word before. "Saturday," she murmured. "Let's see." She tapped a finger on her chin, and if Gavin couldn't tell she already had something planned, then he was blind. "Well, there is the Jumble-O-Rama."

"The what?" Gavin and I asked at the same time.

"The Jumble-O-Rama," Pammy explained. "Have you never heard of it? It's famous. A five-parish jumble sale held up at Swaffham on the last Saturday in June every year. They're known for their quality goods, but you don't want to waste your money right off the mark. It's best to spend all day sussing out the place, getting to know what's there so you can swoop in the last half-hour for the best deals."

Gavin swallowed. "All day?"

"They set up enormous marquees over an entire field." Pammy set her tea down to gesture for effect. "And they're really good about grouping clothes in sizes, although, of course, by afternoon that's sort of out the window." She got up on her knees on the sofa, her excitement rising. "Handbags, shoes, designer dresses, furniture. Mary Berry was seen shopping in the kitchen tent one year. The toy marquee is enough to send any little one into fits."

Gavin put a hand on the back of the sofa to steady himself, took a noisy breath, and let it out slowly. "Yeah, all right, Jumble-O-Rama it is. So, what time do we start out for this?"

Pammy tilted her head to one side as she considered his question. "Well, gates open at nine o'clock, but the queue starts forming by eight. I'd say we should leave here no later than seven."

"In the morning?"

"Seven o'clock," Pammy said, a challenge in her voice. "Saturday morning. All day."

Michael emerged from the bedroom at those words and hurried down the stairs. "I'm not going out on a Saturday morning twitching, if that's what you're talking about."

"No," I said, handing him a mug. "Gavin and Pammy are going to the world's largest jumble sale in Swaffham on Saturday. They have to be on the road by seven o'clock to arrive in time, and they'll be shopping all day."

Michael sputtered and snorted and had to set his tea down before throwing his head back in laughter. "Priceless," he said at last, wiping an imaginary tear from his eye. He slapped Gavin on the arm. "It'll be a grand day out, Lecky."

"Stuff it," Pammy said to her brother with a smile.

Gavin turned to me for sympathy, but I could only raise my eyebrows. His Herculean task had been set.

* * *

"That's quite an accomplishment," I said to Pammy when the men had departed. "Gavin, a jumble sale — I'd've never thought he'd be up for that."

"He's the one said we should share interests."

"And you've certainly done your part." I slung my bag onto my shoulder and slipped on my spare pair of heels.

"You aren't wearing those today?" Pammy nodded to the clodhoppers.

"Certainly not," I said hotly. "It was an emergency, and all Sheila had for me to borrow."

I gazed down at the thick-soled footwear. There was a problem here — although it was a problem I would never breathe a word of to any living soul. Those shoes, looking like barges run aground, were comfortable. I felt as if I had been walking on air. But they weren't for me.

"In fact" — I snatched up the shoes and attempted to cram them in my bag, but found they were bigger than the bag itself — "I need to return them."

True, I remembered that Sheila said she didn't want them back, but I felt a sudden urge to get them out of my sight.

I cast a glance to the sofa. Pammy had pulled the blanket up to her chin and stretched out her legs.

"You told DI Callow you'd be in this morning to sign your statement," I reminded her crisply. "I'm going over there now — you may as well come along."

Pammy reached over and caressed her phone screen, bringing it to life and showing the time. "Ah, Julia" — she yawned — "I'm shattered after yesterday. I'll do it tomorrow. Promise." She reached for her tea. "Will you tell her for me?"

* * *

At the police station in Sudbury, I offered up everything I knew or could speculate about the murder of Bob Brightbill, all of which DI Callow had heard before. She gave me nothing in return.

"How close are you to solving this?" I asked and received a frown for an answer. "Why would you suspect Tony? Was he tired of giving his brother money?"

"We're looking into Tony Brightbill's finances, although at first glance his business looks rock solid. Now," she said, her cool gaze locked on me. "Is there something else you have to tell me?"

Part detective inspector, part mind reader. "Right, well, I . . . need to show you this." I pulled the sleeve up on my cardigan and told her the story.

Tess turned icy. "That's assault, Julia."

"It's the farm, you see, it's all a shambles for him now. I don't think he meant to hurt me."

Of course he didn't mean it, a voice inside me said. *Just like he didn't mean to bash Bob's skull in.*

Tess snapped her notebook closed. "Let's see how far he gets if he tries to use that excuse. 'I didn't mean to' my . . . I'm going back to him today." She glanced round the interview room, empty apart from the two of us. "Now, is Pammy in the lobby?"

"No," I said. "She's exhausted after spending yesterday in the rain looking for a short-toed eagle, and so she stayed back. She said she'd be in tomorrow."

"I haven't invited her to tea," was the DI's retort. An image of the Bakewell tart at the Winch & Blatch café popped into my mind.

But once I'd escaped the police station, I decided against an intermediary stop. If I hurried, I could beat Vesta to opening the TIC.

* * *

We had a traffic jam in front of the Tourist Information Center when I arrived. Vesta rounded the corner, and

Tommy Pears crossed the road toward us carrying a pink bakery box, but before I could say "Good morning" we were surrounded by six women who looked to be in their fifties, all wearing different clothes but each with something red on — a scarf, trainers, a belt. As I unlocked the door, and rattled off greetings, I exchanged looks with Vesta, who took Tommy in hand, guiding her behind the counter and out of the fray.

The women filed in directly behind us and made immediately for the wall of leaflets. As I switched on the lights and turned the sign to *Open*, I said, "You're very welcome to the Fotheringill estate. Is there something I can help you with today?"

"No, love, we're fine," one of them said, and held up a *Shop Smeaton!* leaflet. "Look now, girls, I've got it."

"A day out, is it?" I asked, my breath coming quickly. "You'll find an excellent choice of shops on the high street. Really, the village is teeming with the best in local crafts and clothes. You can find anything you would need or want. Plus we've an old-fashioned sweets shop. Barley sugar, aniseed balls, army and navy — anything you could wish for, and everything made on the premises. The wool shop, Three Bags Full, has a fantastic selection and is run by a real artist."

"My, my," one of them murmured, stretching her neck out to get a better view of our worktable where Tommy had taken a single-layer iced cake out of the box.

"Honey and ginger," she informed them.

"And obviously," I added, "we have a tea room — Nuala's. You can't miss it. Nuala is the best baker in Suffolk. I can recommend every single thing on the menu, because I've tried it all." The women nodded approvingly and marched to the door. I dashed to the counter and went after them, thrusting business cards into their hands. "I'm Julia Lanchester, manager here at the TIC. Please do let me know if you have any questions. And have a lovely day," I called after them.

As the kettle rattled to a boil, clicked off, and wheezed, I put my hand on the glass door and continued to watch the women's retreating figures. "Do you know who I think they are?" I whispered in amazement. "They're the Red Hot Shoppers. They have a website where they rate villages for atmosphere, quality, range of goods, local sourcing, and staff. They go all over East Anglia, and Cambridgeshire, too, I believe. And now they're here! I wonder should I warn anyone?"

I turned to find Vesta setting out plates and Tommy standing to the side, wringing her hands.

"Well, no, perhaps not. I suppose I'll just let matters run their own course," I said. "A cake, Tommy, how lovely."

"It's a thank-you of sorts," she said. "You've been so kind to me, and I noticed the tea room."

"It's a lovely gesture," I said. "Honey and ginger? That's another new one for Nuala — she's getting adventurous. Shall we give it a try?"

"I'm awfully sorry about yesterday," Tommy rushed on. "Being out there with Willow. I waited for her after school, you see, to introduce myself and discuss the poster. And we just seemed to hit it off. Then we got to talking about Bob, and next thing I knew, we were out at the pond."

Vesta put a hand on Tommy's back and smiled. "Willow is a remarkable woman. She understands the world in a different way from most people. You must have a touch of that in you, too, and that's why the two of you get along."

Tommy pushed a wisp of hair off her face, returned the smile, and we were all able to settle with our tea and cake.

"It's shocking, isn't it," Tommy mused. "Bob being this Mr. Brightbill's brother and someone Willow's aunt knew yonks ago. Found here, murdered. Such a lovely man." Tommy's voice trembled.

Willow had sent me a late-night text, explaining she and Lottie were having a long talk, and had ended with: *O Julia, isn't it the most amazing and heartbreaking story you've ever heard?* I had brought Vesta up to speed that morning when I rang to say I might be late in, giving her a digest version of the Brightbill saga. Now, I licked a wodge of icing off my finger as I considered that Tommy Pears was up to speed, too.

"Is Willow all right today?" I asked.

"Mostly. So much has been resolved, yet so much is still in flux." Tommy sipped her tea and added, "Willow asked me to return to the abbey ruins."

"Why?"

"Mossy galls. Apparently one of her students made a small bonfire of the ones she'd collected — he said it was to represent how the grasslands were burned regularly." She shook her head. "They don't know how he got hold of the matches. But now they need more of those robin's pincushions. I told her I'd go out."

"I can do that for her," I offered. "You don't have to go."

"No, it's fine, because I rather feel I need to visit the ruins again. It was the last place I saw Bob."

Oh, fine, now Tommy will be calling up spirits out at the abbey just as Willow tried to do at the pond.

"Well, why don't I go with you. Would that be all right?"

CHAPTER 25

"Are those your walking shoes?" Tommy asked as I changed from heels to clodhoppers at the abbey ruins car park.

"No, certainly not." I glanced down at my feet, which appeared to have grown three sizes. "It's only that I want to save my heels."

Tommy nodded, pushed hair out of her face, and surveyed what we could see of broken walls of the medieval site, now almost covered with the rampant growth of summer.

"Peaceful out here, isn't it?" she asked. "Do you know much of the history?"

"Not enough, but I'm about to. We'll be creating a better experience here at the ruins — provide a map of what the abbey looked like all those centuries ago and tell its story. We'll draw more people out with events. I've already started working on plans for a banquet in the undercroft, a one-day medieval fair with food and entertainment and historical tours of the site." Had I mentioned any of that to Linus?

We strolled through the grounds, and I pointed out as much as I knew — remnants of the arched windows in the cloisters, the chapter house — until we reached Michael's and my private place. In a flash, I was transported to one of our lazy afternoons, all pillows and blankets and each other's arms.

"This is where we had our picnic," Tommy said, her hands on her hips as she surveyed the scene. "The children had a lovely time."

My face went hot — our private paradise invaded. Must keep that in mind.

"Duncan's quite the lepidopterist," Tommy continued. "And Tilly loves anything her brother loves, so Bob set them a competition to see how many different kinds of butterflies could they spot? They went to the edge of the field and got to work. And then Bob said to Noel, 'You'll remember how the brook runs behind the ruins, won't you?' But of course, Noel didn't, because we'd never been here before. 'Ah, then,' Bob said, 'let me take you down and show you where the fish are.'"

"Sounds like a fine time."

Tommy smiled. "Oh, it was. I read a book and fell asleep, and when I awoke, Tilly and Duncan had spotted a common blue and a holly blue, a peacock, a brown hair-streak, and I can't remember how many skippers. Noel and Bob came tramping back from the brook, and Noel said it was time to pack up and go home. That's when Bob said what a lovely family we were."

This was an extended version of the Pearses' day out, although I had remembered the bit about Noel as fisherman.

"When you came back the next Sunday, your husband had his fishing gear with him."

Tommy shook her head, but not in disagreement. "It had been such a struggle to get him to come out here the first time, I don't know why. But I rather dug my heels in about it — family outing, you know. And then returning that next weekend, well, he'd really turned against the place by then. But the children were eager, and a return visit was a small sacrifice to make for us, considering he's gone all week long."

An imperfection in the perfect family? It isn't unheard of. "Noel's work must make it difficult at times for you." But it was none of my business, and so I sought another topic. "Did the children explore the undercroft when you were out here?"

"Duncan did a quick recce looking for signs of bats," Tommy replied, "but the weather was perfect, and Bob set them that butterfly competition. They'd much rather muck about outdoors if at all possible."

I led us out of everyone's favorite picnic spot, and we circled round the undercroft and came upon a scrubby stand of blackthorn and a twisted, half-dead holly.

"What's behind all that?" she asked, nodding to the thick growth.

"Oh, I don't think it's anything."

"Looks as if someone's been here." Tommy pointed with a toe to the ground, where the long grass had been trampled flat.

"Mmm. Deer, possibly. We've roe on the estate. Perhaps a doe leaves her fawn here during the day."

Tommy scanned the undergrowth in the nearby copse. "Do you think we startled her?"

"If we did, I'm sure she'll be back. Unless she only went in deeper." I pushed on a dead holly stem to peer inside the thicket, and saw stone steps leading down to a metal door.

"Where does that go?" Tommy asked, looking over my shoulder.

"I've no idea." I looked round us, trying to get my bearings. "Perhaps the storerooms beneath the undercroft?" I pushed further and stuck myself on a spiny holly leaf.

"Ah!" I pulled my hand out and cursed, sucking on my finger.

"They're even worse when they've dried up," Tommy commiserated.

I carefully prodded a holly stem with one of my well-protected boat feet. It moved freely.

"That's why it's dried up — it's been broken off," I said.

"Do deer graze on holly? They eat roses, I know. Let's hope they've left the mossy galls alone."

* * *

We followed the directions Willow had given Tommy and found ourselves on the far side of a hedgerow where the dog roses continued to bloom and robin's pincushions clung to thorny stems. We started work at either end of the stand. The warm air buzzed with insects, while a nearby blackbird sang, and a distant chiffchaff repeated its name over and over. I discovered harvesting mossy galls calming activity that helped to clear my mind, but I was unsurprised that, as we worked, Tommy returned to the topic of Bob's murder.

"You and the detective inspector seem to be friends," she called over to me. "Do you know how the investigation is going?"

"We are friends away from her police work, but she tells me nothing," I complained. "Not to say that they aren't making progress, because they are. Bob was seen late on that Saturday afternoon. And this is key" — I stuck my head out of the brush — "we have a witness who says Bob told her that he was going off to an appointment with someone." I snipped a gall and dropped it in with the rest, wondering if I'd said more than I should. But really, with Pammy as the witness, it couldn't be that much of a secret.

A thrashing from a nearby thick stand of hazel and field maple brought our hands to a standstill.

"Is it the fawn, do you think?" Tommy asked.

"Mmm."

I started toward the noise to investigate, but a sound from a different direction arrested my movement.

Coo-koo — coo-koo — coo-coo-koo

"Listen!" I whispered. "A cuckoo!"

Coo-koo — coo-coo-koo — coo-koo

"Does it have the hiccups?"

"No, an extra syllable means it's an aberrant call. You hear it after mating season." I pulled my phone out of my bag, set it to record, and held it up high. "Won't Rupert be pleased? Come on, cuckoo — go again. I need evidence you're here."

* * *

"I'll drop these at the school for Willow," Tommy said as we stood at the door of the TIC. She shook the box, and the mossy galls rustled within. "And then I'll be off home. Tilly's asked may she cook our meal this evening. Shepherd's pie."

"Won't you take the rest of that lovely cake with you?" I asked. "I'm sure the children would love it."

Vesta and I sent Tommy away with the remainder of the honey-and-ginger cake and, thinking about lunch, I idly looked in the fridge and found a sandwich.

"Egg and cress," Vesta said. "And some of that pomegranate and elderflower fizzy water you love."

"This is perfection," I sighed, sinking into a chair. "Now, Ms. Widdersham, you are officially off duty. And you've not working tomorrow, either. I'll see you on Saturday. Off you go."

Vesta pressed her lips together as if thinking of a way to counter my command, but when I raised an eyebrow at her, she remembered who was boss. "Ring if you need me," she managed to say as the door closed. I tucked into my lunch.

It took me an hour to finish it, as the afternoon was dotted with the occasional visitor and each time I rose to greet one, I needed to make sure I had neither egg nor cress stuck in my teeth. It grew quiet about four o'clock, and I gratefully switched the kettle on and began rummaging in our biscuit tin. We seemed to be at the tail end of everything again — crumbled Hobnobs, pieces of digestives, broken custard creams — only the shortbread fingers held up well in such conditions. At the bottom, I found the remainder of a package of Jaffa Cakes and wondered when was the last time my dad had visited. I could think of no one else who ate the things.

I set about emptying the tin, eating up most of the broken biscuits as I did so, and washing it out afterward. My phone went off as I dried my hands, and I glanced over to see who was calling.

Miles Sedgwick.

Michael's older brother phoning me — whatever for? Although we were always civil to each other on the rare occasions we met, our polite behavior was a fraud. Miles was smug and self-righteous, and I'd say he found me brash and pushy. So, it was a draw.

"Miles?"

"Julia, how are you?"

"I'm all right. You? How's Maevis? How're the children?"

"Costing me too much as ever. Listen" — *ah, good, he's getting to the point* — "Michael rang me up this morning and asked for a favor."

I couldn't imagine what sort of favor this could be. Michael had worked in the family public relations business for twenty years before becoming Rupert's assistant, so it wasn't as if he needed tips on that front. Was it personal? A fear clutched at my heart — had Michael asked Miles for advice on proposing to me? Was he sending in a second?

"He had a few questions about a former client of ours. Of course, I'm not in the position to reveal private information, but I find that most of the time what we seek is available to the public, only covered in dust as if no one had thought to search in the right corner. You only need to know where to look or whom to ask."

"Tony Brightbill? He asked you about Tara's Tea?"

"He wouldn't exactly say what concerned him," Miles said stiffly, a thread of suspicion in his voice. "It isn't Pammy, is it? Because she was warned—"

"Warned? You *fired* her. I'd say that's a bit more than a warning."

"She cost us a huge account," Miles countered, "that would only have grown in these last two years. It wasn't even that she bollocksed that opening day, it's because she can't keep her hands off—"

"Harmless flirting, Miles. Are you telling me you don't lay it on thick when it comes to your work?"

The air between us shifted, and I heard a dismissive sniff.

"That isn't why I rang, Julia, and so why don't we just get on with this?"

"Yes, let's," I said, and plopped myself in a chair. "And so, it was about Tony Brightbill?"

"And the company's finances. Here's what I know. Tony started Tara's Tea eight years ago, but it wasn't his first business. He'd tried a chain of American-style diners about fifteen years earlier, spent a lot of money, and lost everything. It was family money — the great-grandfather made a fortune in scrap metal."

"So he had no money to start Tara's Tea, or is the Brightbill well bottomless?"

"He borrowed the money from another Brightbill — his brother, Robert."

I held my breath before asking, "How much? How much did he borrow?"

"A million — it was no shabby beginnings for Tara's Tea. He's opened two new shops since we had his account, though, and it looks as if he might be stretched a bit thin at the moment. But I'm sure he has other things on his mind. I read his wife died. I've nothing on the brother, Robert. Quiet sort, I suppose. Stays out of the way and counts his money. Now, what's this about?"

"Tony is in the village looking to steal away our best baker," I said. Not a lie, not at all.

"Ah, well. Is that why Michael asked me to ring you with this information, because it was Fotheringill business? Not that I'm not delighted to talk with you. Or does he have his hands full of birds today?"

I offered a polite laugh and pictured Michael and Gavin on the Cambridgeshire Fens waiting out the short-toed eagle.

Miles had no more desire to prolong our conversation than I did, and so it ended quickly. I immediately rang Tess, reached her voicemail, and spilled the story as I glanced at the time — just gone five o'clock. I really should've locked up by now. Just as I finished the message with "There's motive — it was Bob's money, not his" the bell above the door jingled.

I looked up at my visitor and leapt out of my chair.

"Mr. Brightbill."

"Ms. Lanchester," he said.

Yes, I really should've locked up.

* * *

Five o'clock on a weekday in Smeaton-under-Lyme cars lined the high road like cattle, nose to tail, ambling home. Drivers never looked out their windows, and foot traffic seemed to have dried up — a combination that made me feel isolated in the TIC, alone with a suspect in a murder case.

Had Miles had the time to warn Tony Brightbill we were nosing into his background? Had he said, "Look out for Julia — she'll try to pin something on you?"

"Can I help you, Mr. Brightbill?" I asked. "I'm afraid I was just about to close. End of the day, you know." I stayed where I was behind the table behind the counter, and Brightbill remained just inside the door. I clasped my phone in my hand. Could I dial 999 without him knowing?

"I feel as if I need to explain a bit more about my brother and our relationship. And our family. I realize Lottie told you about Bob, but I don't want you to think that we were an uncaring lot."

Lottie told *her version* of the story — that was what he meant. And now, he was here to offer the Brightbill family's side.

"Oh, *pfft*, families," I said. "We've all got stories, haven't we?"

"When I said Bob came home and I gave him money, it wasn't an act of charity. It was his money I gave him. I was merely his . . . banker, if you will. It was money left to him by our parents. Bob wanted nothing to do with an everyday sort of life, and so this arrangement arose — when he needed a bit to live on, he'd stop by."

I stayed quiet and attempted to sort this out. Bob had piles of money, but no use for it. That made sense. It fit with

Lottie's story about Bob's attitude toward life. He needed only a bit of money to get by and enjoy his life.

"I didn't want you to think I had grown tired of giving him handouts. That wasn't the case."

"Yes," I said. "That is, no. I mean, I understand." My thoughts continued to race while my mouth offered nothing of substance.

"It's his money, in his name."

"Except, of course, you must have power of attorney," I pointed out.

Tony didn't answer, giving me a moment to bite my tongue.

"My family has always taken care of itself," he said. "We've seldom seen the need to ask for outside help."

Not sending your brother to hospital after a head injury, for example. Not going to police with a missing persons report when he vanished.

"Were you in the village the day Bob was killed?" Tony asked.

"Were *you*?"

He huffed in exasperation. "Ms. Lanchester, I want to know what happened to my brother, and Detective Inspector Callow has told me little. This leads me to believe I'm under suspicion, but I want to assure you I don't know who would murder my brother. It was a violent and cruel act" — his voice broke — "and the person who did it needs to be brought to justice. You seem to be involved in every single aspect of life on the Fotheringill estate, and so I come to you. Is there anything you can tell me? Is there anything I can do?"

My phone went off.

I answered in a rush of relief. "Hi, Tess."

"I want your source," DI Callow said.

"I was just about to close up the TIC," I replied in a conversational tone. "And Mr. Brightbill has stopped by."

"Are you all right?" Tess asked urgently.

"Fine." Was I? I stole a look at Tony. He hadn't moved, but had stuck his hands in his trouser pockets and stared at the floor as if he wasn't listening to my side of the conversation. He looked not in the least like a murderer.

"I'll stay on the line while you get rid of him," she said.

I held the phone away from my mouth. "Mr. Brightbill—"

"It's all right," he said, pulling a hand out of his pocket and slapping a card on the counter. "I'm staying locally for now. Will you ring me?"

He didn't wait for an answer, but walked out. I crept up to the window and watched his retreating figure as I threw the lock on the door.

In my mind, I had accused Tony of murder, but now I wasn't so sure. My opinion of his guilt or innocence flip-flopped in the blink of an eye.

"Maybe he decided he didn't want to pay back the million quid he borrowed," I said to Tess. *Flip.*

"He's asking more questions than he's answering," she replied.

"Can't you tell him anything, Tess?" I asked. "He's in such pain." *Flop.*

"He knows how his brother died and when. And, we've been unable to confirm his alibi for that Saturday."

Flip.

"Where did he say he was?"

"A cemetery outside of Doncaster, spending the day at his wife's grave — the anniversary of her death."

Flop.

CHAPTER 26

I found myself loitering outside Three Bags Full on my way home from work. Here was someone who could put me straight about Tony Brightbill, I decided. Lottie hadn't seemed keen on Tony the evening before, but perhaps that had been the initial shock of seeing him after so many years. Now, she'd had a day to think things through, and she might have a more objective outlook.

She stood high on a wooden ladder set against her wall of wool, pulling out skeins and dropping them to the floor, where they bounced and rolled off in different directions. She looked down at me and said, "Julia, all right there?"

"I am," I replied. "And you?"

"I decided it was time for a bit of a clean-out," she said, her head deep in a cubbyhole and her voice muffled. "It's the ones far in the back you forget about, isn't it? I'll have a sale. I don't suppose His Lordship would let me set a table out on the pavement, would he?"

"Well, I don't see why not — you've only to ask."

The top row of yarn cubicles having been emptied, Lottie came down the ladder. When she stepped on terra firma, I noticed she had a crochet hook stuck behind one ear like a pencil and a furrow on her brow.

"I hope I'm not bothering you," I began.

"You're no bother, Julia," she said as she began collecting skeins from the floor and dropping them into a giant basket in the corner. "I've told Willow my story and I've talked with your Detective Inspector Callow, although I'm sure she was disappointed, as I had nothing of substance to offer her."

I chased after a few skeins that had bounced under the counter and tossed them in the basket, while I said, "And all that after your talk with Tony."

"There's a man with a great deal to answer for," she said, her back to me, but the bitterness in her voice coming through quite clear. She sighed. "No, I didn't mean it the way it sounds. It's only that he's the last Brightbill left, and so he must take the brunt of the fallout. That family" — she turned and shook a blood-red skein in the air — "they were always experts at closing ranks. A world unto themselves. Never any need for outsiders, because the family would always take care of things."

"Is he sad about Bob?"

"Yes, I believe he is. Although you'd never know it by looking at him. And he's still grieving for his wife. It can't be easy on him, and I should remember that." She examined the skein she held, hugged it to herself, and exclaimed, "I wish he'd said something." I knew she didn't mean Tony. "Why didn't he just walk in here and say something to me?"

"If Bob had come in . . ." I began and then hesitated.

Lottie's eyes grew dark. "We would've sat down over a drink and told each other stories until we'd found that common ground taken from us all those years ago." Her eyes filled with tears. "And then what? We'll never know now, will we?"

* * *

Pammy waited on the doorstep of the cottage and for the first time, I wondered if we should give her a key. The thought hadn't time to linger long before I banished it.

"You look quite smart," I said. Her black skirt, more mini than micro, was topped with a shimmering blue blouse that moved like liquid.

"Thanks," she said, high color on her cheeks. Inside, she walked to the sofa and whirled round. "So, well, here it is. I have a job. A proper job, not one where my brother only puts up with me and boots me out the minute I—" she stopped and reversed before she went down that road. "A proper job," she repeated. "Assistant manager at a charity shop in Bury Saint Edmunds. Not just any charity shop, mind you — Oxfam!"

"Well done, you," I said and gave her a hug.

"They set an exam as part of the interview," Pammy rushed on. "A table piled high with donated clothes that I had to sort and price. After that, they asked what kind of creative leadership I would bring to the position, and I told them I'd organize a Posh Frock sale — a special evening where we'd save up all the very best clothes and give out free glasses of Prosecco as women shop. Also, I pointed out to them that my entire outfit" — she swept her hand from head to toe — "came from Oxfam shops."

I was speechless in admiration and amazement. It was as if during her time on our sofa, Pammy had been in a chrysalis stage, and in an instant, she had emerged to stretch her wings.

"There's more." Pammy wriggled with excitement. "Another woman at the shop — an older woman, a widow — has a spare room in her house to let and said I could start out there and we would see how it works. I could save up and look for my own place!"

"So, what about you and Gavin?"

"Yeah, Gavin." She grinned and giggled and blushed. "We're, you know, an item. But we aren't moving in together yet. I've learned my lesson there. In fact, I've learned a lot staying here with you and Michael and I know I need to take responsibility for myself and my life. And it starts now."

A call echoed in my mind.

Coo-koo — coo-coo-koo.

In June it changes tune.

As I marveled at how a bit of patience on our part had paid off, Pammy asked, "So, when's Michael home?"

"Not for a long while," I said. "Nightjars."

"Nightjars?" she repeated, wrinkling her nose. "Is he at a pub or something?"

"No." I laughed. "But we should be. How about we go out for a meal, my treat. Stoat and Hare?"

"A bit fancy."

"Not too fancy. The pub is quite cozy, although I suppose the dining room is a step up. Lovely food."

"Burgers?"

"The best."

"I'm in."

* * *

"God, where've you got off to lately?" Peg asked as soon as we'd stepped in the door.

"I know, there's not had a spare minute," I said, "but we couldn't keep away any longer. Do you know Michael's sister Pammy?"

"No," Peg replied. "Lovely to meet you. Would you like a table? We're in a bit of a crush, but I can squeeze you in."

We followed Peg, and I turned to Pammy and whispered, "Could it be there's someone in the village you haven't met?"

She only smiled as she waved to Derry from the garden shop, who stood with a gin and tonic, arm on the bar. Derry raised her head in acknowledgment.

"Will you be all right here?" Peg asked, stopping at a small table set up against a dividing wall in the dining room.

"Perfect." I took the chair facing the rest of the busy room, and Pammy sat across from me with a view over my shoulder of the stairs up to the rooms above and into the bar.

"Peg, has Fred agreed to be the first chef demo at the market?"

"I'd say he's wavering."

"Right then. Hang on," I said to Pammy.

I backtracked into the bar, stuck my head in the kitchen, and jumped out of the way of a server carrying four full plates.

"Sorry. Hiya, Fred," I called.

Peg's husband looked up from a simmering saucepan.

"What about that demo at the market. Next Wednesday?" I asked. "You'll be our first, and you can cook whatever you like."

"What? Oh yeah, right." A server swooped in and stuck a food order on the line. "Sure. Fine. Talk to me tomorrow?"

You see, catch them in a busy moment, and it's easy.

Returning to the dining room, I walked through the bar, and as I passed the staircase, saw a familiar face. Tailored, jewel-toned business suit, cascading chestnut hair — ah, the businesswoman who had been in search of a chemist.

"Hello again," I said and received a blank look. "Sorry, out of uniform. I'm Julia Lanchester, tourist manager. We met on the high street when you were looking for—"

"Contact lens solution! Lovely to see you again," she said warmly, taking my hand in what was a mashup of a shake and a clasp. I remembered she was in sales.

"We're delighted you've returned," I said.

"Yes, as you can see, I'm still quite taken with your village." She nodded a greeting to Peg and continued up the steps.

Peg smiled at her retreating figure, but murmured, "That isn't all she's taken with."

I leaned in to hear more, but Peg said, "Must get to work," turned on her heel, and headed for the bar.

* * *

We might've gone a bit overboard on ordering food, but Pammy and I were both famished. Burger with Stilton for her, stuffed sole for me. We ordered starters, too — she the smoked haddock rarebit, and I, the poached pheasant egg on artichoke ragout. As we waited on the food, we started in on a bottle of the house red, and, now that she was in the loop, I caught Pammy up on the Brightbill investigation, although I went easy on speculating who the murderer might be.

"Can you believe it?" she asked, incredulous. "And Willow's aunt knew him?" She shuddered. "He's a right one, that Tony, but still — his wife dies and now his brother murdered? No one deserves that, do they?" She cut her eyes over her shoulder at the other diners. "He won't be coming in here, will he?"

I assured her he wouldn't, but then he did say he was staying local. I, too, glanced round the room, just to be certain.

The starters arrived, and we moved off the subject of murder. I cut into my egg, and watched the golden yolk ooze out before stabbing a piece.

"Gavin and I have been telling each other about our past relationships," Pammy said.

That must've taken awhile, I thought, and blushed remembering my own past.

"There weren't any great successes," Pammy said, "but then, they weren't all bad." She looked at me over the rim of her glass, a teasing Sedgwick twinkle in her eye. "He spoke quite highly of you."

My hand froze in midair and yolk dripped onto the napkin in my lap.

"*He what?*"

Pammy reached over and patted my hand. "It's all right, Julia. It was a long time ago."

I dropped my head. "Oh, my God."

"And you were both free agents. Remember, we all do a crazy thing every once in a while." She took up her knife and fork and examined her starter before adding, "I've certainly learned my lesson about inappropriate choices."

I sighed and rescued the egg dangling from my fork. Her brother would disagree. Michael considered Gavin a highly inappropriate choice for his sister, although I saw it otherwise. Gavin and Pammy seem to be bringing out the best in each other.

"Yes, well, I suppose you and I have both learned a few lessons."

No response. I looked up to see Pammy staring over my shoulder, a frown on her face.

"You know who I think that is?" she asked. "I think it's that other fellow."

I swallowed before I could ask, "What other fellow?"

"It *is* him," she said, squinting. "I'm sure of it. I recognize him from his hair." She looked back at me. "The fellow I saw out near the church the day Bob died."

I spun round and could see nothing except the back of someone starting up the stairs and a few people milling about at the bottom. When at last they cleared, I had a straight view into the bar, where Guy Pockett — whose hair rose up several inches like a yeast bread — stood alone finishing off a pint and watching us.

CHAPTER 27

"You saw Guy Pockett near the church the day Bob was murdered. Why didn't you—" I had to stop as the server came to clear our starter plates and set down the main courses. When she'd left, I leaned over the table. "Did you talk to him?"

"Yeah, well, I asked if he knew where you lived. And he didn't."

"You saw him near the church," I repeated. Near the church was not that far from the pond. Guy Pockett was observed near the scene of the murder and near the time of the murder. With all my will, I reined in my galloping suspicions. "But, there were loads of people by the church. There had been a wedding, remember?"

"No, it was *after* the wedding. Weren't you all here in the pub? I didn't see anyone else."

True. Vesta and Akash's wedding had ended, and we'd traipsed down to the garden here at the Stoat and Hare. Michael and I had intended to leave the reception a bit early, but instead we'd ended up being among the last remaining, and when we'd strolled down the high street, arriving home about seven o'clock, we found Pammy on our doorstep.

"But why didn't you say anything about him? Why didn't you tell the police?"

"I don't know." Pammy drew her arms to her chest defensively. "I forgot, I suppose. It wasn't about him, was it? I'd seen Bob, and that's what was important. Who cares about some other bloke?"

I nodded back to the bar. "And you're sure he's the one?"

Pammy leaned over, looking past me.

"Well, he's gone now."

I turned. No Guy Pockett in sight.

* * *

I spent the rest of the meal attempting and failing to coerce Pammy into talking with the police immediately. She begged could we finish our meal in peace and wait until the morning when she would go straight to the station in Sudbury and tell DI Callow the news that Guy had been seen near the site of Bob Brightbill's murder.

"He's another witness," I insisted, although in my mind I called him something else. "The police need all the information they can get."

"What's she going to do about it this evening?" Pammy pointed out.

"All right," I conceded. "You can wait until tomorrow — but off you'll go, first thing."

We managed to clean our plates and sat in contented quiet for a few moments before Pammy asked, "How's the crème brulée in this place?"

* * *

And so, when Michael arrived home just minutes after we did and said, "That's a wrap on the nightjars. Who's up for fish and chips?" he was met with a duet of sighs.

"I could do you scrambled eggs on toast?" I offered, and got busy. "But listen now, your sister has something to say."

"What's that, then?" Michael asked.

"You are speaking," Pammy said, nose in the air, "to the new assistant manager of the Oxfam shop in Bury Saint Edmunds."

"Is that right?" he asked, breaking out in a grin.

"And I've sorted out lodgings."

"Not with—"

"No," I rushed in. "With someone from the shop."

"Ah, Pammy, that's grand," Michael said, giving his sister a hug and a kiss on the cheek.

"So, short-toed eagle?" I asked.

Michael poured himself a glass of wine and held up it up. "Sitting pretty on a low branch of a willow as if he'd been waiting for us. Got him cruising over the flats, too, hunting for snakes."

"Congratulations. And how was Gavin?"

"Good." Michael took a slug of wine. "Yeah, he's good in front of the camera, I'll give him that."

"Of course he is," Pammy said, heading upstairs to take first shift in the bathroom.

"And he's looking forward to that jumble sale on Saturday, I can tell you," Michael called after her. Pammy turned and grinned before closing the bedroom door.

"Thanks for ringing Miles," I said over my shoulder as I scraped eggs onto the toast on his plate. Michael started in on his food as I explained what his brother had found for us. "It doesn't look good. Tony could've wanted to be shed of that million-quid loan and done in Bob to be free of it."

"You told Tess?"

I nodded. "But now there's this." I related Pammy's sighting of Guy Pockett. "Was he the one Bob was going to meet?" I sighed. "We're back to Guy slipping off the organic rails — spraying that field with herbicide and wanting to keep it quiet."

Michael's eyes dropped to my arm, where the violet handprint of bruising had mellowed and a hint of yellow-green was beginning to emerge.

"She was having a word with him today," I said.

"She should have more than a word," Michael replied brusquely. "Did you ring her about Pammy's sighting?"

"No. Pammy's going into the station first thing tomorrow. And I'm going to work. I've given Vesta the day off."

* * *

Michael left early the next morning to collect Rupert in Cambridge and make a ten o'clock meeting in Sheffield to plan for the city's upcoming Day of Flowers, Birds, and Bees.

"Didn't you work late last evening?" Pammy had asked her brother as he stood in the doorway. She still wore pajamas, and looked up from hunting through a bag. "And will you work on the weekend again?"

"No work this weekend. I've got other plans," Michael said on his way out.

Fine for some. I worked weekends and wouldn't abandon Vesta to the Saturday crowds.

I hitched my bag up onto my shoulder, ready to head for the TIC, although it was long before opening time. Still, how busy could a Friday morning be? I would be able to enjoy my tea in peace and quiet in a place where milk was not in short supply while Pammy readied to leave for the Sudbury police station. And she'd be leaving soon, wouldn't she?

It didn't look like it. She had been sifting through her possessions for the past half-hour, retrieving a top, pulling it on, and then ripping it off, and moving to another. Microskirts lay scattered across the floor, landing where they had been tossed.

I delayed my departure for work, keeping one eye on Pammy while I pretended to clean out my bag, shoveling detritus onto the counter, including a handful of business cards I'd collected recently. Minty's Tea Room in Brandon, Winch & Blatch, Deena Downey, the businesswoman looking for a chemist.

But at last I could take it no longer.

"You'll be off now to the constabulary, won't you? You promised."

Pammy clasped a T-shirt to her chest, an anguished look on her face. "Will you come with me?" she whispered.

"I can't, Pammy — it's a workday. You'll be fine."

"I'd rather not go alone."

"You've put DI Callow off twice now. I wouldn't chance a third time."

"But that was because I had plans on Wednesday. And yesterday was my interview."

"Why didn't you say that?"

"I didn't want to jinx it." She stood there in her bra and pajama bottoms, her shoulders drooping, fiddling with the sleeve of the top she held. "Look, I've never been in a police station before."

I checked the time and caved. "All right, I'll go with you. But only if we leave immediately, then I can make it back in time to open."

And, hey presto, in the span of five seconds, Pammy had donned a microskirt, pulled on a top that read Brains + Beauty! and a pair of shoes. We were ready.

* * *

"You see, it slipped my mind about the other bloke, because all I did was ask him if he knew where Julia lived, and he didn't. Pretty snippy about it he was, too. But I'd forgotten about that until last evening when we were at the pub and there he was and I remembered. It was because of all this about the murder, you see, and how I could identify Bob for you. You were glad about that, weren't you? That I had seen him? That's helped, hasn't it? So, it isn't as if I've done something wrong." A pause. "Have I?"

We sat across from DI Callow in interview room number one. Pammy's voice had risen higher and higher as she had offered her explanation, until it had drifted off into a whisper at the end.

"You've done nothing wrong," Tess said, and I heard Pammy take a deep breath and let it out. "But you realize we must follow up on every possible lead or witness in the vicinity. And so, you say it was this man, Guy Pockett, you saw the day you arrived?"

Tess pushed a photo across the table showing Guy standing at the door of his cottage looking as if he were in a police lineup.

"No." Pammy shook her head emphatically. "I didn't see him."

"You said you saw Guy Pockett," Tess reminded her.

"No, it was Julia said I saw this Guy Pockett whoever he is."

"Pammy, you said it was the fellow last night at the pub," I reminded her. "The one with the hair."

"Yes," Pammy insisted, jabbing furiously at the photo, "but not that hair. You're the one who said it was this one."

"I didn't!"

"You did!"

"*Quiet!*" Tess's look was hard as glass, but I saw a flicker of what I interpreted as sympathy flash my way. "What man did you see near the church?"

"Well, that's what I'm trying to tell you," Pammy said in an injured tone. "It looks as if there's been a mix-up. Last night, I said the fellow with the hair, and I can see now how that might've been misleading, because Julia thought I meant this hair. But it wasn't."

The DI sighed. "What did the man you saw look like?"

Pammy frowned in concentration. Then she shrugged. "He looked sort of a regular fellow."

"Except for his hair," Tess prompted.

"Yeah," she said, nodding, "he's got this mass of lovely hair. Wish mine was like that. The sort you can just shake out and looks good."

"Color?"

"Mmm, sort of black. Brown — maybe a bit of red in it. But dark, mind you, he's not a ginger."

"How old was he?"

"God, I'm terrible with ages! Thirty-five? Forty-five?"

The questioning continued, and I realized that Pammy could no more describe this fellow than she could a goldfinch. Powers of observation could be learned, and perhaps that's something Gavin could take care of, but at the moment, the struggle to get a clear answer out of her was telling on the DI's face.

"If you had a photo of him," Pammy said, "that would help. I'd know him if I saw him. Like I did with Bob."

Tess's nostrils flared.

"What was he wearing?" I tried.

"Dark trousers, charcoal — H&M, I think. You know, the skinny chinos. His shirt had thin, faded stripes, a pale blue against navy, and he had a jacket on from Topman. Probably two hundred and fifty quid retail all told, but, of course, I could do the same sort of thing for forty pounds at charity shops. You just have to know what you're looking for."

Details at last — just not terribly useful ones.

Pammy signed her statement and swore to the detective inspector she would think hard about this fellow and what he looked like.

"I'll try to locate a police artist to send out to you," Tess told us, "although they're thin on the ground round here. Still, if we can find one, we might be able to work out a likeness."

* * *

"I suppose I don't pay enough attention," Pammy confessed, buckling her seat belt.

"You do pay attention, but only to clothes."

In an attempt to prove me, or herself, wrong, Pammy stared out the window on the short trip from Sudbury and commented on anything remotely avian.

"On the wire, there. It's big and black. No, wait — white, too!"

"Magpie."

"Brown!" she exclaimed. "A little brown bird back there."

"Yes, we don't see too many of those."

"Did you see there on that roof?" she asked as we stopped at a traffic light. "A blackbird, I'm sure. And look! One just flew by us."

"Blackbird on the roof, yes. But it was a dragonfly that just flew past."

"I quite like birds, and I intend to learn all about them," she stated. "And memorize what they sound like. I want to hear a cuckoo. Do they really say *coo-koo*? Where do I go to hear one of those?"

I cut my eyes at her as we pulled into my lockup. "I might be able to help with that."

CHAPTER 28

I had five minutes to open on time. I broke into a trot down the high street, tossing the key to the cottage to Pammy without a thought. "Here you go. I must hurry. If you're going out later, why don't you drop the key by the TIC. All right?"

"Yeah, right, sure." Pammy waved the key as if it were a first-prize ribbon. "Thanks!"

My first visitor of the day, waiting at the door, had become a regular — Tommy Pears. She began with her usual "I hope you don't mind" but I broke in.

"I'm delighted you're here. Have you come to start on the abbey leaflet? I could just do with a cup of tea."

That kept us off the subject of Bob Brightbill's murder, put her to work, and allowed me to attend to business. A glorious late-June Friday morning and time for the international traffic to pick up. By midmorning, I'd dealt with a horde of Germans, a gaggle of Japanese, a squadron of retired American military, and an amorphous cloud of spiritualists who hoped to hold an autumnal equinox event out by the cider orchard in September. I took their details and said I'd be in touch.

All the while, Tommy sat behind me humming lightly as she drew a layout and began sketching. The first moment

I could breathe, I found my cup of tea had gone cold. I filled the kettle to start again.

"That's lovely," I commented, looking over Tommy's shoulder. Her design drew my eye down the page and would fit perfectly with the story I had in mind to tell. She had blocked off spaces for photos and filled in with sketches of abbey life. I pointed to a monk. "That one looks like Sean Connery."

"*The Name of the Rose*," Tommy said. "One of my favorite films. I didn't see it when it came out, of course, but I've got it on DVD now. He made quite a striking religious figure." She wiggled her eyebrows and giggled, and I realized it was the only time I'd seen her truly happy, apart from that first visit with her husband and children.

As I fished the tea bag out of my mug, I heard the jingle — so much for my tea break. But it was only Pammy, who stood just inside the TIC and gazed round her.

"Wow, Julia, this is amazing. It's as if you've got your own shop here."

"Without selling anything," I replied. "Well, except for the odd key chain and pencil. Tea?"

I introduced her to Tommy who, I explained, was "visiting from London" and doing a bit of graphic design for us and, because they would find out themselves, I explained their Bob connection.

"You met him?" Tommy asked. "Wasn't he a lovely man?"

"Yeah." Pammy nodded in sorrow. "He seemed like it. And did Julia tell you, I saw someone else that afternoon nearby and police are hot to track this fellow down because he could be a witness. Only problem is, no one knows who he is."

How convenient she left out the reason no one knew who he was — because she couldn't come up with a decent description. I pitied the poor artist Tess tracked down to help out with that.

Pammy sat down at the table with her tea and I handed her the biscuit tin. "Not much there. I'll make a run to the shop at lunch."

"I could go," Pammy said, as she looked over Tommy's leaflet design. "You did all this? It's fantastic."

"Tommy's quite talented, isn't she? Look, she's done Sean Connery as a monk, and the other day she made a quick sketch of me."

Pammy peered closer, and then her head rose slowly and she locked her eyes on me. "Tommy's an artist," she said, stating the obvious. And the penny dropped.

"Tommy," I said, "I wonder could you do us an enormous favor. Really, it would be doing the police a favor. DI Callow is searching for an artist to work with Pammy on a likeness of the fellow she met, but you are here, and you're quite skilled at catching a person's likeness. Would you mind trying?"

Tommy's face lit up. "Of course I will. I would do anything to help find out who killed Bob."

They got to work, and I went for my phone to ring Tess with the good news, but was diverted by a swarm of Canadians, each wearing a maple leaf lapel pin. The moment they had gone, in came a throng of teenage Spaniards — school trip, I thought. I chased round after them as each one seemed to feel compelled to pick up and put down — in the wrong place — every leaflet, key chain, and pencil in the entire center.

During it all, I tried to eavesdrop on Tommy and Pammy, but heard only snatches of the session. "Oh yeah, that's the hair. But I think his nose was a bit different," Pammy said. This indicated to me they were making progress, and Pammy was actually remembering.

Two adults, who had spent their time in the TIC in lively conversation with each other, now began herding the Spanish students out. I noticed a cluster of women waiting outside on the pavement to come in and recognized them — it was the Red Hot Shoppers returned. I knew they visited a village more than once before posting on the blog. Behind me, I heard Pammy say, "Perfect!" and a chair screeched. I threw a glance over my shoulder to see Tommy, pale and pushing hair off her face.

"Sorry," she said, sounding out of breath. "I have to go now. It's because . . . I have to go." She got to the door along with the last few students, and pushed her way through.

I looked back at Pammy with my eyebrows raised. She shrugged her shoulders.

The TIC filled with the women in red, and I slapped a welcoming smile on my face. "Hello again, and welcome back. What can I help you with today?"

Had their first shopping experience in Smeaton-under-Lyme been a happy one? They were difficult to read — faces remained neutral, and although they asked few questions, they were pointed. How much control did the estate exercise over the people who ran the shops? Were there plans to expand? Which was the oldest shop, and which, the newest?

I told them as much as I could, but added, "I'm sure Lord Fotheringill would love to chat with you. He has such wonderful stories about the village. Shall I give him a ring?"

"No, dear, that won't be necessary. We've lunch booked at the Stoat and Hare, and then we'll be on our way. Thanks ever so much."

They marched out, and I had trouble keeping myself from marching after them and putting my head in every shop to find out how it had all gone. But alas, here came the Swedes.

Pammy slipped out the door, waving at me and mouthing "Shop," and I spent the next half-hour with Swedish ramblers, a marking pen, and a map of all the footpaths on the estate. When I at last bid the walkers goodbye, I saw Pammy across the road, her arms full of sandwiches and packets of biscuits. She glanced up and down the high street, waiting for a break in the traffic, but when it cleared, she froze, her foot hanging off the curb in midair, her attention taken by something out of my sight. Then, in a flash, she bolted across the road and into the TIC.

"It's him!" she whispered furiously. "I saw him. He's out there now."

"What? Who?"

Pammy dashed behind the counter, dropped her armload onto the table and then pushed it all out of the way. Sandwiches and biscuits tumbled to the floor, and papers sailed through the air. She snatched one of them and darted back to me.

"Here," she said, shoving it in my hand. "This is who Tommy drew. That's the bloke I saw on that Saturday, and now he's right outside."

I studied the drawing of the man seen near the Stoat and Hare not far from the churchyard and the pond beyond. The man who could be a witness to Bob's murder. I knew the face, dark hair with curls dropping onto his forehead, narrow nose. As I gazed down at the sketch, the bell above the door jingled, and I looked up to find Noel Pears.

* * *

"Hello," I said to Noel Pears, my face going beet red as I stashed the paper behind my back.

"Where's my wife?" Noel demanded, the affable demeanor I remembered from previous encounters nowhere in sight.

"Your — I have no idea," I said, finding myself disinclined to tell him she'd been in the TIC only a few minutes ago.

Noel huffed, his arms at his side, his hands constantly working. He shifted his eyes to Pammy, who stretched her neck out and tilted her head, staring at him as if he were an exhibit in a zoo.

"Hello," she said.

He frowned at her. "Do I know you?"

We both answered at the same moment.

"Yes," Pammy said.

"No," I said, louder. "She's an intern with us."

Pammy's look suggested I'd lost my reason, but I didn't think it was a good idea for a possible witness to a murder to know the origin of tips in the investigation. Confidentiality or something, wasn't it? Plus, I didn't like Noel Pears' attitude.

"And you just started today," I added, staring Pammy down.

She turned her head coyly to the side and said, "Yeah, that's me, an intern. Are you a tourist? What would you like to see? Want to visit the abbey ruins where all those monks lived about a million years ago? You might see Sean Connery."

He glared at us one at a time. "What's all this about? What are you filling my wife's head with?"

"Mr. Pears," I replied airily, "I have no idea what you're on about, but since you've stopped in, let me ask — have you spoken to the police?"

"Of course I have," he snapped. "They rang the day after Tommy came in here."

"No, I mean have you spoken to them again."

Noel narrowed his eyes at me. "I have nothing else to say to the police about."

"Yes, you do," I persisted, and caught myself about to reveal just what I had kept Pammy from revealing — that we knew exactly where he'd been on that Saturday. "That is, you might. It's about that Sunday, the Sunday you and Tommy and the children all met Bob Brightbill. He was murdered the following weekend, and surely you must realize that any detail or insight you can offer to the police could have an enormous impact on the enquiry. Your wife's been quite helpful."

"Why are you interfering with my family?" he shot back. "Because, I won't stand for that. My wife and my family are very important to me. So just, leave off."

And with that, he stalked out. Pammy rushed to the window and watched.

"He's driving away in some kind of a dark car."

I peered over her shoulder, missed getting his car's number plate, but noticed Pammy's keen powers of observation had returned. "It's a Ford Fiesta, just like yours — it's even the same color." And two a penny on British roads.

"So that's it, is it?" Pammy tugged the paper out my hand and smoothed out the wrinkles. "He's Tommy's husband."

"Look, Pammy, when you and Tommy were working on the sketch, did she draw what you told her to draw or did she—"

"Make it up herself? Dunno." Pammy stared at the paper. "I started her out, but she sort of continued on her own. But, even if she did draw a picture of her own husband, he's still the right person." Her brow furrowed. "But why is he the right person? If they don't live round here, what was he doing at the pub last night? Why was he here on that Saturday? How did he come to be a witness?"

"Possible witness," I reminded her. "Noel is away from home all week — he installs and maintains software for businesses. But Saturday, I don't know. Tommy says he's always home at the weekends."

Pammy crossed her arms and raised an eyebrow. "Away all week, but always home on the weekends? And what does that tell you?"

I held out the sketch to examine the face once again. I needed to check something. The TIC was quiet at the moment — dare I take a risk nipping out?

"Listen, Pammy, would you mind staying here for five minutes on your own? I need to see Peg at the Stoat and Hare."

* * *

I flew out the door, leaving Pammy standing behind the counter, arms stretched to either side and resting on the glass rim like a minister in the pulpit about to launch into the Sunday message.

"Don't worry," she called after me, "I've got this."

The pub teemed with a busy lunch crowd. I scanned the dining room, saw the Red Hot Shoppers at a large round table, and ducked back into the bar — I didn't want them to think I was stalking them. I caught Peg as she barreled out of the kitchen with two plates of crab salad.

"When you have a—"

"Right," she replied and swept off. I waited, surreptitiously checking out the rest of the diners as well as the drinkers in the bar. I saw no one of note.

"I won't keep you," I promised when Peg returned two minutes later. I held out the drawing. "Do you know him?"

"I do indeed," she said.

"He and his family helped identify the man who was killed," I explained.

"His family?"

"His wife and children. They all met Bob — the victim. Well, anyway, the thing is, I saw him outside your door here a few days ago, and he said he'd just nipped in to use the gents'."

"Ha." Peg took a step closer and lowered her voice. "I don't want to be a gossip, but I can tell you he nipped in for a bit more than that. Do you remember the well-dressed woman you were talking with last evening?"

"Yes."

"I'd say she isn't his wife."

"You'd be right."

"For more than a month now," Peg said, "they've been here every midweek — one night, sometimes two."

"Did you ever see him on a Saturday?" My heart was pounding.

She squinted her eyes in thought, until the door opened and in came a quartet of Germans I recognized from the TIC earlier. I exchanged greetings with them, and Peg drew them away toward the dining room.

"Peg?"

Without a pause, she turned and said, "No. Never on a weekend."

CHAPTER 29

I walked outdoors and stood in the middle of Church Lane. My suspicion had been confirmed, and although I told myself that Noel Pears and his midweek trysts with the woman in sales had nothing to do with Bob's murder, it did little to quell my rising fury.

Tommy must suspect something. I could see it now in her uncertain behavior and her recent adoption of the TIC as a second home. I thought how she remembered everything about the family's afternoon at the abbey ruins when they'd met Bob. How he'd set the children to searching for butterflies and left Tommy to nap while he and Noel went down to the brook looking for that good fishing spot. They must've had time for a chat out there. I wondered what they'd talked about.

I punched Tess's number into my phone. "We found our own artist, Tommy Pears," I told her. "She's quite good and sketched the fellow from Pammy's description. And so, we have your witness. Possible witness," I corrected myself hastily. "The trouble is, it's Noel Pears."

"She drew a likeness of her own husband from a description Pammy gave her?"

"Yes, I know it's strange, but Pammy swears she was spot on and that Noel is the fellow she saw. Tommy left a bit upset, and not long after, Noel stopped into the TIC."

"What did he want?"

I walked slowly down Church Lane. "He thinks I'm interfering."

"In what?"

"In his family life. I think he's nervous about being found out." I told the tale and ended with, "I've got the woman's business card in my bag — no wait, at the cottage. I'll get it for you."

"Where did Pears go?"

"Away. In a dark blue Ford Fiesta."

"We have spoken with him. He never said a word about being in the village apart from the family visits."

"A Saturday away from the family wasn't his usual behavior," I told Tess. "Peg says she'd seen him only midweek. But maybe they weren't in a room at the Stoat and Hare every time they met up. It's summer, after all, and good weather. They wouldn't need a hotel room, only a secluded spot. And of course he didn't say, because he didn't want to be found out."

"Murder trumps infidelity, Julia. Look, I'm coming up now. Are you at work?"

"Yes." In theory.

The DI ended the call, and I found myself opposite Nuala's. I could see her in the window serving someone. She looked up and waved.

Isn't it lunchtime? Or past? I was ravenous. Perhaps I'd surprise Pammy with cake for our tea.

I trotted across the road and in the door.

"Afternoon, Julia," Nuala greeted me. She took my arm and guided me away from the tables, into the next room with the glass case of cakes. "They were here this morning for their elevenses."

"Were they?" My mind filled with the myriad of possibilities of "they." The Germans? The Swedes? Noel Pears and Deena Downey?

"The Red Hot Shoppers," Nuala whispered.

I gasped. "How did it go?"

"Three lemon drizzles, a blackberry sponge, my new honey and ginger, and a slice of chocolate cake." Nuala smoothed her apron. "Clean plates when they left."

"That's fantastic," I said. "We'll have to keep a lookout on the blog, but I'm sure you made the best impression. Oh, Nuala, I'm so sorry about interfering, but you know, don't you, we can't do without you? And not just your cakes, it's you. You're a vital part of the village and estate and a good friend and . . ." Nuala looked at me askance. "Oh all right, I'll be quiet about it. You've heard about Tony Brightbill and his brother, haven't you?"

"Lottie told me. It's terrible, isn't it? He seems quite broken up about it," she said, slicing my chocolate cake. "He's been in, of course, and I offered my condolences."

"Yes, well." Enough of Tony Brightbill and Nuala. "You and Linus are talking, aren't you? He's being civil?"

"His Lordship is always civil, Julia, you know that." She turned away and added, "I'm invited to a dinner party this evening at the Hall. People from Historic England are coming. Linus made a particular point of saying how much easier these events were when I was there."

Yes! "Oh, Nuala, I'm so—"

"Now," she said, returning to the business at hand "do you want to take this away?"

"Yes, please. And also, I'll get a slice of something for Pammy. Michael's sister," I explained. "She's been visiting."

"In that case, you'll want the coffee and walnut — it's her favorite."

* * *

Nuala packed in two lemon squares and two pieces of her cherry-and-almond traybake, too. Just in case they were needed. She tied the pink bakery box up with twine for a handle, and I strolled down the pavement, swinging it by my side as if I had not a worry in the world, until it came to me that I'd left Pammy in charge of the TIC. Good God, what had I been thinking?

I dashed into the cottage long enough to get Deena Downey's business card, which I'd left on the kitchen counter in a heap of odds and sods after cleaning out my bag. The heap had slipped off onto the floor, but I didn't see the card anywhere. Had I put it back in my bag?

In a rush, I turned out the contents onto the table, pushing my phone and coin purse to the side in order to sift through the remaining contents. But, no — there it was on the floor, hiding under the ledge of the cupboard. *Deena Downey, sales, VidMetronics*. I dropped the card in my bag, threw my bag onto my shoulder, and made it to the door before I remembered the most important item — the bakery box.

Out on the pavement, I ran, zigzagging between strolling mums with pushchairs. One woman called out, "Good move!" and, not missing a step, I looked over my shoulder and said, "Thanks!" When I turned my attention back to the road ahead, I crashed into Guy Pockett.

He'd stepped out of a shop doorway directly into my path, and I hadn't time to stop. I spun round like a whirligig, as I tried to regain my balance, holding onto the twine of the pink bakery box as if my life depended on it. Guy grabbed for me, and we both tumbled to the pavement. I held my arm straight up, keeping my prize aloft and safe.

"I'm sorry, Julia." Guy jumped up and grabbed my forearm to help me. I felt a dull ache from the bruises still not healed. "Really, I'm sorry," Guy repeated.

He was the picture of calm concern. I pulled my arm away, adjusted my thin cardigan, and tugged my skirt down. "It's all right. It's only that you startled me." And gave me a run in my tights, I noticed.

"I thought you saw me."

"I was in a bit of a rush. Now, if you'll excuse me, Guy, I need to go." I stepped back so that I could give him a wide berth.

"The other day," he persisted. "I didn't mean to hurt you. You know me better than that."

The problem was, I did know him. But surely I had nothing to fear at that moment with the door of the TIC was in sight. And after all, it was a summer Friday with both villagers and visitors meandering about, enjoying the day.

"Well, let's just forget all about that. I really must—"

"I want to show you something," he said, stepping in front of me.

I looked at his empty hands. "Show me what?"

"I found an old Cadbury chocolates tin in the barn. It has a few newspaper cuttings and such. I think it was Bob's."

"Then you should take the tin to the police," I said firmly.

"No. I'm not going to the police. They're trying to fit me up for Bob's murder, and they twist my words round. I'll have none of it." He glanced over his shoulder as if DI Callow listened in. "I've been cautioned once, you see. They tried to charge me with GBH. It was years ago, and they aren't supposed to count it, because it wasn't my fault. The bloke I hit was attacking me. I was self-defense."

GBH — grievous bodily harm. Bob was murdered when someone crushed his skull with a chunk of wood. Tess had warned me off contact with Guy, but she hadn't mentioned this, but of course, I wasn't privy to details in the investigation.

"I want to give you the tin," he said, "and you can do what you like with it. You might want to show it to Ms. Finch at the wool shop. She knew him, right?"

I considered his point and agreed that Lottie would certainly want to see bits of Bob's later life. I knew I would. But didn't any of Bob's possessions belong to Tony now? Well, that was something to sort out later. "Do you have it with you?"

"No, I've left it out at the farm. Will you come by and collect it?"

Did he take me for someone so devoid of common sense that I would go out to his farm alone?

"I don't even know what it is you've found."

"It's like I said — just stuff. It means nothing to me, but it must've meant something to him, don't you think? And there's a little book about birds."

I chewed on the inside of my cheek and thought. "Bring the tin into the TIC."

"Well, yeah, I could do. Maybe tomorrow or Monday. I'm not sure, because I've a great load of work ahead of me, you know."

And I knew how tomorrow could become a week from tomorrow with Guy. Or never. The thing to do would be to tell Tess about this. She'd send DS Natty Glossop out, and the tin would become evidence. And then, of course, I'd never be allowed to see it, and neither would Lottie.

"Well, I—"

"Cecil is coming out later to help me start on a new plan for the farm," Guy added. "He'll be there."

It occurred to me that if I went out to collect the tin, I would be saving the police a journey.

"I suppose I might . . ."

"Yeah, so I'll see you?"

"Mmm," was my only answer. All words and thoughts had been sucked from my brain by what I saw over Guy's shoulder. Down the road and across from the TIC stood Noel Pears and Tony Brightbill, deep in conversation.

CHAPTER 30

Just as in one of those nightmares when you want to move, but can't, I broke away from Guy only to be caught against a surging tide of Spanish students who moved forward as one enormous entity, elbowing me and one another with no apparent awareness. I fought to get through as I peered between bodies to the scene ahead. I saw Noel walk away, heading toward Akash's shop while Tony crossed the road and walked into the TIC where Pammy Sedgwick, the woman who had made a shambles of his tea room's grand opening and who had been fired from the family firm over it, now stood waiting to assist any hapless tourist who walked in.

I broke free at last and sprinted to the finish line, pushing open the door to dead silence.

Pammy, behind the counter, had arms crossed tightly, her face a rigid mask of anger and unease. Across from her stood Tony Brightbill.

"Ah, Ms. Lanchester," he said with relief.

"Julia," Pammy said with icy aloofness, "Mr. Brightbill has just this moment arrived and asked to see you. The TIC has been quiet while you were away, apart from a gentleman who wishes to speak with you regarding access to hand-washing facilities on the estate." Her officious air dissipated as a puzzled expression took over now. "Also, a large black bird looked in the window at me."

Alfie must've finished molting. I'd deal with Health and Safety later.

"Thank you, Pammy. I appreciate you filling in for me, and I have great confidence in your ability to help visitors with their requests."

Oh, really, why not?

Pammy grinned at her victory. "Tea, Mr. Brightbill? No sugar, as I recall."

Tony watched Pammy fill the kettle and switch it on.

"Ms. Sedgwick," he said. "I want to apologize for my behavior while you worked at HMS. I do regret my actions, and I hope they didn't lead to any permanent rift with your family or any problems with subsequent employment."

The kettle began to rattle as it heated. Pammy shifted from one foot to the other, but kept her eyes on Tony and held her head high.

"That's kind of you, Mr. Brightbill, but as it happens, my career has been building since that unfortunate event, and recently, I've been asked to take a managerial position with Oxfam. I'll be starting next week." She examined her nails briefly before adding, "I'm terribly sorry about your wife. And your brother."

"Thank you."

"Mr. Brightbill, how do you know the man you were talking with just now?" I nodded across the road.

Tony glanced out the window as if to remind himself. "My company bought a software package, and he was the one who went out to install it. And he's had to go back again for maintenance. VidMetronics."

VidMetronics — the company name on Deena Downey's business card. So that's how the affair between Noel and Deena started? But that was beside the point.

"I find it hard to believe you'd remember a random bit of software being installed at your company."

His bushy eyebrows shot up. "It seems a rather mundane thing to disbelieve."

"You are company owner of Tara's Tea, you can't know every contract worker coming and going at your offices."

"It's one office, Ms. Lanchester, only one. And we've four people who work there — five when I'm in. The vast majority of my employees are in the tea rooms themselves. So, it isn't as if I don't know what's going on in my own office. I can tell you the day the rubbish is collected if you like." His eyes blazed.

"Are you sure you haven't seen that fellow away from your company's headquarters? You've never seen him here in Smeaton before today?"

"I have no trouble remembering where I've seen the man. Why are you—" He paused for a moment as the kettle reached its apex of clamor, switched off, and wheezed in relief. "Are you saying he has something to do with my brother's death?"

"I am saying nothing of the kind," I replied.

"What do police know something?" Brightbill asked, taking a step toward me.

"How would I know that? Look, if you've got questions, you need to talk with the DI, not come looking for me."

"I came looking for you, Ms. Lanchester," he said, thumping a finger on the counter as his voice rose, "because I get the distinct impression that although you are not part of the police force, you cannot help but insinuate yourself into the middle of things. It's a wonder the two of you" — he nodded to Pammy — "aren't related."

"Am I supposed to take that as an insult?" I sniped at him.

Jingle.

"Is there a problem?" DI Callow asked. "I could hear you both out on the pavement."

"Detective Inspector." Brightbill's charm returned in an instant. "Do you have any information about my brother's death that you can share with me?"

"I would like to talk with you, Mr. Brightbill," Tess replied evenly. "Can we arrange to meet at the hotel here in the village in say" — she checked her watch — "thirty minutes?"

"Yes, thank you. Ladies," he said to the room and left.

"You see," Pammy said, pointing after him. "You see how he can turn. Just like *that*." She snapped her fingers.

* * *

I attended to tourists while Pammy dropped her voice to a conspiratorial whisper and told Tess about Tommy drawing a sketch of her own husband. In spare moments, I filled in with details of Noel's affair with Deena Downey, and as I did, Pammy grew subdued.

"You can confirm it with Peg when you go to meet Tony Brightbill," I said.

The DI stood and prepared to take the drawing with her.

"Wait," I said. "We need a copy."

"You already know what he looks like."

"Oh, come on, Tess. At least let me take a photo." She allowed me to pull out my phone and snap. "There, you see. It might come in handy." Although I couldn't really see how. It was only that I wanted to keep hold of some bit of the enquiry, and Tess didn't seem to be in the sharing mood.

The DI filed away the sketch in her portfolio and said, "We'll contact this VidMetronics for Noel Pears's schedule and find out where he's supposed to be today. And I've Sergeant Glossop and DC Flynn in the village — they'll keep an eye out. Also, I want to see Tommy Pears again."

"She was really shaken up. Can you let me talk with her first? Please." I wasn't above begging. "I'll tell her to phone you. Anyway, I'd say she's gone back to Dagenham by now — end of the school day, you know. She'll need to be home for the children. And after all, you have an appointment with Tony Brightbill."

Callow nodded her permission.

Having made this minor inroad, I rashly tried for more. "And what about him? Do you have new evidence? Is that what you're going to talk with him about?"

The DI cut her eyes at Pammy, who leaned over the counter to listen.

With a shake of her head, Tess began. "We have CCTV footage that shows Tony Brightbill at motorway services on the M18 near Doncaster — that's a three-hour journey at best. He went into the M&S, bought a cold lasagna, which he claimed he took home and put in the microwave. He has his own security system at the gate of his house, which he has shared with us. It backs up his story, showing he arrived home just before eight o'clock. And speaking of CCTV, this enquiry would be going more smoothly if the earl would—"

"A fascinating discussion," I interrupted, "which I know you will want to have with Linus. Now, why didn't you tell me Guy had form?"

"He had a caution eight years ago, but it was removed — taken off his record."

"What's his alibi for the time span you have for Bob's death?"

Tess studied me, I'm sure weighing the danger of handing over the information.

"He was working in his fields until about seven o'clock — seen from the next farm over — after which time he went to Royal Oak and stayed until eleven. Then, back to his cottage."

"Doesn't account for his whole weekend, does it?" I asked. I shouldn't have asked it aloud.

"Julia, you know not to approach Guy Pockett."

"Do you really think I would attempt to interrogate Guy concerning his whereabouts the day Bob was killed?" I asked blithely, praying she didn't notice how I qualified my statement. "I know better than that."

* * *

Pammy hadn't said a word since explaining to Tess about Tommy's sketch. After the DI departed, she slumped in a chair at the table, hands in her lap.

"Makes me quite ill seeing the other side of it," she said. "Tommy finding out what her husband has been up to." She whisked away a tear. "Julia, the man I was seeing, that I was living with — he really did tell me he was getting a divorce. But wasn't I the fool to believe him?"

I gave her a quick hug. "That's finished now and all for the better. Things are looking up, aren't they?" That got a smile out of her. "And now you are officially relieved of your TIC duties, Pammy. Thanks for filling in." We packed up a sandwich and her slice of coffee-and-walnut cake, and I handed her the cottage key as a reward. "I might have an errand after I close up, so don't worry if you step out."

She studied the key in her hand. "Gavin took a day shift at the pub, but he'll be free for a bit until he has to go back again." She smiled. "He said he'd pop down between and perhaps we'd go for a meal."

"Extra hours — my, isn't that industrious of him?"

"You think he did it, don't you?" Pammy asked. "Tony Brightbill. You think Tony killed his own brother and Noel Pears saw it and now Tony may suspect there's a witness. Mr. Can't-Keep-It-In-His-Trousers had better be careful."

I laughed. "I don't know. At the moment, Noel Pears should be far more worried about lying to Detective Inspector Callow."

"His game is up," Pammy declared. "He must know that."

CHAPTER 31

The second half of the afternoon I spent alone, as tourists found their own way round the estate without any help from me. Just as well. I needed to think about the people and events surrounding Bob's murder. DI Callow would say it was none of my concern, but it was, because those people existed in my world, swirling round me like the cotton fluff from a poplar caught in the breeze.

I rang Tommy, but had to leave a message. I dutifully ate half a chicken sandwich, before proceeding to the afternoon's main course, my slice of Nuala's fantastic chocolate cake. The kettle switched off as my phone rang.

"I've my feather identification exam this afternoon," Michael said when I answered. "As soon as Rupert finishes the radio interview he's recording. I was hoping you could help me cheat."

"Oh, I'd be delighted," I replied, putting him on speaker as I made my tea. "Here's a helpful hint. If it's extremely long and blue and the very end looks as if it has an eye painted on it — it's a peacock feather."

"That's the way it's going to be, is it?" he asked, and I could hear the smile in his voice. "How are you faring without Vesta?"

"Not bad. It's turned quiet. But when I had to dash out earlier, I had a ready substitute. Your sister."

"You let Pammy loose on a load of unsuspecting tourists?"

"She managed just fine. She was even civil to Tony Brightbill." I settled at the table and filled Michael in on the day's news — Tommy's surprising sketch of her husband, Noel's affair, and seeing Noel and Tony in conversation.

"I don't know, Michael, it's as if all the evidence and clues and witnesses and suspects are just a heap of spare parts dumped on the floor at Tess's feet, and she's supposed to make something from it. I don't know how she does her job."

"That's just it," he reminded me sternly, "it's *her* job."

"Yes," I muttered.

"But you can't stop thinking about it. So tell me."

It was what I needed — to say it all aloud. I sat up straight and shifted my idling mind into gear. "All right. Guy. He needed to keep Bob quiet about the field being sprayed, or he'd lose his organic status."

"And he's violent," Michael added.

"But there's Tony," I said. "His finances are stretched thin, and he didn't want to pay Bob's huge loan back."

"Did Bob demand repayment?"

"I don't know. Did Bob have a solicitor? You wouldn't think."

"And Tony's got an alibi, according to Tess."

"Are you defending him?"

"Talk me out of it."

"He could've doctored his own CCTV tapes if he knew an expert. He could've hired someone to kill Bob." A thunderbolt of a thought struck me. "That's it — he hired Noel Pears to kill Bob. That's how they know each other! Apart from the software installation, that is."

"Noel Pears is a software engineer *and* a hired gun?"

I huffed. "All right, a bit far-fetched. But Noel Pears might be a witness to something or someone. The fact that he's kept quiet because he didn't want his affair revealed makes him a cad. Worse. But now he'll have to confess his omission when Tess puts the screws to him."

"What about Lottie?"

"Whyever would Lottie kill Bob?"

"He abandoned her all those years ago, a young woman madly in love, and the anger has been building. Suddenly, he's back in her life. What else would she do?"

I thought of Lottie's sad-happy face as she told her childhood story. Wistful, not revengeful, as if she had started dreaming about what her life would've been if Bob Brightbill hadn't fallen out of that tree.

"No, I don't buy it. If she would harm anyone, it would be Tony."

"How about this," Michael offered. "The spirit of one of your monks from the abbey floated over to the pond and did it. That would be fantastic publicity for your medieval banquet and ghost tours."

I had taken an enormous bite of cake at that moment, and spluttered a laugh.

"Tea and cake?" he asked, a well-informed guess.

"Mmm."

He was quiet for a moment, and then said, "I remember you eating chocolate cake in Nuala's that first time."

I sighed at the memory of one of our earliest encounters. "I thought you were smug and inefficient. And you didn't even tell me I had chocolate icing smeared on my face."

"I confess now, it was all I could do to keep from leaning over the table and licking it off."

"I wish you weren't on the phone," I confessed.

"We'll have time soon enough. I'm taking you off tomorrow."

"Off?" An electric thrill ran through me. "Off where?"

"I'm not saying. It's a surprise."

"A surprise!" I squealed. "Will you blindfold me?"

"Blindfolds don't work with you, remember?"

"Not fair," I said, well remembering the instance. "It wasn't my fault I could see out the bottom — you didn't tie it on well enough."

* * *

I boxed up the lemon squares and cherry-and-almond traybake and closed the TIC, all the while drifting along in a dream world as I imagined being whisked off Somewhere Special the next day. Where would Michael take me? At this point, it could be a dingy hotel in Peterborough, and I'd be happy as long as it was only the two of us. Of course, I hoped it wasn't a dingy hotel.

Reality began to weasel its way into my dream. I couldn't leave Vesta alone on a Saturday. What if the Spanish students returned at the same moment the Germans and Swedes walked in? What if a swarm of bicyclists arrived needing a circular route round the estate? No, I couldn't. But it would've been lovely.

Standing out on the pavement, I considered my options. There was no need to go directly home, because Pammy might be entertaining Gavin, so I darted across the road and to the corner, into Akash's shop for a cool drink.

"Isn't it wonderful about Pammy's new job?" Gwen asked.

After that, I nipped into the chemist for a pair of tights and heard the same comment, then I dawdled long enough outside Sugar for My Honey for Helen to put her head out and say she planned to send Pammy off to Oxfam with a pound of mixed candies for her first day.

As happy as I was for Pammy, my thoughts were all on Guy Pockett as I talked myself into and then out of going to his farm to collect the tin he said belonged to Bob.

I shouldn't do it. I got out my phone to ring Tess and let her take care of the matter. But then, I tried to imagine what sorts of things Bob had collected. More eggshells? Or something more personal? I would go. I dropped my phone in my bag, but my sleeve pulled up and I saw the tip of a bruise, now a bright shade that would match the breast of a yellow wagtail. *No, leave it to the police.* Out came the phone again. I found myself standing in front of Three Bags Full and wondered if Willow were upstairs. And if she were, would her new best friend be with her? I dropped my phone back into my bag and walked in.

Two women stood chatting near a display of tams while Lottie demonstrated what I heard her call the "eyelet stitch scarf" to a third. When she saw me, she nodded to the stairs in the back, and I slipped past the women and went up.

I hesitated in the doorway as Willow carried a pot of tea from the kitchen into the sitting room while Tommy perched on the edge of the sofa.

"Hello," I said. "I hope I'm not disturbing, but Lottie said to come up. I've brought something for your tea." I held the bakery box aloft.

Tommy leapt to her feet.

"You see, Tommy, I told you she'd be by," Willow said with an enormous smile. "Come in, Julia." She sat and poured out three cups.

"I'm sorry I ran out earlier," Tommy said to me. Her ponytail sagged, and her face had no color, except for bright red cheeks, like spots of rouge.

I shook my head. "You don't need to apologize. You had a shock. My, you've stayed in the village later than usual — is everything all right with the children?"

"Oh yes," Tommy said with relief. "My mother's taken them to her flat for the evening. Always a treat when their Nan's in charge, because it involves a movie and being able to eat pizza on the sofa."

"Well, then," I said, unwilling to bring up Noel's name, "I'm so glad you're here with Willow. We were a bit concerned, you know."

"Who was concerned?"

"Me. Pammy." *The police.* "Pammy was so grateful that you were able to—" *catch your husband lying about his whereabouts?* Hmmm, must tread carefully.

"He shouldn't have been here on that Saturday," Tommy said. "He told me he was going to Grimsby in Lincolnshire, because an important customer had insisted he sort out a problem, weekend or no. A lie. And it wasn't the first. He couldn't keep away from her, I suppose. They were meeting here in your village, weren't they?"

Relieved I wasn't the first to mention the affair, I still stumbled over my words. "I really don't know any details."

Tommy took a deep breath, but it caught halfway in and she cleared her throat. "I think I've known for a while that he was seeing someone else, only I didn't want to admit it to myself. Another woman in his department tried to drop a heavy hint not too long ago, but I ignored her. When Pammy began to describe the person she saw here on that Saturday, it was if my suspicions were coming out the end of my pencil and showing me what I could no longer avoid." Her voice wobbled, and she sank onto the sofa.

Willow put a hand on her arm. "It's a hard truth, and you're amazingly brave to face it."

Tommy sniffed. "But this is my problem, Julia, not yours. Your detective inspector wants to know if Noel was a witness to Bob's murder."

Noel was a despicable, lying lowlife, but he still could assist in the enquiry. "It's quite possible he saw someone or something. DI Callow is eager to talk with him."

The phone on the coffee table vibrated, and Tommy lifted an eyebrow at it. "There he is again. He's been ringing all day, but I haven't answered."

"One of those was mine," I said. "And you might have one from the DI as well."

Tommy's brow furrowed. "Sorry, I just assumed they were all Noel. I know I'll have to face him, but I can't do it now. And he keeps leaving messages saying 'I love you.

We need to talk.' I stopped listening. He knows I know." Tommy picked up her cup and saucer, but they rattled violently, and so she set them down again. "I came here to the shop after I left you, Julia, and Lottie sent me upstairs, told me I could stay as long as I needed to. Wasn't that kind of her? I sat there" — she nodded to the front window that overlooked the high street — "and it was so peaceful. Until I saw Noel walk by a couple of hours ago."

I looked out to see the Friday traffic moving like treacle and the few people on the pavement outpacing the cars. A couple of hours ago was well after Noel had stormed out of the TIC. I didn't like to think of him skulking round our village the rest of the afternoon. Had Tess not found him yet, explaining to him a witness had put him in the village the day Bob was murdered?

"Just as well you stayed here," I said and returned to my cup of tea. "So, what have you two been up to? Oh, wait. I mean . . . I didn't mean to imply . . ."

"We aren't planning a visit to the pond, if that's what you mean," Willow said, and I reddened because that's exactly what I had meant. "Bob didn't want us to, so, no need to worry."

Right, no need to worry.

"And I promised Cecil."

Better.

"Well, that's grand. So, Cecil. I hear he's going to get Guy Pockett back on the straight and narrow."

"Yes, he's taken on Guy as a personal project. He's out at the farm now," Willow said.

That was the all clear I needed. No one could object to me visiting Guy when another person was present. "Excellent. Well, I'd best be off."

"All right, then. Lovely to see you, Julia," Willow said. "Thanks for the cakes. And you rest assured that Auntie and I are taking care of Tommy." She frowned. "Where's Pammy?"

"I'd say she's with Gavin. He's between shifts at his pub, and said he'd pop round. Why?"

Willow brightened. "No reason. It's only, we hoped she wasn't alone. Otherwise, we would've asked her up for tea."

That would be an interesting trio — or quartet, if they counted Bob. Did they?

CHAPTER 32

I eased the nose of my Fiat out into traffic and joined the parade, creeping along with the others up the high street toward the end of the village. It took forever. I stuck my elbow out the open window and inhaled the scent of summer — warm with a miasma of green and floral scents mixed with car exhaust. As we crept by the turnoff to Church Lane, I glanced over to the Stoat and Hare and noticed Tony Brightbill standing outside the door, his eyes on me. He made no acknowledgment — not a wave or a lifting of the head in greeting — only watched as I continued to inch my way out of the village. I stared straight ahead, but glanced in my side mirror, and noticed Lottie walk up to Tony. I kept my eyes on them as they spoke, but when the car behind me honked, I realized traffic had moved along and I hadn't. I edged forward.

Tess had finished talking with him, I suppose, absolving him of his brother's murder. But did the DI know of Tony's connection to Noel? I think not. It could be nothing, but it might be something. I would ring her later. Brightbill still made me nervous. I got a final glimpse of the pavement in front of the pub and saw it was empty. Was Tony now harassing Lottie Finch? Or perhaps it was the other way round and Lottie would have it out with him for the way his family treated her all those years ago.

Once I reached my turnoff at the north end of the village, I relaxed. I picked up speed along the empty lane, passing the car park for the abbey ruins and continuing to the track that led to Guy's farm, where I hit a hole so deep that my head bounced off the roof of the car. I slowed, but not much. I preferred to arrive while Cecil, my buffer, would still be in attendance.

But Cecil's Peugeot, on loan from Linus, who preferred the bicycle for local travel, wasn't parked at the farm. I shut off the engine at the edge of the yard and sat in my car, debating my options — go or stay? — while I watched the curtains in the cottage for any sign of life. I lingered just long enough to be seen, for here came Guy from round the corner of a stone shed carrying a long-handled hoe.

"Where's Cecil?" I asked from the window of my car. "Has he gone already?"

"Running late, but he's on his way." Guy waited. "It's in the barn — the tin. Come on, and I'll fetch it."

How about if he fetched it and brought it out to me? But I would look both silly and suspicious if I remained in the car. And after all, Cecil was on his way.

I got out and followed Guy across the yard, keeping myself at as great a distance as I could. He walked into the shady barn, where thin shafts of sunlight came through the gaps between boards. I stayed in the open doorway, where a few lazy flies buzzed round and round, and brought to mind Willow's flies. The air smelled of sweet hay and manure. A swallow swooped down from the rafters and straight over my head, showing off his pale underside and red throat. He flew out of the barn toward the field across the way. I watched as he soared over the disaster that organic farmer Guy had created when he'd sprayed the expanse with a chemical herbicide. No insects for you there, little swallow — keep looking.

Guy stopped in the far back corner and stuck his arm between bales of hay stacked as high as the loft. He pulled out a tin, and as he approached me said, "He'd hidden it away well."

I stepped back out into the yard and kept my eye on the hoe in Guy's hand. He noticed, hesitated, and then hung it carefully between two pegs on the wall by the door. "I wouldn't do anything, Julia, but I know it's my own fault you think I would."

His apology sounded sincere, and he looked suitably ashamed, hanging his head, his face gone pink, but I would continue to take care.

"No, it's all right, Guy. Thanks." I took the tin from him. It was dented and rusted, the scratched lid adorned with a painting of dahlias overflowing a basket and "Cadbury Milk Chocolates" written in script. It was in poor shape for a collectible. Bob probably had found it on a rubbish heap, knowing it still made a useful storage container. Had his life been a string of old rusted tins with memories held inside?

"Do you want to come in and sit down while you look, or are you taking it straight away?" Guy asked.

"I'll take it, it's just . . ." I couldn't wait and popped the tin on the spot. Inside, just as Guy had said, were newspaper cuttings. I read the headlines. *Cuckoos Endangered — Migration Routes to Blame? Burton Fleming — Yorkshire's Hedgehog Village* and *A Girl and Her Rook — The Bird That Cracked the Case.*

"I read that one — that's our Alfie," Guy said with pride, pointing to the photo.

"Our Alfie" was how everyone on the estate referred to the rook. "Yeah, there he is," I said with a smile. The next cutting, dated October of the previous year, read *Nature's Art — A Woolly Piece of Work* and described a tapestry, now hanging in the Tate Britain, created by Lottie Finch, proprietor of Three Bags Full in the Suffolk village of Smeaton-under-Lyme. So, this was how he had found her and Lottie never knew.

"So you see," Guy said, "what would the police care about that?"

I spotted a small book under the clippings. "Oh look!" I cried. "It's just like mine." It was *The Observer's Book of*

British Birds. I'd bought my used copy for a pound at a church jumble sale when I was twelve. Had Bob carried his round since childhood, or had it been a later acquisition? I felt close to him at that moment, as if I could turn to the page of his favorite bird and read along with him. He'd probably memorized most of the descriptions. I know I had.

"I thought you'd like that," Guy said.

I didn't answer, because I'd just seen what lay below the book at the bottom of the tin — an old leaflet that had been folded and straightened out again, its corners tattered as if it had been carried round in someone's pocket. It had the distinctly soporific title of The Fotheringill Estate Abbey: Eight Hundred Years of History.

"He must've come in the TIC, and we didn't notice," I said with a stab of guilt. "But when it's busy, people can pop in, find what they want, and leave before we ever see them. Still, I feel terrible."

"I don't know how you keep track of as many people as you do," Guy said, and I appreciated the allowance.

I heard the crunch of gravel and saw Cecil's car bounce into the yard and stop.

"Anyway," Guy said, "Bob was a bit secretive. I never did know where he slept. I asked once, and all he said was that he said he'd found a good spot, a place where no one had slept for donkey's years."

"Hello, Julia," Cecil said as he eased his tall frame out of the car. This was an official visit. I knew that as Linus's son and heir to the Fotheringill estate, Cecil had worked hard at developing the skills he needed to deal with tenants.

"Hello, Cecil." A tiny thought darted into my mind — should I tell him I'd just seen Willow and Tommy together, or would he immediately think they were having a séance upstairs at Lottie's? The thought darted out again.

"Haven't seen you in a few days," Cecil said. "How is it everything going?"

The enquiry into the murder of Bob Brightbill was what he meant, but we must speak in code when in the presence of a suspect. Was Guy still a suspect? But look, he'd held onto Bob's special tin just to show me.

"No one tells me much of anything, I'm afraid." I clutched the tin to my chest. "Well, I'll be on my way. Thanks, Guy."

"Right, Pockett," Cecil said as the two men headed for the cottage, "ready to get to work?"

I walked out to my car, reading through the old abbey leaflet. Apart from pretty dreary writing, I couldn't see it held a clue for me.

Guy stuck his head out the cottage door.

"Centuries," he called.

"Sorry?"

"Bob. He didn't say donkey's years, he said a place no one had slept in *centuries*. That's a bit daft, isn't it?"

Guy went back in, and I stared at the leaflet in my hand. Bob Brightbill had been living at the abbey. I jumped in my car and bounced off.

* * *

The abbey car park was empty as usual. I pulled on the hand brake and looked at my feet and then at the passenger-side floorboard, which was taken up by Sheila's shoes. I'd worn them when touring around the ruins with Tommy, and they'd been perfect, their enormous flat soles providing stability no matter what the terrain. Not like these work shoes — spike heels that sank into the ground and slipped off stones. I glared at my feet and found I'd already kicked my heels off and put Sheila's shoes on. It wasn't as if there was anyone to notice what I was wearing, but just in case I did see another person and needed to make a quick change, I dropped my heels into my bag.

Now, to suss out just where Bob had been sleeping. The police had searched the place and found no sign of a campsite, so where had Bob hidden himself away? Was there a particular stone in one of the remaining bits of building that, when removed, would reveal his bedroll and tent? Would we need to knock down the rest of the abbey to find out?

I hitched my bag up on my shoulder and walked the path, realizing I'd visited the abbey more often in the last week than I had in the last year. I stopped to survey the remnants of ancient walls outlining refectory, chapter house, and all those other buildings and rooms. I walked through the undercroft, the only place that still had a ceiling, and examined the corners. Perhaps Bob had actually kipped outdoors, but nearby. Under a hedge? Down by the brook? I came out the other end of the undercroft, circled back the way Tommy and I had, and stopped near the no-longer-secluded spot for picnics.

My phone dinged with a text from Michael.

Feather exam flying success. Home soon.

I replied *Celebration 2 ensue.*

I took one step before another text came in — this one from Linus.

Julia, I hope I'm not disturbing you, but it's vital you ring me the minute you receive this. As you probably know, I've asked Nuala to be at my side during th

The text broke off probably from Linus accidentally hitting "send." Another one followed immediately.

this evening's dinner with English Heritage. You remember this dinner will open up discussions of the estate's involvement in — well, perhaps we can go over th

Linus longed for the days of proper letter writing and had yet to embrace the brevity of today's communications. Here he came again.

I want to communicate my feelings to her, but am worried that if I frighten her, she will bolt. Does that sounds crass? What about a gift? I thought perhaps som

I sensed his frustration, but would he ever get to the point? And then, as if he'd heard me, a text came in accompanied by a photo.

Would this be appropriate?

It was a scarf upon which danced the blue and green shades of the sea intertwined with streaks of rose red and accented by gold swirls. Most likely silk and hand-painted. It was gorgeous.

Exhausted from reading this missive from His Lordship, I dashed off a reply. *Perfect. Good on you. Have a lovely evening.*

Ding — a text from Vesta. *Where's Pammy?*

Ding — a text from Willow. *Where's Pammy?*

Ding — a text from Gavin. *Where's Pammy?*

Pammy Sedgwick, the most sought-after woman in the village, I grumbled. But if anyone should know where she was, it was Gavin. I rang him.

"Where's Pammy?" he answered.

"Why does everyone think I know where Pammy is?" I snapped. "Look, I thought she was with you. Are you at the cottage?"

"No, I'm working."

"You're meant to be off and go back later."

"I took a third shift."

"Gavin, you can't work three straight shifts." He'd gone from not being able to keep a job to working round the clock. "What's this about?"

"I'm skint, that's what it's about. And tomorrow's the world's largest jumble sale, and it's important to Pammy." The pub noise behind him increased and he dropped his voice, so I had to strain to hear. "I thought, if she found something special, something she really wanted, I'd buy it for her."

"Ah, Gavin, that's so sweet."

"Yeah, well," he replied. "The problem is, I don't want to tell her I've taken extra work. I want it to be a surprise. And so I sent her a text to say I couldn't see her this evening. I've heard nothing back."

Bad move — although, really, Gavin had come so far in such a short time, he could be forgiven for one misstep, couldn't he?

"Your intentions are admirable. Amazing, really. But you can see how she might not like that, because it looks as if you're canceling for what she sees is no good reason. You'll have to tell her why, and then she'll be fine about it."

"I have told her. After two more texts and nothing back from her, I rang, but she didn't answer, and I had to leave a message. I explained everything and said I was sorry, but still nothing. I can't stand this."

Didn't Pammy believe him? Perhaps she had seen this pattern before in another man, and it triggered an automatic response or, lack thereof.

"Right, listen, Gavin, I'll ring her and see what's up. She's just sitting at the cottage. I'm sure it'll all be settled in no time, and she'll be looking forward to seeing you at seven o'clock in the morning."

I tried her, and as I waited for her to answer, a faint noise drifted toward me from somewhere nearby. But I couldn't quite identify it, and when I tried to listen again, a breeze started up, rustling leaves and grass and drowning out the sound just as Pammy's voicemail started.

"You can't give up on Gavin over this, Pammy. He's doing it all for you. Why don't you give him a ring. All right? Talk later."

There now — had I taken care of business? I stared at my phone, daring it to ding at me again. Silence. Right, now I can think. I scanned my surroundings.

What had Bob said to the Pears family the day they met? Perhaps he had given a clue about where he slept. I thought hard on what Tommy had told me about their visit. Bob had been kind, knowledgeable about the area, and seemed to perceive what each family member needed most. He had quickly caught on to the fact that their son, Duncan, was a naturalist, and had set him and his sister an enjoyable task. Bob had allowed Mum to rest — Tommy had seemed content with reading and a nap — while he had taken Dad off to fish.

Bob had mistakenly thought the family was familiar with the abbey ruins from a previous visit. Isn't that what Tommy had said? "You remember how the brook runs behind the ruins," he'd said to Noel. At least, it was something like that.

But the Pears family had never been to the site — they had never been to the estate.

But now we know one of them had. Noel Pears and his midweek trysts had been going on for a month or more according to Peg, and that could place Noel on the estate at least a fortnight before Bob was murdered. Noel and his lover had met up at the Stoat and Hare, but could they have met elsewhere on the estate, too? After all, we'd had such a long stretch of lovely, warm summer weather, why not take it outdoors?

Bob had been right. He *had* seen Noel Pears at the abbey ruins before the family visit.

"They were together here, weren't they, Bob?" I asked aloud. "You saw Noel and Deena."

The world went black.

CHAPTER 33

Someone shoved me and I fell forward. I took a breath, but the blackness covered not only my eyes, but also my mouth and nose. I grabbed at it, and it made a rustling sound — plastic, like a bin bag. My hands were knocked away and I was pushed down, and a knee pressed on my back, holding me on the ground. My arms and legs waving helplessly as I tried and failed to reach behind me and grab my assailant. I heard the ripping sound of duct tape coming off a roll, and then it was wrapped round my neck, securing the bin bag.

I struggled and rocked and shouted, but my voice went nowhere, only inside the bag, my air supply virtually cut off. I was going to smother. I flung my arms round, and my assailant grunted with the effort to keep me still. As I flailed, I knocked into my handbag on the ground beside me. I grabbed blindly for anything that could help, and found a shoe. My hand closed over it.

Using my left shoulder to ward him off, I began battering the body I couldn't see with the spike heel of my shoe — *bang-bang-bang* — striking blindly, hoping to inflict damage. I must've got several good jabs in, because he shouted in pain before he wrenched the shoe from my hand and yanked me to my feet. I shouted for help, and he hissed, "Shut up, just shut up," and struck me.

He couldn't see my face anymore than I could see his, and the blow hit my chin, but still caused me to cry out — a small cry as I was nearly out of air. As he wrapped duct tape to bind my wrists, I gasped, "Can't breathe."

He frog-marched me off and I felt myself slipping, losing consciousness, until we walked directly into a patch of holly. The dead leaves stabbed and caught at me and brought me to my senses. I knew where we were — at the top of the steps Tommy and I had seen. The steps that led down to a centuries-old iron door. I heard the dry, scratching sounds of dead branches being moved.

And I knew who my captor was.

"Noel," I panted. "It's Noel, isn't it?"

He nudged me forward, and I stumbled down the first few steps before he caught me with one hand and ripped a hole in the bag. I gasped, gulping in air.

"What are you doing, Noel? How will this help?" I pleaded, turning my head right, left, up, and down to get him in view through the gap. I caught a glimpse of his curly hair plastered to his forehead with sweat, and eyes that didn't seem to focus. I saw red slashes the size of a spike heel on his cheek and forehead, and one at the corner of his eye that had drawn blood.

"What use could it be, Noel, to bring me down here?" Isn't that right, shouldn't I use his name — say it over and over? *I know you* — that's what it tells him. Would it help or hurt? "They'll find me, you know they will. Wouldn't it be better if you went to the police now instead of forcing them to chase you down?"

I kept it up, babbling innocuous questions and comments, as he pushed me down the stairs, only my solid boat shoes and his tight grip kept me from plunging headfirst. We reached the bottom, and I could see the iron door stood ajar. Noel put his shoulder to it and it scraped across the stone floor, opening onto a black corridor. I blinked at the darkness and noticed a thin shaft of horizontal light high up and far in the distance. The air felt cool and dry — were we in the storerooms below the undercroft? Is this where Bob had lived?

He propelled me toward the light, and we came to the end of the corridor and another door. Noel shoved me through and into more darkness. I fell hard on my knees and before I could recover, he seized yanked me up by my bound hands and dragged me to the wall where he wrapped more tape securing my wrists to a heavy iron ring attached to the wall. I sank down, unable to stand but twisting my arms as I did so. A small miracle — my bottom landed on a tall square stone. Noel fell back against the door, panting.

"Noel," I said, "I still can't breathe. Please, please, won't you—"

He lunged at me and I cried out, but he only tore at the bag until it sat like a ruffled plastic collar round my neck.

"Won't do you much good," Noel said. "There's no one about."

"What good is any of this, Noel?" I begged. "What will Tommy think?" I heard a groan across from me. "My God — is she here? What have you done with her?"

"You shut up about my wife!" He shouted in my face. "The both of you, shut up! I love my Tommy, don't you understand that? This has nothing to do with her or my family. He didn't see that either, did he? You're all interfering in affairs" — he hesitated, as if realizing his poor choice of words — "in things that are none of your bloody business."

"Selfish git." The voice across from me slurred her words. "Lout. Brute."

"Pammy?" I yelped in astonishment.

"I won't let you two ruin my marriage," Noel said.

"No," Pammy replied, "you're doing a proper job of that all on your own."

No wonder Pammy hadn't answered her phone. But how in the world did she get here?

"You killed Bob, because he knew," I gasped, tugging against the tape to test the strength of Noel's wrapping. It quite secure. I twisted as I spoke, trying to get a sense of our surroundings, and noticed another horizontal shaft of light high on the wall above Pammy. The dust of the ages settled on me, and I sneezed before saying, "You bashed in his skull."

"I didn't want to do that," Noel argued. "It was his own fault, putting his nose in where it didn't belong. My family was none of his business."

"You were deceiving your wife and your children. And you were found out."

"I never wanted to bring them to this bloody place, but I couldn't think of a reason not to come. I'm soft that way. I'd do anything for my family."

"Oh yeah, you're Father of the Year, you are," Pammy spat.

"What was he doing lurking about, spying on people?" Noel jeered. "We thought it was only the two of us, that no one else was near. But he saw us, and he just laughed and said, 'Good day for it.' I didn't think anything of it until our Sunday family outing. Tommy insisted this spot would be perfect and the kids caught the idea from her, and I told myself surely that old tramp had gone off and would be wandering the countryside far, far away."

"He wasn't a tramp," I snapped. "He was an intelligent man who cared about nature. He was a citizen scientist, studying plants and animals and—"

"Couldn't he have done that in Norfolk?" Noel shouted. "But no. I show up with my family, and here he is, just as he'd been when . . . They all thought he was brilliant, but he made a wrong move, taking me down to the brook and telling me he knew what I was up to. Asking me was I being fair to my wife, and how was I going to make this right. He threatened me, pure and simple!" Noel's voice echoed in the dead space.

"Threatened your sweet setup, you mean," Pammy said. "I can't believe we're forced to listen to this load of codswallop."

"Well, then," Noel said, "I'll just leave you to yourselves."

"Why did you meet him at the pond?" I asked in a rush. My eyes had adjusted to the darkness, and I could make out the space now. I saw Pammy across from me, slumped against the wall, her hands, too, wrapped and tied to an iron ring. The room appeared empty. I didn't like Noel being there, yet what would happen when he left?

He grew still. "The family loved this spot and had determined before we'd even left that day they wanted to return the next week. Another fine Sunday," he said bitterly. "I couldn't talk them out of it, not without saying why. And I just knew when we returned, he would be here. And he would tell Tommy. I couldn't let him do that — I had to convince him not to do it. So, I drove out early the day before, on the Saturday, and came here and waited for him to appear. I didn't know where he stayed or if he was sleeping rough, but it was all I knew to do. I waited hours. There was no one about. Until at last, here he came, out from behind those bushes at the top of the stairs, as if he owned the place."

"If you planned to kill him, why didn't you do it here?" Pammy asked.

"I didn't *plan* to kill him," Noel said, "I only wanted to make sure he moved along, was well out of the way when I came back with Tommy and our children. But he wouldn't talk to me. Of all things, he said he had a wedding to attend, and he'd meet me over by the churchyard later. Giving *me* orders, and there was nothing I could do, because all at once a great load of ramblers came out of the field, acted surprised to see the place, and settled down for a picnic. Bloody walkers," he spat. "I tried to follow him, but he took off across the fields on a bicycle, and so I thought, fine with you, I'll see you at the churchyard."

"Reverend Eccles said he saw Bob outside the church that afternoon," I said. "I think he wanted to get a glimpse of Lottie, and he hoped she would be at Vesta and Akash's wedding."

"Poor sausage," Pammy said in a mournful tone.

"I saw him among the gravestones. I tried to reason with him, but he only talked about lichen and orchids and linnets, and then he walked away, out toward the pond. I followed him. I picked up a broken limb along the way." Noel looked down at his empty hand. "I only wanted to stop him."

He didn't have the branch in his hand now, but I could well imagine he could find another. I shuddered. "There are witnesses, you know. Not us — other people saw you. Other people saw Bob. What will you do about them?"

In the dim light, Noel looked for one of us to the other. He shook his head. "No, it's you two that are the problem. You" — he pointed at Pammy — "stopping and asking directions on that Saturday, and you" — he stabbed his finger at me — "you filmed me."

"I what? Are you mad?"

"You brought Tommy out here. You deceived her into thinking you were looking at birds. You held your phone up and you filmed me. Yesterday. Here. You and Tommy. You were trying to catch me out, weren't you?"

It took a moment before I knew what he was talking about. "The world doesn't revolve around you, Noel — I was recording the call of a cuckoo." But had I caught him in my video? Would police find my phone and see it?

"A cuckoo?" Pammy asked. "Do you have one that lives nearby?"

"People know we're here," I said to Noel in my best TIC manager voice. "Including the police. You did know that DI Callow has her entire team out searching the estate for you. And for us. We're expected. In fact, we're late."

"I don't believe that," Noel said. "No one knows you're here."

"I happened to be at a nearby farm before I stopped here. This will be the first place they'll think of to look for me. And Pammy."

"That's a lie, and you don't even do it well," he snapped. "To be convincing, you need to set up the same pattern, you see. If you're mostly found where you said you would be, then it doesn't matter when you aren't — no one will check, because they'll believe you are."

I blinked at his nonsense. "Are you giving lessons on how to cheat on your wife?"

"You have to think," he continued. "Ask yourself 'Where should I be?'"

That gave me pause. I should be at the cottage by now. Michael had probably arrived. Wouldn't he wonder where I was, and would he try to contact me? My phone, lost somewhere outside, would ring and I wouldn't answer, just as Pammy hadn't answered Gavin. And no one knew I had stopped at the abbey ruins.

"You'll stay here," Noel said, as if settling an argument. "You'll stay until I sort out what to do with you two. No one comes to this place. And if they did, who would hear you? You sit tight."

He walked out. The metal door creaked closed, echoing in the darkness, and I heard metal against metal as he slid a bar across followed by the *snick* of a lock and the twirl of a dial. We were alone.

CHAPTER 34

The combination lock was a bit of overkill, I thought — as if we could break free and try an escape. I yanked at my duct-tape shackles.

"We'll be here forever, won't we?" Pammy asked. For the first time, the anger had leaked out of her voice, and it quavered.

"They'll find us," I insisted.

"Who? How? He's right — no one comes here."

"People do come to visit the abbey ruins. Just not that many of them." What time was it? Probably seven o'clock by now. "If not this evening, then tomorrow. Saturday is always busy on the estate."

I strained my ears, but heard nothing, only the silence of the centuries. The air smelled of cold earth and dusty stone, and I could quite imagine the ghost of a monk floating by. I shivered.

"How did he catch you?" Pammy asked after a moment.

"I'm not a trout," I said. Pammy laughed, and that made me feel better. I explained about the tin and what I'd figured out. "I came here to have a shufti, as they say — look round for where Bob might've set up house. And I remembered Tommy saying Bob had acted as if Noel had been here before. And he had. At the moment I realized it, Noel grabbed me. How about you?"

"A wrong turn," she answered glumly. "I was in the cottage, and it was about four o'clock, and I thought I'd nip out and give Gwen the news of my job."

"And Helen. And the chemist. They're all quite happy for you."

"Yeah, well. On my way back to the cottage, I saw Noel driving up the high street. What's he still doing here, I thought. Isn't he in trouble? Shouldn't someone find out where he's going? And before I could think anything else, I got in my car and followed him. It was exciting at first — like a car chase, you know, only slower, because of the traffic. He drove straight out of the village, and turned into the lane, and so, I did, too, but then there were no other cars about, and I looked obvious. When he drove past the car park here and pulled in behind some bushes, I kept going a bit further, before I did the same."

"You should've phoned Tess immediately."

"I thought I should find out what he was doing — make sure it was worth phoning the police. I crept out and sneaked up to a pile of stones, but before I made it any further he appeared from nowhere and grabbed me. I got loose, but I fell and hit my head and I got all woozy and he dragged me here."

"Did he hurt you?"

"No, although I tried my best to hurt him. I might've got a good kick in, I don't know. Mind you," she added, "I've a right lump on my head. And I don't have my bag — he must've taken it."

"I think it's out there. That's what I heard when I called you — I heard your phone ringing from somewhere nearby."

"We're completely cut off," Pammy whimpered.

"I talked to Gavin just before Noel got me. He's been trying to reach you."

She sniffed. "He thinks I've stood him up, doesn't he?"

"Not quite. He's still slaving away at the pub."

Pammy clicked her tongue. "He works too hard, that one."

There's a comment I never thought I'd hear about Gavin Lecky.

We were silent. I tugged again at my restraints, but the tape round my wrists was so tight I couldn't bend my fingers down close enough to pick at it. My arms were bent back at an awkward angle and were beginning to ache.

I sighed heavily and shifted my bottom on the stone, thankful that I was sitting, although I could feel the cold seeping through my skirt. I stared at the shaft of light, trying to gauge the time of day. I'd never noticed these thin ground-level windows from the outside, but my exploration of the abbey ruins had been cursory at best. Occasionally, students would come out from the University of East Anglia to admire the piles of stones and the low vaulted ceiling of the undercroft, but no one had ever made a fuss over underground rooms. Perhaps those slits had been ventilation and a bit of daylight for the monks and their supplies. Over time, the soil might've been pushed up against the outer walls, and when the hollies and blackthorns grew, their roots held the soil in place against the opening, reducing the size of the windows. Who would even notice them now?

Panic began to overtake me, and I inhaled deep, even gulps of the dank air to refocus. Had Bob slept in this chamber? I peered into the dark corners, looking for signs of habitation.

"Does Tess suspect it's Noel, do you think?" Pammy asked at last.

"Tess suspects everyone," I replied. "She'll zero in on Noel in no time, if she hasn't already. He's not long for freedom."

"What if he doesn't tell them we're here?"

"They'll find us."

"Maybe, but how long will it take them. Days? Weeks?" She sobbed. "It isn't going to be pretty, is it — the end?"

"Pammy! Don't be so dramatic." I spoke with more force than I needed, but I had to convince myself, too. "The problem is, this entire case was all about the abbey ruins, but we were distracted because Bob was found at the pond near the church. You'd think if he was going to tell Willow anything, it would've been about Noel and the abbey."

"He? You mean Bob? Are you saying Bob talks to Willow?"

"I'm saying nothing of the kind. It's just that Willow gets . . . feelings."

"Right, well," Pammy said, sounding considerably brighter, "then won't she have a feeling about us?"

"She did about you," I said. "When I stopped at Lottie's shop after work, she asked me if you were alone. And then I got all these texts from people asking where you were." How odd. Had Bob sent out the spirit version of a police BOLO — Be On the Look Out for? We could only hope.

"Must be nice to live in a village like this," Pammy remarked. "Where you all keep an eye on each other."

"Yes," I sighed.

In the ensuing quiet, I found myself growing sleepy. I rested my head back against the wall and closed my eyes. Were the police looking for us? Was Michael driving round the estate searching for my car? Wouldn't they question everyone? How long would that take? No one knew Pammy had driven off after Noel, and no one knew that after I left Guy Pockett's farm, I came to the ruins. But eventually they would surely piece it together. And they would think to search the grounds.

The thin shaft of light went out.

"What happened?" Pammy cried.

"Nothing happened," I said. "The sun must've gone down behind the trees, that's all."

"Night. We'll be in the pitch black for hours and hours." Pammy's voice trembled. "Oh Julia, what do I do if I need to have a wee?"

I shivered as I realized Pammy was right — this night would seem forever.

"You do what you have to," I said.

* * *

No stars, no moon, no sound. Nothingness.

Disturbing images floated through my mind. I stood with Michael in the sunny back garden at our Pipit Cottage as he protected me from a cuckoo the size of an elephant. I sat perched on the corner of my dad's desk as he explained I had an endangered lichen growing on my face, and he would now use me as an example of biodiversity. I was seven and playing upstairs with Bee on a rainy day, and I heard Mum calling up to say a young fellow named Bob Brightbill had moved into the beech hedge along the drive. And next, I was living in the darkness of a badger's sett, and I heard the animal digging his way in.

"What's that?"

I woke with a jerk, breathing hard and staring into the dark.

"Pammy?"

"What is that?" Pammy asked again, her voice shaking.

"Did you hear something?" I asked.

"No . . . it's . . ." I heard her thrashing, and the iron ring she had been lashed to squeaked in resistance. "I think something's crawling on me. A spider. Yes, yes, a spider and it's crawling up my arm!"

She screamed — high-pitched and at a volume guaranteed to shatter my eardrums. It echoed round the space and went on and on, filling my head until I thought I, too, would scream. I shook my head back and forth as if I could shake the sound away, but did it so violently, I hit my nose against the stone wall and yelled out in pain. At last, it was quiet — apart from my ears ringing — but I heard Pammy take a deep and ragged breath, and I feared she would start again.

"Pammy, don't, please!"

She paid me no mind. I should've marveled at her ability to start and end on a note so high and loud and sharp it shredded every nerve in my body.

"Get it off! Get it off!" she howled, before launching into another inhuman shriek.

If she kept this up, I would be driven crazy long before we were dead.

She paused to inhale, and that's when I heard them. Voices. Or had I gone deaf and was imagining it?

"Get it off!" Pammy wailed.

"Listen!" I shot back at her. "Be quiet and listen!"

She gasped and held her breath. Silence, blessed silence — and in the silence, someone shouted words I could not understand.

"He's coming back." Pammy's voice was flooded with fear. "He's coming back to kill us. He'll use the same branch he used on Bob. He'll bash our skulls in and then he'll burn it and there'll be no evidence and—"

I opened my mouth to comfort her, but my throat constricted as I heard noises outside the door.

"Pammy!"

But that voice came from above. We listened — I, for one, afraid to believe what was happening.

Dirt sifted down from the thin horizontal slit high up on the wall as the soil was dug away like a badger digs a sett. I watched as the opening grew and behind it lights flashed across the darkness. I could see movement.

"Pammy?" Gavin yelled again.

"Julia?" Michael called.

"*Yes!*" we screamed. "We're here!" I could see two heads with halos of bright lights behind them.

The door rattled, and Pammy squealed.

"It's the police," Gavin shouted. "I'm coming down."

He disappeared. Michael's face filled the gap — I recognized the outline of his hair, always a bit shaggy.

"Julia! Are you all right?"

"I'm all right!" But I choked as I said it, unable to keep back a torrent of tears. "I'm all right." I wept.

I could see Michael in silhouette as he kept at the soil until the opening widened and he could shove his head and a shoulder through.

"I'm not waiting any longer," he shouted. "There is no perfect moment!" His voice cracked. "No, *this* is the perfect moment!" He thrust his arm through the hole and held open his hand.

"Julia, will you marry me?"

CHAPTER 35

"Yes," I said. "Yes, yes, yes." Police lamps lit up the abbey ruins as if we were on a movie set and uniforms and detectives were cast and crew — but we were the stars, Michael and I, as we stood in the grass amid the bustle. "Ask me again," I demanded as I accepted his handkerchief and wiped my bloody nose.

He held me tightly round the waist as if I might fly away, which I thought quite possible, I was so filled with happiness.

"Julia Ruby Craddock Lanchester," he said, his lips caressing my cheek, "will you marry me?"

"Yes," I murmured. "Yes, yes, yes."

Pammy and I had been freed only moments before. The police had broken the padlock and cut through our duct-tape chains while Michael and Gavin both tried to assist and both got in the way. The four of us — a mad, happy stumbling mass of emotions — had run out and up the stairs, knocking into Tess, DS Glossop, and DC Flynn on their way down. We had spilled out onto the grass in the evening air perfumed with honeysuckle and light still in the western sky, after which my entire attention had been consumed by Michael's proposal. I didn't think I could ever hear it enough times. We stood in the center of our favorite picnic spot — its reputation now changed forever — while Pammy and

Gavin took possession of a smooth, wide stone. She sat across his lap with one arm round his shoulders and he had arms holding tight to her waist.

"I don't have a ring," Michael said with a worried look. "It's only that I thought we could choose it together. You might have a few ideas."

Gold with a vintage look — a filigree design with an oval diamond surrounded by — this was Bee's idea — a ring of tiny sapphires.

"Yes, we'll shop together."

DI Callow appeared, calling us back to the moment. She spoke to a uniform and then approached us.

"How are the two of you? Would you like that off, Julia?" She nodded to my bin-bag collar, still attached with duct tape.

"Yes, please." I held still while Tess cut the tape with a penknife.

"Do either of you need to see a doctor?" she asked.

"Nah," Pammy said in a cavalier fashion. "We're all right, aren't we, Julia?"

I rubbed my neck and took stock. Our wrists were raw and marked with wide red bands from where the tape had been pulled off, and we were coated in dirt. I had a bloody nose and another ruined pair of tights. My ears were still ringing and I was sure Pammy would come up bruised from her thrashing.

"We're fine," I replied. "Except, what about your head, Pammy?"

"What'd he do to you?" Gavin growled.

"I fell and got this," Pammy said, placing Gavin's hand on the lump just above her forehead.

"Right, you're off to hospital," he replied, standing with her in his arms.

"Wait," she said and giggled. "I want to know what happened."

"Yes, me, too," I said. "I can see how you would think of the abbey, but how did you know we were down below?"

"Are you joking?" Michael asked, the corner of his mouth tugging up into a grin. "I grew up with that scream of Pammy's. She let loose every time she thought there might be even the faintest possibility of a spider in her room. I'd know the sound anywhere."

"There *was* a spider down there and it *was* crawling on me," Pammy insisted. "But I have to say, I'm rather glad of the little bugger now."

Gavin sat back down. "Weren't you frightened by it all?"

"Nah, we weren't scared. Were we, Julia?"

"Well, we were a bit uneasy." It's easy to be brave in hindsight.

"When we arrived," Michael said, a bleak look passing over his face, "even before the scream, we knew you were somewhere nearby — at least we hoped. Because of what I found."

At that moment, DS Glossop joined the impromptu debriefing and held up a plastic bag with one of my spike heels in it. The memory came back strong, and I knew the feel of the shoe in my hand as I battered Noel's face.

"I hit him with it."

"Ah, so that's how he came to appear pockmarked." Glossop grinned.

"You found him?" I asked.

"Oh, yes," Tess replied. "As it happens, there was a minor road-traffic incident at the north end of the village involving Noel Pears and Mr. Sedgwick here."

"It was the other bloke's fault," Gavin insisted. "I'm a witness."

"Thank you, Mr. Lecky."

"You and Gavin?" I asked Michael, bewildered. "Car crash? Noel?"

Michael took over. "Lecky came to the cottage as I was ringing round trying to find you. He was looking for Pammy. I rang Peg at the Stoat and Hare, who told me police were out on the pavement talking with Tony. She said Lottie was there, as well as Willow and Tommy. We went straight up."

"Tony Brightbill and Lottie watched me pass by earlier," I said. "But how could they know where I was going?"

"Mr. Brightbill had seen Pears drive by not long before, followed close on by Ms. Sedgwick. He thought it a good idea to notify the police — as you should've," Tess said grimly, with a glance to the couple seated on the rocks.

"I was about to ring you," Pammy said. "I only wanted to know where he was going."

"You had just been at the Stoat and Hare earlier," I pointed out to Tess, "talking with Tony."

"Well, I returned when Mr. Brightbill rang. Ms. Wynn-Finch, too, had phoned us with a tip," the DI said. "She told me she had a feeling you might've gone out to Guy Pockett's farm and could I please check on both you and Ms. Sedgwick."

I vowed to myself never again to dismiss Willow's vibes, feelings, or intuitions.

"Guy had found another old tin," I said. "This one held newspaper cuttings Bob had collected. But I didn't mention going out to the farm to Willow."

"Bob must've told her." Pammy's stage whisper caught the ears of the entire crime scene, and there was silence.

"We were all of us gathered in front of the pub when I rang Guy Pockett," DS Glossop offered. "He mentioned your fascination with an old leaflet about the abbey. We came straight out, although Mr. Sedgwick and Mr. Lecky were in the lead car."

"It wasn't meant to be a convoy," DI Callow said with ice in her voice. "It was police business."

"Good thing we did go first," Gavin said happily. "That Pears bloke pulled out of the lane right in front of us. Sedgwick had no chance to avoid him."

"Where did he think he was going in such a rush?" Glossop asked no one in particular.

But Pammy and I locked our eyes on each other. We knew where Noel was going — far away, leaving us locked up for well and good. Or so he thought.

Tess sighed. "Mr. Sedgwick clipped the back corner of Pears' Fiesta on the passenger's side, and both cars came to a stop in the middle of the road. He seemed a bit dazed. Our police cars narrowly avoided the two cars, cutting to the left and right. It meant Pears was pretty much surrounded when he leapt out."

"Berk," Gavin commented. Pammy snorted and hid her face in Gavin's shoulder.

"When he jumped out," Michael said, "I'd no idea who he was."

"I have a photo of Tommy's sketch on my phone," I said. "Wherever that is. Want to see it?"

"The impact popped open the boot of his car," Callow explained. "When we realized who the driver was, we had reasonable grounds for a search. Inside the boot, we found a piece of a branch wrapped in plastic. It's already on its way to forensics to check for blood and tissue."

"He was saving the murder weapon — did he think it was a souvenir?" I felt queasy, remembering the damage it had done to Bob's skull.

Michael's grip on me tightened. "We thought — we were afraid he might've used it again."

"We would never have let him, would we, Julia?" Pammy said with defiance.

"We were tied up," Pammy. Remember?"

"I don't think he had plans to use it again," Tess told us. "Most likely he was too panicked to get rid of it. Afraid someone might see."

I swayed slightly, and Michael caught me. "I'm all right," I lied, but he led me over to another low piece of wall and tried out the stones. They held and we sat.

DC Flynn appeared with a large flask of tea and a stack of paper cups and began pouring.

"Is this from the station?" I asked.

"God no, I wouldn't drink that stuff," Moira replied.

I accepted a cup gratefully — a good, strong, sugary brew.

"Why did Tony Brightbill think it odd that Pammy was following Noel out of the village?" I asked.

"Mr. Brightbill said he got the idea from you earlier today." Tess said. "The way you reacted to seeing him talk with Pears made Brightbill think he was somehow involved in the murder." I saw a smile creep up on her. "He said you don't have a terribly good poker face."

CHAPTER 36

"And he thrust his arm through the slit and reached his hand down and said, 'Julia, marry me.'" As I spoke the words, the story caught at my heart on this eleventh or possibly twelfth telling as much as it had when it happened. "And his eyes were the color of cornflowers."

"You couldn't see his eyes — it was too dark," Pammy pointed out, pausing on her way out the cottage door with both hands full of plastic bags.

"I could see his eyes," I said with force, "and they were the color of cornflowers."

"It's better to go along with her if at all possible," Bianca warned, her voice emanating from my phone on the coffee table as she had indulgently listened to my tale for the third time.

"So I've learned," Pammy replied.

To my consternation, Bee and Pammy had become quite chummy in the four days since Michael proposed, even though they had yet to meet face-to-face.

"Have you set the date?" Bianca asked.

I reached for my tea. "Probably early December. We've got to get through migration first, and then all the winter birds arriving, and of course, we have to wait until I'm finished with the Christmas Market."

"Hope you can fit the wedding in. Couldn't someone else take care of any of that?"

"You know how Dad is in autumn," I said. Migration is huge to an ornithologist, and Rupert always had a busy television schedule October and November.

"And his younger daughter has to do everything herself, as well."

"I daresay you inherited your fair share of that trait," I said. "Aren't you president of the parent groups for each of your children's classes all at the same time?"

We had reached a stalemate. "Tomorrow, we'll talk about your dress," Bee said. "Bye now."

Pammy returned from packing the last bits and bobs into her Ford Fiesta.

"You haven't finished your tea," I said. "And Michael's not here yet."

She settled at one end of the sofa with me at the other.

"You should've had another night at that posh hotel," she said. "I'd've got myself packed up all right. After all, here it is Monday — your day off."

Regardless of the events of Friday evening, Michael had whisked me off on Saturday morning as he'd said he would. We had spent two nights in a former country manor now a luxurious hotel near Colchester with its own shops and spa and a lovely restaurant and country walks. We had stayed there once before — a fleeting night more than a year before — and had promised ourselves we'd go back. Neither of us was about to let Noel Pears get in the way of that. And, DI Callow gave us permission to wait until after the weekend to sign our statements.

Pammy and Gavin carried through with their plans as well — the Jumble-O-Rama at Swaffham. Pammy's plastic-bag population might've increased slightly, but how could I fault her when she offered me a gorgeous billowing summer frock she'd found late in the day at a shockingly low price? I gasped when I saw the name on the label. She had looked quite pleased and would accept no money for it. Gavin had been a trouper. It didn't hurt that on his wanderings round the event, he had spotted a cattle egret in the next field.

I much preferred to tie up loose ends, and so between mud masks and massages and room service when we couldn't bear to leave our quarters, I'd been able to chase down the details I needed by ringing everyone involved. I learned the dinner at Hoggin Hall with the English Heritage folk had gone quite well — perhaps even better than that, because even over the phone I do believe I could tell Nuala was blushing when I asked for more personal particulars. Good.

As I'd driven by the Stoat and Hare on Friday, I'd seen Lottie Finch walk up to talk with Tony Brightbill about Bob. It was because Tony had heard from Bob's solicitor — he did have one, after all — who had seen the death notice that morning. Tony learned that his brother had split his entire fortune among a variety of nature organizations, including the Royal Society for the Protection of Birds and every county division of the Wildlife Trust in Britain. Bob had named Lottie his executor.

This news came from Willow, who reported Tony seemed relieved to have the family money matters settled. "I think he would've given it away himself if Bob had left it to him." Lottie was being cautious in her dealings with Tony, still resentful all these years later, about how his family had treated her. "But," Willow insisted, "Bob believes they'll become friends eventually."

Willow also reported Tommy and her children would move out of London and perhaps to Suffolk, where she might ply her trade of graphic designer in peace. If that happened, I'd say we'd be putting a fair bit of work her way. First off, I would commission a sketch from her — a likeness of Bob Brightbill we would run in the newsletter as he posthumously received the first OFE, Order of the Fotheringill Estate. Perhaps Lottie could accept the award in his name at a ceremony — would she mind? — and the local papers could attend. Must mention this to Linus before I make any concrete plans.

I tried my best not to think the worst of Deena Downey, but without much success. Tess told me that when questioned, Deena remembered the fellow who'd seen her with Noel at the abbey ruins, but hadn't thought anything else about it. She swore she hadn't a clue what Noel had done. Her alibi for the weekend of Bob's murder was confirmed — it had been her birthday, and she was home celebrating with her husband and three daughters. Deena agreed to cooperate fully with police on the case, but asked if the DI could see fit not to mention her involvement to her husband. Callow made no promises.

As Pammy and I finished our tea, Michael arrived home, and the three of us made our way outside to the pavement. Pammy stood next to her car, which had been carefully packed with every single one of her plastic shopping bags, leaving her just enough space to see out the back window. She wore a microskirt and a rosy pink top with the words *It's All Good!* written in shimmering gold.

Elbows at her side, she lifted her hands, palms up, and said, "Well, wish me luck."

We hugged and kissed and said we knew she would make the best assistant manager any Oxfam shop had ever seen. She climbed in her car and had started the engine when I shouted, "Hang on a tick!" I dashed back inside and came out with Sheila's clodhopper shoes. "Here you go — I've cleaned them up a bit."

"Thanks, Julia. They'll go in pride of place on the shoe shelf. Maybe I'll write up a tag that tells what they've been through, and we'll fetch a record price."

We watched her drive off to Bury Saint Edmunds — twelve miles up the road — and her new position and new digs. Michael stood behind me, his arms wrapped round my waist. I rested my head against his cheek.

And July she flies away.

THE END

AUTHOR'S NOTE

Continued thanks to my writing group — Kara Pomeroy, Louise Creighton, and Joan Shott — as well as my agent, Colleen Mohyde; my editor, Kate Miciak; and the staff at Alibi. Their attention to story and detail make all the difference.

In my research for *Farewell, My Cuckoo* and all Birds of a Feather mysteries, I relied on the experts and bird lovers of The Royal Society for the Protection of Birds (www.rspb.org.uk) — of which I am a proud member!

ADDITIONAL NOTE

Many thanks to Joffe Books, publishing director Kate Lyall Grant, and to my agent Christina Hogrebe (Jane Rotrosen Agency) for re-publishing my Birds of a Feather series!

THE JOFFE BOOKS STORY

We began in 2014 when Jasper agreed to publish his mum's much-rejected romance novel and it became a bestseller.

Since then we've grown into the largest independent publisher in the UK. We're extremely proud to publish some of the very best writers in the world, including Joy Ellis, Faith Martin, Caro Ramsay, Helen Forrester, Simon Brett and Robert Goddard. Everyone at Joffe Books loves reading and we never forget that it all begins with the magic of an author telling a story.

We are proud to publish talented first-time authors, as well as established writers whose books we love introducing to a new generation of readers.

We won Trade Publisher of the Year at the Independent Publishing Awards in 2023. We have been shortlisted for Independent Publisher of the Year at the British Book Awards for the last four years, and were shortlisted for the Diversity and Inclusivity Award at the 2022 Independent Publishing Awards. In 2023 we were shortlisted for Publisher of the Year at the RNA Industry Awards.

We built this company with your help, and we love to hear from you, so please email us about absolutely anything bookish at feedback@joffebooks.com

If you want to receive free books every Friday and hear about all our new releases, join our mailing list: www.joffebooks.com/contact

And when you tell your friends about us, just remember: it's pronounced Joffe as in coffee or toffee!

ALSO BY MARTY WINGATE

BIRDS OF A FEATHER SERIES
Book 1: THE RHYME OF THE MAGPIE
Book 2: EMPTY NEST
Book 3: EVERY TRICK IN THE ROOK
Book 4: FAREWELL, MY CUCKOO

THE POTTING SHED MYSTERIES
Book 1: THE GARDEN PLOT
Book 2: THE RED BOOK OF PRIMROSE HOUSE
Book 3: BETWEEN A ROCK AND A HARD PLACE
Book 4: THE SKELETON GARDEN
Book 5: THE BLUEBONNET BETRAYAL
Book 6: BEST-LAID PLANTS
Book 7: MIDSUMMER MAYHEM
Book 7.5: CHRISTMAS AT GREENOAK
Book 8: BITTERSWEET HERBS

Printed in France by Amazon
Brétigny-sur-Orge, FR